A Case of Wine

Steve Schach & Sharon Stein

Wandering in the Words Press

To request permission, visit
www.wanderinginthewordspress.com.

All characters in this book are fictitious, and any resemblance to real persons, living or dead, is coincidental.

PUBLISHED BY WANDERING IN THE WORDS PRESS

ISBN:
Print: 978-1-7332126-8-7
Digital: 978-1-7332126-0-1

First Edition

In Memory of
Johan Koeslag
1940 – 2018

Professor Johan Koeslag—brilliant researcher, physician, biologist, world-famous physiologist, keen amateur ornithologist and geologist, and author of over eighty refereed articles in research journals, eleven with Steve as a co-author—was an insightful early reader of our books, including this one. But above all, he was a wonderful person and a really good friend.

Professionally, his greatest strength was his refusal to believe something just because someone else said so. Instead, he determined the truth for himself. This attitude led to some of his most outstanding and original research ideas.

But Johan was more than just an outstanding thinker and researcher. He was a fun person to be with. Doing research with Johan wasn't work, it was pleasure.

On July 15, 2018, an intruder murdered Johan in his home in Cape Town, South Africa.

Also by Steve Schach

Old Bach Is Come
Highly Satisfactory
A Matter of Trust

Also by Steve Schach and Sharon Stein

Coopers Island
Bakerloo Line
Double Two
The Book Buyer
Crossword Traitor

CHAPTER ONE

The powerful explosion totally destroyed Goran's Bottle Shop. After the red-brown dust had settled, the remains of the two-story structure looked like a photograph from the First World War; the ruins eerily resembled the broken shell of a building in the middle of No Man's Land that the artillery on both sides had viciously pounded for weeks. The blast reduced the shady trees on Queen Maude Avenue in suburban Willowbrook, on Sydney's lush green Upper North Shore, to blackened stumps. Even the incessant harsh screeching of the cockatoos and lorikeets ceased for five minutes, perhaps out of respect for the dead; the body of Goran Pekić, sole proprietor and licensee, was now just charred bone shards. And there was no trace of the contents of the thousands of bottles of beer, wine, and spirits that had graced the crowded shelves of Goran's Bottle Shop.

＊

My name is Damon Ogilvy. I was born in Australia. I grew up on a sheep farm about an hour's drive from a country town called Mullajumba: population eighty-seven people and tens of thousands of sheep.

I used to work as a lawyer in a one-person practice in Katoomba, a town in the Blue Mountains about sixty miles west of Sydney. Nearly ten thousand people live there, but unfortunately not enough of them came to my office to seek legal advice. And many of those who did never returned because I managed to upset them with my incredible lack of tact. My mother used to say, "Damon opens his mouth only to change feet."

I tried to find a way to earn additional money on the side and was delighted to discover that in Australia you could become a certified financial planner by doing an eight-day crash course and obtaining a diploma known as Regulatory Guide 146, or RG146 for short. Believe it or not, you didn't even need a high school education, let alone a university degree, work experience, or professional accreditation. Offering financial planning services in addition to legal advice improved my own financial situation somewhat, but I still couldn't accumulate quite enough money for a down payment to buy my own home, the great Australian dream; housing prices are unimaginably high in Australia, even outside the major cities.

One day, a client named Barnett Mornay came to see me for financial advice. His wife's brother desperately needed funds to pay for a top lawyer to try to keep him out of jail for tax evasion. To attempt to raise some money, his brother-in-law offered to sell Barnett ownership of a gold mine in Western Australia that had never yielded more than a few ounces of the precious metal. I glanced through the documents Barnett had brought me.

"Your brother-in-law is asking for fifty thousand dollars for the gold mine and the mineral rights. The running expenses are currently about ten thousand dollars a month. That's far too much for a mine that doesn't look as if it's going to produce much more gold."

"That's true," Barnett said, "but the geologist's report describes the mine as 'highly promising.'"

"Well, surely you can find a bank to lend you fifty thousand to buy a 'highly promising' gold mine?"

"Not exactly. The banks tell me that they've lost millions and millions lending money to buy 'highly promising' and 'extremely encouraging' mines. As far as I can tell, they rate geologists even lower than used-car salesmen. In fact, one banker said that he trusts politicians more than geologists, which is saying something. I've managed to raise twenty-five thousand, but I can't find the rest. And my wife says that if I don't come up with the fifty thousand dollars, she's going to divorce me."

I knew nothing about gold mines or how to borrow money to invest in one. But I didn't want my client to realize I was totally out of my depth. So I replied as confidently as I could, "Leave the papers with me, and I'll sort this all out."

When Barnett had left, I looked through the documents more carefully, and I noticed that typed under the indecipherable signature of the geologist who'd issued the report was the name H. Czolgosz. I'd attended boarding school with a painfully shy boy named Herbert Czolgosz, and wondered if it was the same person. The only other time I've ever encountered that rather unusual name was when I read that the man who'd assassinated William McKinley, President of the United States, was one Leon Czolgosz, so I thought it might be worth phoning the number on the top of the report.

Not surprising, "H. Czolgosz" turned out to be my old schoolmate, as laconic and withdrawn as ever. After a few minutes of excruciating small talk, consisting of my questions about what he'd been doing and his mumbled one-word responses, I asked him about the report he'd issued. Herbert suddenly came out of his shell and started enthusing about the mine. He kept going on about how this was the most promising mine of its kind that he'd ever evaluated and how he'd struggled to keep his report on a low key for fear of being accused of unprofessional exaggeration. During our school days, Herbert had been the supreme introvert, but now, stemming the passionate, almost frenzied flow of words was impossible. Eventually, I managed to bring the conversation to a close.

An ethical financial adviser always acts in the best interests of one's client. Accordingly, I should immediately have contacted Barnett, told him what I'd just learned, and then helped him to the utmost of my ability to raise the additional funds he needed to buy the mine from his brother-in-law. Instead, I put down the phone and decided to use the information I'd obtained on my client's behalf to enrich myself at his expense.

Lying on the desk in front of me was the key to a fortune. As you know, I was as short of money as Barnett was. But by that night I'd managed to persuade various family members and friends to lend me enough money to offer Barnett twenty-five thousand dollars for a half-share in the mine. He instantly agreed, thanking me over and over again for saving his marriage. Six weeks later, the two men working on our mine found a vein of almost pure gold, a deposit so rich that it seemed as if it could singlehandedly catapult Australia from being the second largest gold producer in the world into unchallenged first place.

Sadly for us, further exploration of the mine proved considerably less promising. Heartbreakingly fast, the vein petered out to nothing. But news of the strike spread rapidly, and Table Mountain Proprietary—now TMP—bought all rights to the mine from us for twelve million dollars each. For TMP, twenty-four million dollars was just rounding error in their balance sheet; the company was willing to throw away chump change on the remote off-chance that there might just be more gold deeper in the ground. But for Barnett and me, it was the opportunity for us to live the lifestyles we'd always wanted.

Barnett used his money from the gold strike and the sale of the mine to go into the oil business. He now fancied himself as a prospector. Much to my amazement, his Indonesian oil wells turned to gold; the man undeniably had the Midas touch. His larcenous brother-in-law, however, was sentenced to four years in prison, despite the oily-tongued pleading of his high-priced Queen's Counsel.

With my share of the largesse, I bought a large penthouse in The Rocks, with an unobstructed vista of Sydney Harbour. Then I gave up the hole-in-the-wall office I was renting in Katoomba and moved my financial planning practice to a corner suite with a harbor view in a fancy office building on Pitt Street, a few blocks from my new penthouse. I hired an older, highly experienced personal assistant named Mrs. Dickenson. And I advertised my services in the appropriate glossy magazines.

As a consequence of the move from small-town Katoomba to a fashionable office in downtown Sydney, my clientele changed from shopkeepers and retirees to wealthy businessmen running large companies. My income increased beyond my wildest dreams; the commissions that financial planners in Australia receive are often extortionate.

After a few months I bought a luxury car and hired a man named Bruce to be my chauffeur. Back home in Mullajumba no one bothered about driver's licenses. When I was twelve, my father taught me to drive our pickup truck, what we call a *ute* here in Australia; I think it's short for "utility vehicle." A year later, I graduated from the ute to our tractor. Eventually, he allowed me to drive our family sedan, a second-hand Holden VK Commodore. But I never traveled the three hundred miles to the nearest center where I could take a driving test. And now, at the age of thirty-nine, there was no way I was going to drive around Sydney as a learner driver in a car festooned with L-plates—hence Bruce.

Life was good. Each morning I woke up and spent at least ten minutes on my balcony watching the maritime traffic in one of the most beautiful harbors in the world. If I needed to visit a client at his or her place of business, I had Bruce at my disposal; I no longer had the hassle of trying to find a taxi to take me from my office to a client in an outlying area of Sydney, let alone the almost impossible task of summoning another taxi to take me back afterwards. In the evenings, Bruce would drive me to the latest restaurant that the food editor of *The New South Wales Daily* had recommended. And in case you're wondering about the name of that newspaper, Sydney is located in the state of New South Wales, but no one has ever been able to find out why Captain James Cook called it that when he encountered the east coast of Australia on 19 April, 1770.

For the next three years I dispensed financial guidance to my numerous grateful clients. During that period, the Australia stock market rocketed upward, as did the value of real estate. In addition, the price of coal, iron ore, and gold—Australia's three largest exports—also soared. Consequently, virtually every venture I suggested to my clients did extremely well. Even though I understood little or nothing about the economy and I had no insight into specific investments, people eagerly sought what they thought was my wise advice. I had a weekly column in *The New South Wales Daily*, and in my role as an all-knowing pundit, I appeared regularly on television.

But at the back of my mind a small voice kept telling me that I'd acted dishonestly in my dealings with Barnett Mornay. I'd broken no laws, but the fact of the matter was that I hadn't acted as an ethical financial adviser. The life I was leading enabled me to silence my conscience most of the time. But sometimes I woke up in the small hours of the morning, racked with guilt as a consequence of my unprofessional conduct back in Katoomba.

What made it worse for me was that Barnett was totally oblivious of what I'd really done. He and I became close friends, and almost every time we met, he told me how grateful he was that I'd bought half the mine, thereby saving his marriage as well as making him an extremely wealthy man.

Soon after I opened my Sydney office, a man named Sebastian Ormsby came to see me for financial planning advice. I'd told him to buy as many shares as he could in four coal mines. In view of the steep climb in the price of the fossil fuel in the intervening three years, my suggestion had turned coal into gold. Now Sebastian came to see me a second time. He'd just sold one of his companies. He had a million dollars to invest and wanted me to recommend an investment. A week before his latest visit, I'd attended a seminar at which a team of slick promoters had strongly pushed a scheme in which investors put their money into Limerick Creek Station, a vast sheep farm. Sebastian knew about my agricultural background. Consequently, when I told him to put his million dollars into the livestock project, he rushed to follow my sage advice.

Sebastian naturally assumed that I'd done my homework. But I hadn't. The only piece of paper I'd read was one of the many glossy handouts the promoters had distributed at the seminar, urging advisors to instruct their clients to take out a large mortgage on their homes to be able to invest even more money in that wonderful sheep farm. Accordingly, not only did I tell Sebastian to put his million dollars in the scheme, but I also strongly encouraged him to obtain a million-dollar mortgage on his palatial waterfront house to enable him to invest two million dollars in all.

"I want to get into this investment scheme right away," he insisted. "Here's my check for one million dollars. And as soon as I have that mortgage, I'll give you the second million to invest for me. From what you've told me this morning, even if your sheep farm is only half as good as your coal mines, Limerick Creek Station will set me up for life."

Sebastian didn't know it, but he was about to invest only one million, eight hundred thousand dollars in sheep; the promoters were paying financial planners a commission of ten percent. For just over an hour's work, I'd get two hundred thousand dollars of Sebastian's money. However, in view of the information that the promoters had shared regarding the limitless potential of Limerick Creek Station, this seemed a small price for Sebastian to pay for what was unquestionably the investment opportunity of a lifetime.

Sebastian left, bursting with gratitude for my sound advice. I got up from my desk to take his check to the promoters' office two or three blocks away in Pitt Street, when an awful thought crossed my mind.

I sat down again and started conducting the due diligence that I should've performed before my meeting with Sebastian. I meticulously read the prospectus and all the other papers I'd received at the seminar. And then I made a few phone calls.

Unlike almost every other financial planner in Australia, I actually knew something about sheep farming. In fact, I was an expert on the subject. And now I was absolutely certain that Limerick Creek Station was a Ponzi scheme. That meant that when the fraudulent investment operation eventually collapsed, as inevitably had to happen, Sebastian would lose every cent of his two million dollars. And he'd lose his home as well if he couldn't pay the interest on his mortgage. Instead of turning sheep to gold, my client was about to become a lamb to the slaughter. And Damon Ogilvy, the sheep farmer's son, had unwittingly pulled the wool over Sebastian's eyes and fleeced him.

I immediately called Sebastian. While waiting for him to answer his phone, I realized I'd acted unethically once again. The promised ten percent commission had blinded me, and I'd neglected my duty as a financial adviser.

"Sebastian, it's Damon. You haven't applied for a mortgage yet, have you?"

"Damon, how nice to hear from you! Actually, you've caught me at the bank. They're giving me an unsecured loan for a million dollars, at a ruinous rate of interest, of course. But they'll convert it into a mortgage on my home as soon as possible. I'm just about to sign the papers, after which I'm coming straight to your office with the second check. This investment is too good to miss. I want to be in it right now."

"Don't you sign anything! Tear up the loan application, just as I've ripped up your check. The sheep scheme is a fraud."

"A fraud? What do you mean? I don't understand. Didn't you just strongly recommend those sheep without any reservations whatsoever?"

"Yes, and now I'm doubly strongly unrecommending them. There are no sheep. There's no vast farm, either. Those eye-catching color photographs in the portfolio I showed you—huge flocks grazing on boundless rolling hills—are computer-generated images. The whole thing is a Ponzi scheme; they're paying dividends to early investors out of the investments of later investors. And when enough people have poured funds into their crooked operation, they'll take the money and run.

"And one other thing, Sebastian. I'm afraid that you're going to have to find a new financial adviser.

As of now, I'm out of the game. Permanently. I'm very sorry."

And I hung up the phone. Having finally realized that I wasn't strong enough to resist temptation, for the first time in three years I felt good about myself.

***

I had more than enough money to retire and do nothing for the rest of my days, but I wanted to do *something*. The question was: What? I realized that I hadn't taken a holiday in years, and I'd never been outside Australia. They say that travel broadens the mind, and I hoped that visiting a foreign country might lead to an idea for an interesting new occupation. It didn't take me long to decide to see a bit of the world.

I flew to Paris. There I experienced *haute cuisine*, the food served in "high level" French restaurants. My taste buds told me in no uncertain terms that what I wanted to be was a full-time gourmet, and I spent the next two weeks enjoying all that Paris has to offer in the way of superlative food and drink.

One evening, I was seated at my inevitable table for just one. That night I had chosen to eat at La Poule d'Argent, arguably the top three-star restaurant in Paris. While waiting for my meal to be served, I was playing *Angry Birds* on my iPhone. Suddenly I heard a light laugh. I looked to my right, and seated next to me, also at a table for one, was a woman playing *Angry Birds* on her iPhone. She was attractive, with an oval-shaped face and shoulder-length, dark brown hair swept up at the ends. Her eyes were an unusual shade of amber; I'd never seen eyes of quite that color before. Her clothing, her complexion, the string of pearls around her neck, even her demeanor proclaimed indisputably that she was English. She seemed to be roughly my age.

Despite her innate British reserve, we started talking: first about our shared taste in video games, then about our shared love of *haute cuisine*. Next thing I knew, we'd asked the waiters to move our tables together. Her name was Janet Maitland. She lived in Manchester, but for three weeks every year she came to Paris for the food.

I know exactly what you're thinking, that I'm going to tell you that it was love at first sight. But you'd be wrong. Instead, something equally unusual occurred. I'd never believed that a deep platonic friendship between a man and a woman was possible, but somehow it happened between Janet and me. We spent every minute together, visiting the sights of Paris during the day and dining together at night. We hit it off in every way except one: there was nothing physical between us. For twenty years I'd dated women to whom I'd been strongly attracted, only to discover over breakfast the next morning that we had almost nothing in common. Now it was the other way around.

Janet told me she knew she wanted to be a police officer from the time she was ten years old. Her father and mother, both successful plastic surgeons, wanted her to follow in their medical footsteps, but they soon realized that Janet was utterly committed to a career in law enforcement. After leaving school she enrolled at Bruche Police National Training Centre, the first step in her meteoric rise through the ranks of the Greater Manchester Police, from Police Constable to Detective Superintendent in only twenty years.

Two days before she was due to return to Manchester, Janet made it clear she felt the same way about me as I did about her. That is, we'd become best friends and confidants, but nothing more. She stated that she wasn't at all happy with the idea of my returning to Sydney, some ten thousand miles away from Manchester, and instead she came up with an interesting suggestion.

"You said you wanted to become full-time gourmet."

I agreed.

"Being a gourmet is a hobby, not a profession," Janet said. "And I don't want to give up my job as a police officer. Why don't you move to Manchester, and we'll find something for you to do while I continue to work as a detective?"

I thought about that for a while, and then I said, "We both love great food. Why don't you come and live in Sydney, the home of many, many fabulous restaurants? And I've just decided what I want to be: a private investigator."

My counterproposal for our joint future was simplicity itself. It would be easy to put an imposing wooden desk and a comfortable large leather chair for Janet into my huge corner office in downtown Sydney overlooking the harbor, and we'd set ourselves up as private investigators. And clients would flock to our business, because we'd solve their problems quickly and discreetly. Until the fees started pouring in, fees that we'd split fifty-fifty, I'd pay Janet a salary comparable to what she'd been earning as a police detective in Manchester. In return, she'd teach me investigative skills.

It took Janet only a few short weeks to sort out her affairs in Manchester. She told me later that at her farewell party speaker after speaker, ranging in rank from raw recruits to Sir Sylvester Ponty, Police Commissioner of Greater Manchester, declared how much she meant to them on both a personal and a professional level. She gave up her rented apartment and put her furniture into storage. Janet had no trouble at all obtaining a visa that entitled her to live and work in Australia. As soon as she'd received it, she flew to Sydney.

Our reunion at Kingsford-Smith International Airport was one of the happiest days of my life. I took her straight to my large penthouse in The Rocks and showed her how, with the aid of additional doors that I'd had installed, the unit now consisted of three distinct parts: her home, my home, and our shared living area. Janet was delighted with the layout, and agreed that living in my penthouse, or more correctly now, *our* penthouse, was an excellent idea.

Bruce, my driver, agreed to stay on and to drive us to restaurants for our meals. Initially, all went well. The day after Janet's arrival here we lodged our applications to become licensed private investigators, or more correctly, "commercial agents and private inquiry agents." As stipulated in the regulations, a Justice of the Peace, in this instance my good friend Barnett Mornay, witnessed our signatures.

Five days after submitting her application, Janet received her license, together with a handwritten letter from Colonel Arnold Waterfinger, the head of New South Wales Security Licensing and Enforcement Directorate, or SLED. The colonel waxed enthusiastically about Janet's impeccable record of twenty years of sterling service with the Greater Manchester Police, as attested by Sir Sylvester Ponty. Colonel Waterfinger's letter concluded on a note of warm welcome. Nearly a month later, my license was issued. Much to my disgust, there was no letter from Colonel Waterfinger, handwritten or otherwise.

The fly in the ointment was obtaining a New South Wales driver's license for Janet. The written regulations of the Roads and Maritime Services are clear: If you've had a British driver's license for more than three years, the RMS will immediately issue you with a New South Wales driver's license. But the unwritten regulations of the RMS are equally clear: every RMS employee is required to make life as difficult as possible for everyone, without exception.

Janet and I went to the RMS branch in Castlereagh Street, four blocks from my office. Janet filled in the correct form, then took a number from the machine and waited. And waited. And waited. Eventually, her number appeared on the screen and she walked over to window number sixteen, where Malvina du Plessis was sitting. She calmly took Janet's papers and spent ten minutes assiduously trying to find a reason to reject her application. But everything looked perfect, and in desperation she used reason #183: illegible expiry date on Janet's British driver's license. To Janet, and to anyone other than Malvina du Plessis, the date was clear as crystal, so Janet quietly asked to see Malvina's supervisor. Lying through her teeth, Malvina du Plessis insisted that she was the supervisor on duty that afternoon. Janet and I left in a rage, but there was absolutely nothing either of us could do.

If at a later date we returned to the Castlereagh Street RMS, we both realized, Malvina might once again be the next available clerk when Janet's number was called. The problem was easily solved; later that day we went to the RMS branch near Sydney Airport, and she received her license ten minutes after entering the building. It's true that the murky photograph on her new license didn't resemble Janet or, for that matter, any other human being, alive or dead. But Janet now had a driver's license and a private investigator license. We were ready to go into business.

CHAPTER TWO

We decided to advertise widely but discreetly. I certainly had the money to pay for flashy billboards and TV advertisements with scantily clad models singing and dancing, but we both felt that this would be inappropriate for a firm of discreet private investigators committed to treating everything their clients tell them in the strictest possible confidence. Instead, we placed small classified advertisements on the back pages of free local newspapers like *The Inner West Courier*, *The Liverpool Leader*, and *The Lavender Bay Daily*, which, despite its name, is published weekly and contains news from North Sydney and other surrounding suburbs as well. By the way, just in case you decide to follow our lead and advertise in such papers at some future time, be advised that the word *free* in "free local newspapers" appertains to the readers of those papers—advertising in them definitely isn't free.

Within twenty-four hours of placing our ads, two clients contacted us. An elderly man shuffled slowly into our office. Abundant, beautifully groomed, snowy-white hair topped his head, and a Saville Row tailor had undoubtedly made his navy-blue pinstripe suit, albeit at least fifteen or twenty years before. He wore a striped silk rep Old Etonian tie. He told us that he wanted us to find his wife; she'd walked out on him twenty-two years before. With my customary lack of tact, I was about to ask him why he'd waited that long before trying to find her. Janet, however, took no chances. Suspecting, correctly, that I might say something that would upset our client, she quickly jumped in first and pointed out, in the nicest possible way, that following a cold trail like that would probably cost him a small fortune, with Buckley's chance of success; in other words, none at all. After nearly an hour of persuasion, Janet managed to convince him that it would be better for him if he simply tried to forget that he'd ever been married.

The other client was a much younger man, fashionably dressed in an Ermenegildo Zegna "Su Misura" suit in a gray Prince of Wales check pattern, white bespoke Charvet shirt, and a brown silk Jacquard tie. He wanted to know how he could walk out on his wife without leaving a trail that she could follow to claim alimony and child support. Before I could even think about how to respond, Janet all but lost her temper and quickly showed him to the door in a considerably less than friendly manner.

This was totally unlike Janet's otherwise invariable politeness and kindness. And I wasn't the only person who was taken aback by her reaction; I noticed that Mrs. Dickenson, our personal assistant, was frowning in puzzlement. I wondered if Janet's father had perhaps abandoned the family. Or, I thought, the fact that a beautiful woman like Janet was unattached might somehow be connected to a past incident in which a man had jilted her. But despite my usual insensitivity, even I was able to appreciate that Janet's manner said, *Stay well away, and don't ask me any questions of any kind whatsoever.* Just for once, I managed to keep my mouth tightly shut.

A week went by. Nary a client came. We wondered if maybe we should've advertised in a less restrained way. We even wrote a radio-advertising jingle, which I thought was rather good. When we sang it *a capella* to Mrs. Dickenson, she simply turned tail and rushed out of our office, carefully closing the door behind her. I'd like to think that both the words and the music of our composition had deeply moved her but she didn't want us to see the tears of admiration in her eyes. However, I strongly suspect that she wanted to guffaw in the privacy of her own office and not let us see her uncontrollable tears of laughter.

The following Tuesday morning we walked the few blocks from our penthouse to our office in Pitt Street. We took the lift to the nineteenth floor as usual. I opened the door leading from the corridor to our rooms and stood back to allow Janet to enter first into Mrs. Dickenson's office. We greeted Mrs. Dickenson, and I followed Janet through the outer office into the inner office she shared with me. But before I could close the door of our office behind me, the door to the corridor opened again and a middle-aged woman rushed in with a newspaper in her left hand. Blithely ignoring Mrs. Dickenson, she bolted into our room.

"Are you the detectives who advertised in *The Upper North Shore Reporter?*"

"Certainly!" Janet answered, with more enthusiasm in her voice than I'd heard for the last week.

The woman was clearly extremely agitated. She'd been crying, she seemed to have hastily thrown on her clothes, and what little makeup she wore she'd applied equally hurriedly and carelessly. I could see that she was trying to speak, but her highly emotional state prevented her from saying anything. I'm only too aware of my extreme lack of tact, so I wisely followed our client's example and said nothing either.

Janet, on the other hand, knew exactly what to do. She escorted our visitor to a comfortable chair, brought her a glass of water, and asked in a motherly voice, "Now, how can we help you?"

The woman pulled herself together, cleared her throat, and in a voice racked with agony she blurted out the words: "My husband. The police have arrested him for murder. But he didn't do it. He didn't do it."

Seeing Janet in action, I began to understand why she'd received her private investigator license that quickly and with a letter from Colonel Waterfinger to boot, handwritten no less. She calmed our client and managed to extract her story.

I know that you're waiting with bated breath to hear what our client told us. The problem was that she was highly emotional and in no fit state to talk coherently. She frequently repeated herself, every few minutes she went off on a tangent, and she even contradicted herself more than once. And it didn't help matters that she regularly broke into deep sobbing. As a result, what I'm about to tell you is a properly organized description of the facts rather than a verbatim transcript of her sometimes-unintelligible remarks.

Our client, Mrs. Martha Wigram, was born in Port Macquarie in 1970. She worked as a paralegal in the Sydney office of an American white-shoe law firm for a few years. Then, at a Christmas party in 1995, she met Geoffrey Wigram, a mining engineer based in Broken Hill who'd come to Sydney to visit an elderly aunt. It was a genuine case of love at first sight; they married after a brief but intense courtship. They bought a house on Queen Maude Avenue in Willowbrook. Geoffrey commuted by air to and from Broken Hill to pursue his mining career. Martha continued to work at her legal job, which she loved as much as Geoffrey enjoyed his. They tried endlessly to start a family but to no avail. Despite the strains this put on their marriage, they were extremely happy together.

In March 2000, Goran Pekić bought the place next door, a single-story house like the Wigram home and all the others on that avenue. Within a few days, Pekić lodged a development application to add an upper story. The Wigrams had no objection. After all, the space between their home and the Pekić family's was sufficiently large that the second story wouldn't adversely impinge on their property; as the real estate lawyers say, there would be no loss of amenity. In fact, none of the neighbors had the slightest objection. On the contrary, they all felt that the presence of a two-story home on the corner of Queen Maude Avenue and Haversham Lane would increase everyone's property values on both streets. That the development application sailed through the approval process without a dissenting vote came as no surprise to anyone.

A really big surprise, however, came when the alterations were complete. The resulting structure turned out to consist of a bottle shop (a liquor store) on the ground floor and a home for the Pekić family on the floor above. The building was far larger than indicated on the plans. Furthermore, as a whole, it in no way resembled the structure that the local council had approved. Lastly, the presence of the bottle shop was utterly beyond the pale, because no commercial buildings of any kind are permitted in the suburb of Willowbrook.

An even bigger surprise came when the Wigrams and their neighbors objected vociferously to Goran Pekić's building alteration; they found that the authorities totally ignored them. The State of New South Wales had just held an election. The outcome of the voting was that power was transferred from the Progressive Party to the Federalist Party, and the response of the newly triumphant Feds to almost any complaint was essentially, "Blame the [expletive deleted] Proggies." Eventually, however, the Wigrams received a letter from a clerk in the New South Wales Department of Planning and Environment informing them that Pekić's alleged violation of the Willowbrook environmental plan was undeniably an issue at the local governmental level, not the state level.

At the local level, however, every protest emanating from Queen Maude Avenue was completely ignored. For some reason that no one could fathom, Goran Pekić led a charmed life. One widely held theory was that he'd bribed a top official in the local government. However, to acquire absolutely impenetrable armor that could shield him from all protests, Pekić would've had to spend hundreds of thousands of dollars, funds that he apparently didn't have.

An uneasy truce reigned for the next few years. The neighbors living on Queen Maude Avenue and Haversham Lane totally boycotted Goran's Bottle Shop, and they pointedly crossed the street if they saw him walking towards them. But other than that, Willowbrook returned to its pre-Pekić existence.

Then came the second development application. This time, Pekić wanted to convert part of his thriving bottle shop into a wine bar. The reactions of his neighbors fell into two camps. The minority, evidently followers of the "give him enough rope to hang himself" school of philosophy, declared that the men and women of Willowbrook are beer drinkers, and that a wine bar would bankrupt Pekić within weeks. The vast majority, however, were predictably outraged. It wasn't bad enough, they stormed, that Pekić had managed to insinuate a bottle shop into their corner of a residential suburb; now he wanted a wine bar as well. The neighbors organized a meeting in the Wigrams's home, the attendees drew up and signed a petition, and they retained a real-estate lawyer to explore and exercise every possible avenue of protest. And yet the second development application sailed through as easily as the first.

When the alterations were complete, the residents of Queen Maude Avenue and Haversham Lane were horrified to find that, instead of a wine bar occupying half of the area of the bottle shop, Goran's premises now featured a huge café. The area where the wine bar was supposed to go housed a small portion of the café, but a large, new structure erected next to the bottle shop held the rest. A third, and comparatively minor, section of the café encroached on the footpath of Queen Maude Avenue. Pekić had placed four miniscule tables, each with two small cast-iron chairs, on the wide walkway where they couldn't possibly impede pedestrian traffic.

The neighborhood erupted in protest. But the outcome was as before; Pekić continued to lead a charmed life. Remonstration at the state level again led nowhere. The local government officials channeled all objections into an administrative black hole from which no response of any kind has ever emanated. The feral howls of anger from Queen Maude Avenue went unheard.

Pekić's next step was to stealthily increase the number and size of the tables on the footpath. Eventually, walking through the vast forest of tables and chairs that now grew on Haversham Lane as well as on Queen Maude Avenue became impossible; pedestrians had to cross the road to get past Goran's café and bottle shop.

All protests having failed for the second time, a second uneasy truce ensued. As the months passed, the Wigrams and their neighbors assumed that Pekić had achieved all his entrepreneurial ambitions. Their boycott tacitly continued, and life went on.

Then came the third development application. This time Goran stated that he wanted to add another story to his main building. The bottle shop and the café would remain on the ground floor; the middle floor would contain a restaurant; and the Pekić family would live on the new top floor. The residents of Queen Maude Avenue and Haversham Lane were horrified. They held protest meetings that culminated in a document setting out the many reasons why the third development application was untenable and had to be rejected. These included the following: creeping development, the noise impact, the impassability of the footpaths, traffic congestion, and parking issues. But the main issue they raised was noncompliance with regulations. For example, the existing two-story building was already higher than the maximum permitted on either of the two streets, and its current floor-to-space ratio far exceeded the allowable maximum, never mind the proposed three-story building.

The neighbors knew that they had a cast-iron case and that there was no way whatsoever that the local council could possibly approve the third development application. But they were realists, and therefore they knew with absolute and total certainty that the council would give the application the green light. They also knew that the resulting structure wouldn't merely consist of a third story added to the main building of Pekić's palace. And finally, they knew that once again their protests would lead nowhere.

In their anger and frustration, they held a meeting the night before the Zongiri Council, the local body responsible for Willowbrook, was due to consider Pekić's proposal. Tempers rose. The chair of the meeting, Pekić's next-door neighbor Geoffrey Wigram, was unable to calm his friends and neighbors. In fact, he became equally inflamed, and finally shouted out: "If that [expletive deleted] Pekić's development application is approved, I will personally murder him."

The next day, the Zongiri Council approved the development.

Two days later a massive explosion occurred, and Goran Pekić and his bottle shop ceased to exist.

CHAPTER THREE

After drinking a cup of strong coffee that Mrs. Dickenson made for her on our office La Marzocco espresso machine, Mrs. Wigram managed to pull herself together. She told us that she suspected why, some days after the explosion, Detective Inspector Peter Lucas had arrested her husband for the murder of Goran Pekić. "As I told you, Geoffrey publicly said he'd murder Goran. Also, a bomb killed Goran, and Geoffrey is a mining engineer with access to explosives of all kinds. And finally, as Goran's next-door neighbors we were the people that Goran's commercial enterprises affected the most."

She went on to explain the circumstances of the arrest. "Inspector Lucas came to our house in the evening, accompanied by Detective Sergeant Velma Davidson. Geoffrey had just returned from a week at Broken Hill and I'd arrived home five minutes earlier. Inspector Lucas rang the bell. We invited them in. Inspector Lucas then said that he and Sergeant Davidson would like to ask my husband and me a few questions. Of course we said yes, and the four of us sat down in the lounge room.

"Inspector Lucas opened the proceedings by asking Geoffrey if he could pick his brains as a mining engineer," Mrs. Wigram continued. "Geoffrey readily agreed to this. Lucas then asked him what kind of explosive had been used to blow up the next-door building. Geoffrey said that he had no idea. He explained that he hadn't been there when the blast occurred; in fact, he'd left for Broken Hill the previous morning. Geoffrey then suggested that the police employ a forensic explosives expert to go through the wreckage in the crater and determine what sort of device the perpetrator had used to demolish the building. He stated that Professor Edmund Munk of the Western Australia School of Mines in Kalgoorlie was considered to be a world expert in the field but that Australia's extensive mining industry had bred other authorities who were perhaps equally knowledgeable forensic explosive experts. Lucas just nodded.

"Then he asked Geoffrey what sort of casing would've been used for the bomb. Again Geoffrey pleaded ignorance. Without knowing what kind of explosive had been used, he stated, there was no way he could even hazard a guess as to how it was stored or how it was detonated. Again he suggested that the police should hire a forensic explosives expert to sift through the rubble and find traces of the bomb casing. In fact, once the expert had found a piece of the casing, chemical analysis might well lead to the positive identification of the explosive. Again Inspector Lucas nodded.

"Now Inspector Lucas asked whether a timer could've set off the bomb. Geoffrey replied that a timer of some sort could trigger almost any explosion. He asked if they'd found remnants of a timer in the wreckage. Lucas just grunted.

"Then the inspector's voice took on a nasty tone. 'It may interest you to know,' he said, 'that for the past week we've been sifting and resifting through the rubble of Goran's Bottle Shop for clues. To date we've found nothing that has proved to be the least bit helpful—just pieces of glass, charred crown corks, screw tops, and burnt scraps of cardboard boxes. In other words, the only items we've found in the wreckage are the sorts of thing that would be found in every bottle shop. We've found no trace of any explosive, no hint of any casing, and no vestige of any timer.'

"Then Inspector Lucas went on. 'We called in Professor Munk. He concluded that the explosion was the work of a highly trained explosives expert, someone clever enough to design a bomb that destroyed its own casing, detonator, and timer. Not only are you capable of doing this, you had motive and opportunity. Geoffrey Wigram, I arrest you for the murder of Goran Pekić.'"

Having completed her description of the arrest, Martha Wigram again started to weep copiously.

On hearing this account, Janet threw up her hands in surrender. "In the Greater Manchester Police," she said, "we used clues to determine whom to arrest. Inspector Lucas, however, uses an absence of clues to decide who's responsible for a crime. This is monstrous!"

"What do you mean?" Martha asked through her tears.

"Well, in Manchester we'd arrest a suspect only if there was sufficient evidence to convince us that the suspect was guilty. In this case, there's no evidence whatsoever as to what type of explosive the bomber used or how he or she detonated the explosion. Inspector Lucas seems to think that this absolute lack of evidence proves that your husband was responsible for the blast. This is total rubbish!"

Martha Wigram smiled wanly and continued her story. "After the police took Geoffrey away in handcuffs, I phoned the senior partner in the law firm where I work. He's not a criminal lawyer, but he immediately put me in touch with Arthur Trumble, a top lawyer who handles cases such as Geoffrey's. Now I understand why Mr. Trumble was so angry with the police. He said that he'd go to court as soon as possible to secure my husband's release, even though the police are strongly opposing the bail application. In the meantime, he suggested that I contact a private investigator to find out who killed Goran, because the police clearly aren't up to it."

I didn't know what to say, and Janet was uncharacteristically silent, too. Then she asked Martha if she happened to have Inspector Lucas's card. Martha nodded and shuffled through her large tan handbag, which seemed to contain everything including the proverbial kitchen sink. After a minute or two, she located a card and handed it to Janet.

Janet looked at the card, and her face lit up. "Martha," she said, "You told us that the Inspector's name was Peter Lucas. Actually, it's Petar Lukas. Do you see what that means?"

Because neither Martha nor I had the faintest idea what Janet was getting at, we both just sat there, waiting for her to go on.

"Peter Lucas is a typical English name but Petar Lukas is a Slavic name, probably Serbian."

"And therefore?" I asked.

"Well, Goran Pekić is almost certainly a Serbian name. What we have is a Serb, Pekić, who has a friend in extremely high places in local government. This friend lets Goran ride roughshod over any and all planning regulations and protects him from every consequence of his illegal building activities. And it looks like we have a second Serb, Lukas, who has violated the most fundamental principles of police work by arresting a man who almost certainly is innocent of the murder of the first Serb, Pekić. There's something strange going on here."

Martha Wigram had perked up considerably when she heard Janet describe her husband as "almost certainly innocent."

Janet went on, "Martha, you have three different people working to free your husband. Your lawyer, Arthur Trumble, will undoubtedly use every legal stratagem he can to force the authorities to drop the charges against Geoffrey as soon as possible. And Damon and I will find out if there's some sort of Serbian connection in this case, and if there is, whether that would explain what's going on here. I want you to go home and get some rest. I'm sure that between the three of us we'll succeed in getting your husband out of jail quickly."

We escorted Martha to the door and immediately started to work on the case.

"Can you get me the names of the senior planners who are responsible for Willowbrook?" Janet asked.

"Why don't we just look on the internet?" I suggested.

We found the website of the Zongiri Council, clicked on the planning link, and found a page with four names on it. The senior planner was called Zlatan Narjanović.

"Got it!" Janet crowed. "Zlatan is a Slavic name; you're probably more familiar with the Hungarian equivalent, Zoltán."

I nodded. I was just about to tell her that I'd heard of the Hungarian composer Zoltán Kodály and that I loved watching late-night TV reruns of the old Hollywood movies of Zoltán Korda, especially *Sanders of the River* and *The Four Feathers*, when Janet interrupted me.

"I'm wrong, I'm wrong. Yes, Zlatan is a Slavic name, but it isn't Serbian; it's a Bosnian name, because it's ethnically neutral."

"What on earth are you talking about?" I asked. Perhaps I spoke more rudely that I should have, but Janet was so excited by her discovery that she didn't take umbrage.

"There are three nationalities in Bosnia: Serbs, Croats, and Bosnian Muslims, otherwise known as Bosniaks. The name 'Zlatan' isn't a Serb name, a Croat name, or a Bosniak name; it's just a name. In a part of the world where nationalistic fervor leads all too often to ethnic cleansing or even genocide, giving a boy a neutral name like Zlatan could save his life."

"I still don't see it," I said. "I know that Bosnia and Serbia are neighboring countries, and both were part of the former Yugoslavia. In fact, Bosnia's real name is 'Bosnia and Herzegovina,' but not many Australians call it that. Why is it important that the name 'Zlatan' is Bosnian and not Serbian?"

"One word: Srebrenica."

And the penny dropped. In July 1995, units of the Bosnian Serb Army massacred over eight thousand unarmed Bosniak prisoners in and around the town of Srebrenica in Bosnia. The Secretary-General of the United Nations later described the Srebrenica genocide as the worst crime on European soil since the end of the Second World War.

"Are you saying," I asked Janet, "that senior planner Zlatan Narjanović, Detective Inspector Petar Lukas, and the late Goran Pekić were all somehow involved in the Srebrenica genocide, and that after the Bosnian War they immigrated to Australia, along with many of their fellow countrymen who had nothing whatsoever to do with the massacre?"

"I'm not positive yet, but it would cover all the facts. Suppose that Zlatan Narjanović was somehow complicit in the massacre and that Goran Pekić knew this and blackmailed him. Mrs. Wigram said that there was a rumor that Goran had bribed a high official, but she doubted that he had enough money for that. Instead, what if Goran knew about Zlatan Narjanović's role in the genocide and threatened to report him to the International Criminal Tribunal for the Former Yugoslavia in The Hague? Already over a hundred Serbs, Croats, and Bosniaks, including former generals and prime ministers, have been tried and sentenced for crimes against humanity. The penalty for genocide is a really long prison sentence, sometimes a life term; the Tribunal doesn't hand out light punishments. If I'm right, Goran had an unbreakable hold over Zlatan Narjanović—if that's his real name—and that would explain why Goran could get away with almost anything in the planning or building line."

"And what about Inspector Petar Lukas?" I asked.

"His actions tell me that he wanted the murder case to be 'solved' as quickly and quietly as possible, without anyone uncovering the Srebrenica connection. He wouldn't care if Geoffrey Wigram were subsequently found to be not guilty, or even if the Director of Public Prosecutions insisted on dropping the charge in the first place; the bombing would then just end up in the Cold Case File.

"My guess," Janet continued, "is that Lukas, too, was involved in the genocide, but possibly in a somewhat less reprehensible way than Zlatan Narjanović; perhaps Narjanović gave the orders, and Lukas helped to carry them out. I don't think Petar Lukas fears the Tribunal, but if his role in the massacre were to be exposed, he'd surely be deported from Australia to Bosnia, where he'd face a decidedly unpleasant future in a Bosnian jail."

"And how do you propose to verify your hypothesis?"

"It's very simple. I'll send photographs of Petar Lukas and Zlatan Narjanović to the Tribunal and ask their investigators to determine whether Lukas and Narjanović were complicit in the genocide. And even though he's dead, I'll also send a photograph of

Goran Pekić, because we need to know his role, too. It shouldn't take too long to get a response."

Janet contacted *The Upper North Shore Reporter*, the free weekly paper in which Martha Wigram had seen our advertisement, and asked the photography editor if she had pictures of Goran Pekić, Petar Lukas, and Zlatan Narjanović. For obvious reasons, there were many pictures of Pekić on file. The editor also had a shot of Lukas taken at the crime scene on Queen Maude Avenue and one of Narjanović taken at a Zongiri Council meeting. And she declared that the free newspaper would be delighted to sell Janet a copy of each photo for an exorbitant fee.

Janet emailed the photographs to The Hague, and within two days she had a reply: Zlatan Narjanović had been positively identified as a unit commander who called himself Major Falcon, who was wanted for war crimes and crimes against humanity for complicity in ordering the massacre at Srebrenica. Furthermore, there was ironclad evidence that Petar Lukas had indeed taken an active role in the Srebrenica genocide, being personally responsible for the shooting of dozens of unarmed Bosniak men and boys. The photograph of Goran Pekić didn't match that of any known participants in the massacre. However, it was still possible that Pekić had been at Srebrenica but that none of the survivors had seen him there.

At this point, the case was taken out of our hands. The Court in The Hague contacted the Australian Department of Foreign Affairs and Trade. Petar Lukas and Zlatan Narjanović were arrested within twenty-four hours, and Geoffrey Wigram was released a day after that. A few weeks later Lukas was deported to Bosnia to face trial there, and Narjanović found himself imprisoned in a cell in The Hague, awaiting trial on charges of genocide and crimes against humanity.

That was the good news. The bad news was there was still a dark cloud of suspicion hanging over Geoffrey Wigram's head; no matter what anyone said, the facts were that he had the opportunity, he had the motive, and he had the skill to murder Goran Pekić. In addition, no one had yet solved the murder of Goran Pekić. As private investigators extraordinaire, Janet and I now took it upon ourselves to find the real killer.

CHAPTER FOUR

The initial step in solving a murder, Janet explained to me, is almost always to visit the scene of the crime. Even though she now possessed a driver's license, we quickly discovered that having permission to drive a car didn't solve the problem of finding somewhere to park it once we'd arrived at our destination. We decided that the best way to cope with the chronic shortage of parking places in Sydney was to ask Bruce to stay on as our driver, and the following day I asked him to drive us to Willowbrook.

We travelled across the Sydney Harbour Bridge from Millers Point in The Rocks area to Milsons Point on the Lower North Shore. From there I suggested to our driver that we take the Pacific Highway. Bruce politely reminded me that the Pacific Highway— known in these parts as the Horrific Highway—is a dense, overgrown, concrete jungle of endless traffic lights with the occasional brief clearing booby-trapped with a viper's nest of speed cameras, but I felt that Janet needed to experience the contrast between the Pacific Highway and the rest of the glorious North Shore. Nearly an hour later I apologized to Bruce for disregarding his advice as we finally left the Pacific Highway and drove into Willowbrook.

If I had to describe Sydney's North Shore in just one word, I'd have to say: verdant and lush. Yes, I know that's three words, but the sheer beauty of the area cannot possibly be crammed into just one. There are green spaces all over the place, including forests, nature reserves, and national parks; and many of the streets are lined with huge shade trees. Householders take great pride in their gardens; large colorful flowerbeds surround even the apartment buildings. Several areas of the Upper North Shore are exceptionally lovely, but none have the genuine charm of Willowbrook. From the time it was founded in 1894, its residents have striven to turn Willowbrook into a model garden suburb.

As we neared the corner of Queen Maude Avenue and Haversham Lane, the trees were suddenly transformed from umbrageous green giants into stunted, sharp black spikes. We could drive no further. The police had erected a barrier across the roadway because the explosion had propelled several pieces of Pekić's building into the street, and the crime investigators had still not completed their work there. We got out of the car only to find that the police had cordoned off the whole area with endless lines of yellow and black tape; we couldn't possibly get anywhere close to the scene of the crime. From where we stood, we could see a crater, presumably the site of the blast itself. Tall piles of debris surrounded it on all sides.

I pointed out to Janet that, fortunately, the major thrust of the explosion seemed to have been upwards rather than outwards; the surrounding houses didn't seem to have been damaged.

"I'm sure that the shock wave broke numerous windows," she said, "but glass is quick and easy to replace. Nevertheless, you're right; there doesn't seem to have been much structural damage to the neighboring properties."

We walked around the perimeter of the restricted area. Goran's Bottle Shop looked the same from all angles: just a pile of rubble. The only insight into the crime that we could glean was that the explosion had been enormous; the perpetrators had clearly wanted to ensure that Goran and his bottle shop would be reduced to fragments.

I suggested to Janet that we interview the neighbors. Her reaction surprised me.

"Thanks to Colonel Herbert Waterfinger, the head of SLED, we certainly are licensed investigators. But we don't have a client."

"Isn't Martha Wigram our client?" I asked.

"No longer. She engaged us to get her husband released from prison. But once he was out, thanks to us, that was that. Our contract with her came to an end."

"But, as you said, we're investigators. Surely we can investigate?"

"Not without a client," Janet explained. "Our current status is inquisitive busybodies or, as you Aussies say, stickybeaks. We certainly don't want to get on the wrong side of the Australian authorities and possibly even lose our licenses."

I reactivated the cells in the lawyer part of my brain, dormant for the past three or four years, and came up with an idea. "Can't we go back to the Wigrams and ask them to hire us, for a nominal fee of one dollar, this time to find the actual murderer?"

"Now that's a good idea. Let's go around to their house. Martha is surely at her law office, but Geoffrey may not yet have resumed his work at Broken Hill."

We walked to the Wigram's bungalow and I pressed the bell. A clanging echoed through the house but no one came to the door. I tried again, with the same futile result. Geoffrey wasn't home.

And that was that. Frustrated by our inability to get close to the crime scene and barred from interviewing the neighbors, we stayed on the North Shore and treated ourselves to lunch at George of Lane Cove, one of Sydney's finest seafood restaurants.

"What's good to eat here?" Janet asked.

"Their speciality is grilled Moreton Bay bugs."

Janet didn't look at all happy. "I didn't come here to eat insects."

"Sorry, I forgot you've been in Sydney for only a short time. The official name of the shellfish is 'flathead lobster.' They catch them in Moreton Bay, in Queensland, hence the Australian name. If you like lobster, you'll love the bugs."

And over plates of wild Moreton Bay bugs, we analyzed the murder of Goran Pekić as methodically as we could.

"Who wanted to kill him?" I asked, and then proceeded to answer my own question. "It seems to me that there are two lines we could pursue: The Willowbrook angle and the Bosnian angle."

Seeing that Janet was too intimately involved with eating her flathead lobsters to respond, I continued. "Every man and woman in Willowbrook hated Goran for destroying the residential nature of their suburb. I'd imagine that those who lived closer to his establishments on the corner of Queen Maude Avenue and Haversham Lane would have the strongest motive, but it's quite possible that a quiet man leading a quiet life on a quiet back street of Willowbrook suddenly snapped and decided to murder Goran."

Not even a plate of grilled wild Moreton Bay bugs with garlic butter could suppress Janet's detective instinct. Spurred into speech, she said, "Are you telling me that this hypothetical quiet man of yours had the necessary knowledge to construct a bomb that exploded in such a way that it left no trace of its casing, detonator, or timer? I doubt it. It would take a mining engineer like Geoffrey Wigram to build such a device, and even he might not have the necessary skills." And with that, she returned to her bugs.

"I'm sure that the police are investigating the explosives knowledge of every inhabitant of Willowbrook."

"Well, that's what they tried before, and that's why they arrested Geoffrey Wigram," Janet said.

"Actually, that's a slight misstatement of the facts, but never mind. What about the Bosnian angle?"

"That's somewhat trickier," Janet said. "We're still not sure exactly what part, if any, Pekić played in the Srebrenica massacre. Suppose that Pekić knew that Zlatan Narjanović gave the orders to kill the Bosniak prisoners. And suppose further that the reason Pekić was aware of Zlatan's role was because he was there and participated in the genocide. In that case, every Bosnian Muslim living in Sydney would have a motive to kill Pekić. But why am I restricting myself to Sydney? If Pekić was a war criminal, every Bosniak anywhere in the world with a family member who was mercilessly slaughtered at Srebrenica would also want to blow Pekić up. And if such a person had fought in the Bosnian War, he might well have a knowledge of explosives."

"Agreed," I said, "But you've overlooked another angle. Even if Pekić wasn't involved in the Srebrenica massacre, he could still have learned, perhaps by accident, that Zlatan Narjanović had been Major Falcon, a wanted war criminal. Perhaps Zlatan had reached his limit and wasn't prepared to allow Goran Pekić to blackmail him any longer, and therefore he arranged for someone to kill Goran. Zlatan must've realized that he might well be considered a prime suspect. To protect himself, he could've contacted a former member of his unit in the Bosnian Serb Army and flown him to Sydney to murder Pekić. If that's indeed what happened, the actual murderer is surely safely back home in Bosnia and the man who commissioned the murder is locked up in The Hague. And we're no better off if Zlatan Narjanović himself constructed and planted the bomb, because he'll spend the rest of his life in jail in Europe and the murder will be filed as 'unsolved,' with Geoffrey living under a perpetual cloud of suspicion."

"What you're saying," Janet replied, "is that our list of possible suspects includes everyone who lives or has ever lived in Willowbrook who has a knowledge of explosives, plus every Bosniak and every Bosnian Serb now living anywhere in the world with that knowledge. But why restrict ourselves to such a small number of suspects? There were also foreign participants in the Bosnian War: Serbians, Montenegrins, and even Americans. In fact, I wouldn't be in the least bit surprised to learn that some of my fellow British citizens fought on both sides of the conflict."

She finished her glass of Pierro Margaret River Chardonnay and continued. "I think the best way to find the murderer would be to fly to Bosnia and talk to participants in the 1995 War. However, there are two obstacles to that plan. Neither of us speaks Serbo-Croatian, and the locals are unlikely to divulge too much to an Australian and a British detective and their interpreter. More importantly, asking questions about the Srebrenica massacre is unlikely to endear us to many people. In fact, there's a distinct likelihood that something really, really unpleasant will happen to us, along the lines of what happened to Goran Pekić.

"In my opinion," Janet concluded, "This is a job for the police. There's no way that the two of us could possibly find the murderer."

"Could we collaborate with the police?" I asked. "In this morning's *New South Wales Daily* there was a short interview with a Detective Chief Inspector named Walter Tregethick who now leads the investigation."

"I doubt if the New South Wales Police Force would be prepared to work with us," Janet said. "We showed up Petar Lukas as a rogue cop. Speaking as a former police officer, many police officers tend to say nothing about a colleague's misconduct or crimes, even if he or she is an exceptionally evil person; we call it the Blue Code of Silence. Also, our investigation made the police look foolish; it'll be a long time before they forget the editorial in *The New South Wales Daily* that castigated the police for arresting Geoffrey Wigram because there was no evidence. No, I think we should drop the whole thing."

I felt bad for Geoffrey and Martha Wigram, but there was nothing I could do without Janet's whole-hearted collaboration; on my own, I was useless. I decided to console myself with a nice dessert. When the waiter came around with the menus, I suggested to Janet that we try the Crêpe Suzette, accompanied by a bottle of champagne, the 1990 Krug Clos du Mesnil.

I'm not sure whether the waiter handled the bottle too roughly or if he simply had no idea how to open a bottle of vintage champagne. Whatever the reason, there was a loud pop followed by a crack as the cork flew off the top of the bottle and into the ceiling, succeeded by a hissing noise as champagne bubbled out of the bottle onto the floor. The waiter was most apologetic, and Janet wasn't too happy at the waste of the golden liquid. I was about to say something inexcusably tactless to the waiter that undoubtedly would've upset him and certainly spoiled the whole mood of the delightful lunch, when I suddenly realized how Goran Pekić was killed.

Before I could say anything, however, the maître d' wheeled the Crêpe Suzette cart to the table. I didn't want to spoil Janet's pleasure. Rather, I exercised the most unexpected self-control and kept silent while he prepared the sauce in the chafing dish, added the crêpes, then ignited the Grand Marnier and served the dish with the blue flames still flickering. Janet then ate every morsel on her plate and finished her share of the Krug. She looked supremely content.

While all this was going on, I ate my dessert and drank my champagne without tasting anything at all. My blood pressure was rising dangerously, my equanimity was falling rapidly, but there was no way I'd interrupt my best friend Janet's gastronomic orgy by discussing something as mundane as murder.

Eventually, she sat back in her chair with a beatific smile on her face. Now was the time for my moment of triumph.

"Janet," I said, "I think I know how Goran Pekić was killed."

In her eyes I could see the conflict between her two great interests: detection and food. Detection won. The smile slowly disappeared, and she raised one eyebrow interrogatively.

"Do you remember what the police found in the ruins?" I asked. "There were burnt remnants of glass, screw tops, crown corks, and cardboard, and that was all."

"And what does that tell you?"

"What if the explosive was in a wine bottle? That would explain why they haven't found any other evidence. When Pekić opened the bottle, the liquid explosive was exposed to air and the bomb went off."

"Wait a minute," Janet said. "What's the name of this liquid explosive that ignites on contact with air?"

"I've no idea, but there must be such a thing, otherwise my explanation would be wrong."

Janet laughed convulsively; I began to wonder if she'd ever be able to stop. Then she took out her iPhone, accessed the internet, and typed the phrase *liquid explosive* into the Wikipedia search box. She read for few seconds, and while still smiling at my remark, she asked, "What's a hypergolic liquid?"

"I don't have a clue," I said. "Just click on the link, and we'll find out."

The broad grin on Janet's face disappeared in a flash as she read out the sentence: "Although not hypergolic in the strict sense (but rather pyrophoric), triethylborane, which ignites spontaneously in the presence of air—"

She paused. Then she smiled again and said, "Well, Damon, you were quite right, there's at least one liquid explosive that ignites on contact with air."

I smiled modestly. But we both knew that my idea was due to the waiter's clumsy handling of the bottle of vintage Krug rather than any deep thinking on my part. And it was also thanks to my readiness, without the slightest prior knowledge, to hypothesize the existence of a liquid that explodes as soon as it's exposed to air.

"So," Janet said, "one possibility is that the murderer handed Pekić a wine bottle that contained triethylborane. If that's what happened, the next step would be for us to find out who gave the bottle to him. How do you propose to accomplish that?"

I thought for a minute. "If the murderer handed the bottle to Goran, there was the risk that Goran would invite the killer to drink the wine with him. We know that didn't happen, because the police found the remains of only one body in the ruins. So the murderer must've arranged for someone to deliver the bottle to Goran. We'd have to go through all the relevant delivery records for the period to find the killer.

"Janet," I went on, "you no longer work for the Greater Manchester Police. Using forensic evidence to determine whether the killer used triethylborane is definitely a job for the New South Wales Police Force, not us. And we can't possibly check thousands of delivery records. Tomorrow morning we'll go and see Inspector Tregethick, tell him about triethylborane, and then leave him to solve the case.

"By the way, what does *pyrophoric* mean?"

CHAPTER FIVE

The next morning, a uniformed constable escorted us into Detective Chief Inspector Walter Tregethick's office at New South Wales Police Force headquarters at 1 Charles Street, Parramatta. It was a case of déjà vu all over again; I felt that I'd seen Tregethick before. Then I realized why. Walter Tregethick looked just like the cricketers you see in those old sepia-colored photographs of Australian cricket teams of the 1880s and 1890s. He was tall, with longish black hair parted in the middle and cut symmetrically to the same length on both sides. He had a black chevron moustache. And his face was exactly like the faces in those old team photographs: altogether serious, unsmiling, and wooden.

Tregethick's unfriendliness was palpable. He didn't shake hands with us. He reluctantly invited us to take a seat on the opposite side of his desk, settled himself into a worn leather office chair, and said nothing. The silence was deafening. Finally, Janet took the bull by the horns. "We're here because we think we know how Goran Pekić may have been murdered."

"Oh? And how was that?"

"A wine bottle was delivered to him. Only the bottle didn't contain wine, it contained triethylborane. And when Goran opened the bottle, the triethylborane was exposed to the air and exploded, killing Goran and destroying the building. That was why you didn't find a bomb casing or timer; the explosive device consisted of a glass bottle containing triethylborane and its screw top, and that's all."

Janet's brief explanation was met with further silence.

Tregethick finally spoke again. "And why do you think that someone may have murdered him that way?"

"It's the only explanation we can find that fits the facts," Janet said.

Silence descended again, for much longer than before. Then Detective Chief Inspector Tregethick turned to Janet. "And how do you spell that explosive liquid?"

Tregethick slowly wrote the name on a small pad in front of him, in meticulously formed block capitals, using an old-fashioned fountain pen. Then he picked up the phone on his desk and pressed a red button. "Paula? Get me Professor Edmund Munk on the phone. Yes, he's in Kalgoorlie."

After a wait of about forty-five seconds, Tregethick spoke again. "Professor? It's Tregethick in Sydney. Look, I've got two people here who claim that Pekić may have been killed when he opened a wine bottle containing triethylborane. Is that possible?"

There was yet another long silence while Detective Chief Inspector Tregethick listened to Professor Munk. Then he asked, "And is there a more powerful explosive of that class?" Finally, he thanked the academic and hung up the phone.

He turned to Janet. "There's a problem with your explanation. There's no question that if Goran had opened a wine bottle containing triethylborane it would've killed him immediately, but the resulting damage to Goran's Bottle Shop would've been a lot less extensive than what actually occurred. Professor Munk told me that he doesn't know of a liquid similar to triethylborane that packs a larger punch. That tells me that a bottle of liquid explosive wouldn't have been enough to demolish the building.

"However, Munk did say that a bottle of triethylborane might've been the fuse for setting off a larger bomb. But where's your evidence for this larger device?"

From the time we'd walked into his office, Tregethick had completely ignored me. Now I spoke up. "Detective Chief Inspector, what if someone delivered a case of wine bottles to Goran, with all twelve bottles containing triethylborane. Would that have been enough to destroy the whole building?"

Tregethick once more ignored me, picked up his phone, pressed the red button, and instructed the unseen Paula to put him through to Professor Munk again. This time the conversation was much briefer. After he'd put down the phone, Tregethick turned to me. "Munk says that a dozen bottles of triethylborane would do it." And for the first time, there was an absence of coldness in the Detective Chief Inspector's voice.

I was going to ask Tregethick, *And where do we go to from here?*

But I realized that he'd say something like, We *are not going anywhere from here; this is a job for the police.*

For once having thought before I spoke, I said nothing, and again a thick cloak of silence enveloped the three of us.

It seemed that Tregethick was about to tell us that the interview was over. By showing up Petar Lukas as a rogue cop, we'd apparently permanently damaged relations between the New South Wales constabulary and ourselves. But then Tregethick seemed to realize that we were more use to him as collaborators than enemies. He smiled briefly. His smile instantly destroyed his resemblance to a cricketer from the Victorian Age and started to create a bond between us. Janet and I smiled back.

"And where do we go to from here?" Detective Chief Inspector Walter Tregethick asked. He suggested that we discuss the case over a cup of coffee. Disdaining the liquid served at police headquarters, he took us to a nearby café overlooking the Parramatta ferry wharf. A RiverCat ferry was just leaving, the catamaran crammed with tourists from East Asia looking forward to the hour-long ride to Circular Quay down the photogenic Parramatta River.

When the waiter had brought our coffees to our table, Walter Tregethick spoke. "And suppose you wanted to deliver a case of wine bottles containing triethylborane to Goran's Bottle Shop. How would you go about it?"

"There's no problem there," I said. "Wine wholesalers surely deliver wine to every bottle shop all the time."

"And how would you get the explosive inside the bottles?" Walter asked.

I thought for a few moments. "I take your point," I said. "Goran would've been suspicious unless the cardboard case looked genuine and unless the bottles inside the case appeared to be genuine bottles of wine. In addition, you have to know what you're doing when you play around with triethylborane. Furthermore, there can be no air whatsoever in the bottle. On the other hand, if Goran had noticed that the wine bottles were filled to the very top, with no air gap at all, he might've become suspicious. That means that the bomb maker had to be able to introduce an inert gas like argon into the bottles of triethylborane. I'm no chemist, but it seems to me that the person who made the bottle bombs had to be an explosives expert with specialized proficiency in dealing with pyrophoric liquids, that is, liquids that ignite spontaneously when exposed to air. And he or she also had to be able to work with argon gas. We're dealing with an extremely knowledgeable and competent explosives expert."

"We need to ask Professor Munk whether participants in the Bosnian War might've acquired these skills," Janet added. "Personally, I've never heard of anyone using triethylborane for military purposes. But then again, until last night I hadn't even heard of triethylborane. Come to think of it, warfare is dangerous enough without having to deal with the hazards of pyrophoric liquids. My guess is that we can ignore the Bosnian connection, at least for now. This bomb seems to have been an extremely specialized type of explosive device; if we can find the bomb maker, we can probably find the murderer."

"Just what do we know about triethylborane?" I asked. "Can you buy it in shops? Is it used for farming or manufacturing or something? We need to know a lot more about triethylborane before we can find the explosives expert. Walter, do you have a contact in a university chemistry department who can help us?"

"Professor Messmer has assisted the police in the past. If you've finished your coffee, let's go back to my office and we can talk to her on speaker."

We walked back to Police Headquarters. Walter asked the still unseen Paula to phone Professor Messmer at Macquarie University. A minute or two later, we heard a jolly voice with a heavy German accent asking, "Juliana Messmer here. How can I assist you?"

Walter explained the purpose of our call.

"*Ach ja*, I can certainly help you," Professor Messmer said. "Triethylborane is used in rockets to ignite the fuel. If, as you say, triethylborane was used to commit a crime, you need to look for a rocket scientist. Houston, we have a problem!"

"And what about argon gas? How hard is it to work with argon?" Walter asked.

"It's extremely easy because argon is almost totally inert. All you need to do is buy a cylinder of argon. And that's easy. Argon is used in some fire extinguishers, in many industrial processes, it's even used to slaughter chickens. The hard part is handling the triethylborane. Argon gas is no big deal; you might even say it's not rocket science!" And with a loud peal of girlish laughter, Professor Messmer terminated the conversation.

"What she's saying," Janet said, with a heavy dose of sarcasm in her voice, "is that all we have to do now is arrest every rocket scientist living in Willowbrook."

"That's not funny," I insisted. "We're dealing with a murderer with no conscience. It was extremely lucky that the bomb exploded at about a quarter past three in the afternoon, when Goran was the only person inside the main building. The lunch rush at the café was over and the afternoon tea drinkers hadn't arrived yet. Mrs. Pekić and the café staff were sitting outside at a table on the footpath, relaxing in the sun for a few minutes. We've seen the scale of the explosion; it was horrendous. By some miracle, no one other than Pekić was hurt. But if the triethylborane had gone off at, say, lunchtime, it would've been a different story entirely."

"I'll get one team to scour Willowbrook for rocket scientists, chemists, and explosives experts," Walter said. "And there's another important line of inquiry we need to pursue: how was the case of wine bottles delivered? Damon, I'm inclined to reject your suggestion that the case came from a wine wholesaler. The murderer had to ensure that Goran opened one of the bottles of triethylborane. It seems to me that if a wholesaler delivered a case of wine bottles to Goran's Bottle Shop he'd just unpack the case and put the dozen bottles on a shelf, just as he presumably did with every other case of wine that wholesalers delivered to his bottle shop.

"My guess is that a courier service like Federal Express or DHL or perhaps the Australian Post Office delivered the case, addressed to Goran Pekić personally. After all, Australians order tens of thousands of cases of wine over the internet every year, perhaps hundreds of thousands. Provided that the case containing the dozen bottles of triethylborane looked on the outside like a regular case of wine, a courier would've delivered it in the usual way. I'll get another police team to find all deliveries to Goran's premises for the week preceding the explosion. When we find who made the delivery, we can determine who sent the case. That should lead directly to the murderer."

"Is there anything we can do?" I asked.

"You've been tremendously helpful already," Walter said. "You located a wanted war criminal as well as a Bosnian Serb who'll stand trial in Bosnia for murdering Bosniak prisoners. You also suggested that triethylborane was the explosive used and that a dozen bottles of the liquid were utilized. I'll concede that we haven't yet found any traces of triethylborane, but the concept of an explosive pyrophoric liquid seems to fit the facts as we know them. Thank you very much for all you've done. But what we need now is monotonous, methodical police work. We need large numbers of men and women to contact every courier service in Australia; your outstanding detective skills would be wasted on such a task. I suggest you leave the case with me and I'll contact you as soon as we get our hands on some solid evidence."

Walter's encomium was a major improvement on the icy reception we'd received earlier that morning and boded well for future cooperation with the police, not just in this case, but also in future cases. Feeling that we'd indeed accomplished something, we asked Bruce to return us to downtown Sydney.

CHAPTER SIX

Aweek went by without our hearing anything from Detective Chief Inspector Walter Tregethick. I wanted to phone him, but Janet counseled patience.

"If Walter has any information," Janet assured me, "he'll undoubtedly get in touch with us. And he certainly doesn't seem to be the kind of person who enjoys being nagged."

After another week had gone by and we'd still heard nothing from the New South Wales Police Force, Janet reluctantly agreed to telephone Walter.

"We're at a dead end," Walter told the two of us over speakerphone. "We contacted every courier service in Australia. We went back a week but no one delivered a case of wine bottles addressed to Goran Pekić. Then we went back a further three months but with the same negative result.

"We contacted the various wine wholesalers. Together they deliver nearly a hundred of cases of wine every week to Goran's Bottle Shop. Not surprisingly, they're all positive that every drop of wine they've ever delivered to the bottle shop was the real McCoy, and they insist that they've never sent anything to Pekić in his personal capacity.

"Eventually, in desperation, we approached all two thousand, five hundred commercial wine producers, as well as the many companies that ship wine by mail. Again we found nothing.

"It's absolutely frustrating. The only hypothesis that fits all the facts is that Pekić himself received a case of wine bottles that contained triethylborane. But no wine organization has sent a case to Goran and no delivery organization has delivered a case to him. We're almost at the point at which we're going to have to abandon the whole investigation."

This was extremely disconcerting. Janet and I were certain that we'd cracked the case, but there were no facts whatsoever to back up our theory. I suggested to her that we visit our favorite pastry shop, located in the suburb of Putney, and console ourselves that way.

Janet immediately agreed. I summoned our driver. When Bruce texted me to say he was outside our building, we said goodbye to Mrs. Dickenson, and I opened the door to the corridor. There I encountered a courier carrying a case of wine.

"The office next door is locked," he informed me. "Could I please leave this case of wine with you? Would you mind signing for it and, when they come back, telling them that you have it for them?"

Instead of responding to the courier, I turned to Janet and shouted, "I've got it! I know what happened to the wine!"

The courier, a young man wearing a bright orange high-visibility polo shirt and blue jeans, his hair in a ponytail, was taken aback. He didn't know whether to leave the wine in our office or try to find someone more co-operative than I appeared to be. Seeing him waiver, I told him to leave the case of wine with Mrs. Dickenson. I asked her to sign the receipt and then leave a note for the intended recipients in the next office.

Turning to Janet, I said, "We're off to see Walter again."

I phoned Walter's office and fortunately he was there. I told him we'd be at his office on Charles Street in about forty-five minutes. We got into the car, and I asked Bruce to go to Parramatta, not Putney. Our driver is used to my ways and didn't comment on the sudden change of plan.

As we entered the car, Janet stated that even though she was bursting with curiosity she viewed Walter as an equal member of our team and she felt it would be more appropriate for me to reveal my discovery to her and Walter at the same time. I wasn't too happy with that, but I saw her point and I held my peace once again.

When we were seated in his office, I turned to Walter. "Have you ever ordered wine over the internet?" I asked him.

"Certainly," he said. "And just about everyone I know has also done that. It's generally cheaper than going to a bottle shop. And what with the appalling traffic congestion in Sydney—it took you nearly an hour and a half to drive the fifteen miles from your office to mine—and the abysmal lack of parking, having your vino delivered is definitely more convenient. And it's often the only way to lay your hands on certain wines in short supply."

"And are you always home when they deliver your wine?" I asked.

"No, I'm never there. They deliver wine on weekdays during normal working hours, when I'm here at the office or at a crime scene."

"Then how do you get your wine?" I continued.

"Well, it would be a truly bad idea if the delivery person left the case at the front door. Petty theft isn't a really big thing here, but no one but a certifiably insane fruit loop would leave a case of wine unattended on a doorstep anywhere in Australia, let alone without a signature."

"And therefore?" I prompted.

"And therefore the courier leaves the case with a neighbor who's at home and can sign for it. The neighbor phones me in the evening, and I go to their house and pick up my wine."

"Exactly!" I said. "Goran Pekić was an all-round nogoodnik and everyone hated him. As a result, we've been assuming that the killer intended the exploding wine for him. But what if the murderer actually intended the bottles of triethylborane for someone else, a Willowbrook resident who was at work, and the courier delivered the case to Goran because he knew that there'd be someone in Goran's Bottle Shop who could sign for it? My theory is that Goran decided to keep the case for a couple of weeks without informing the owner. And if no one came to claim the wine after that time, I've no doubt that Goran would drink it himself. But when he opened the case and took out a bottle to sample the vino, he signed and sealed his own death warrant.

"I'll bet," I continued, "there's no Bosnian connection of any kind. It's certainly true we unmasked two Srebrenica murderers, and almost certainly a blackmailer as well, as a consequence of our investigating the explosion. But my guess is that none of that had anything to do with the bomb itself. Goran Pekić took the case of explosive liquid from the courier and signed for it. If only he'd been a nicer person, eventually he would've contacted the real recipient, who would've picked it up. But Goran was, among many other unpleasant things, a thief. He decided to hold onto the delivery, and the whole thing blew up in his face, pun intended.

"Walter, I suggest that you tell your team to contact the courier services again. But this time ask them about a case of wine bottles delivered about two weeks before the explosion, addressed to a home within five hundred yards of Goran's Bottle Shop, probably a home on Queen Maude Avenue or Haversham Lane."

Neither Janet nor Walter said a word. Notwithstanding their collective experience as detectives and their many professional successes, my latest theory had bewildered them. Whether it was because I'd suggested that the Srebrenica genocide was now a red herring or whether my claim that Goran Pekić was a not-so-innocent bystander rather than the intended murder victim had stunned them, they both seemed reluctant to respond.

After a long silence, Walter spoke up. "Leave it with me. If you're right, we should have an answer within twenty-four hours." We all shook hands, and Janet and I left Walter's office. Bruce drove us from Parramatta to Putney Pastry Paradise, where Janet and I each chose a pastry and slowly savored it.

***

The next morning, Janet and I arrived at work before Mrs. Dickenson. We were both relieved to see that the case of wine was no longer in her office; to us, a case of wine now meant nothing but big trouble.

We sat down at our respective desks. Two minutes later Detective Chief Inspector Tregethick called me on my iPhone; he sounded excited.

"Damon, please put Janet on speakerphone."

I pressed the correct button.

"Damon, you were 100 percent right. Fifteen days before the explosion, a case of a dozen bottles was sent from Port Botany Imported Wines to an address in Queen Maude Street, four or five houses away from Goran's Bottle Shop."

I smiled and waited for Walter to continue.

"The courier service was La Perouse Delivery Service, a small company that handles deliveries within the greater Sydney area for businesses in the vicinity of Port Botany, including Port Botany Imported Wines. The signature we retrieved from the courier's hand-held delivery device is illegible, but it certainly doesn't correspond in any way to the neat signature of the intended recipient."

"And who was the addressee?"

"I'm afraid I can't tell you that; as I'm sure you know, we have strict confidentiality rules in this country. But I can tell you that the case is getting exceedingly complex. I contacted the local area commander at Port Botany police station, and she told me that the Sydney drug squad is extremely interested in Port Botany Imported Wines. At one stage, they were convinced that the Italian Mafia was sending cocaine to Port Botany Imported Wines together with their shipments from Italian wineries. The drug squad searched every inch of the last two containers that Port Botany Imported Wines received but to no avail. They just can't work out how the cocaine gets from Italy to Sydney. A month ago, the drug squad caught a known druggie in Newtown trying to sell cocaine that they suspect came from Port Botany Imported Wines. However, the druggie isn't talking, and there's no way of tying the cocaine to Port Botany Imported Wines. All in all, it's a most unsatisfactory state of affairs.

"And now for some really interesting news. Two days ago, yet another Italian wine shipment consigned to Port Botany Imported Wines arrived in the port. The drug squad and customs agents went through the container with a fine-toothed comb, but with the usual outcome: bupkis. They were resigned to releasing the shipment today.

"But with the latest information connecting Port Botany Imported Wines to the murder at Goran's Bottle Shop, we've been able to get a search warrant for the Port Botany Imported Wines warehouse. The duty magistrate asked one or two routine questions, but then signed the warrant without further ado— quite unlike her usual behavior.

"That means that the container will be released at once. If it's picked up this morning, we'll raid the premises this evening. We hope we'll find cocaine.

Even better, we hope we'll find the solution to the Willowbrook mystery."

The idea of taking part in the police raid really appealed to me, and I was sure that Janet, as a former police officer, would definitely want to participate. I turned to Walter and asked him if Janet and I could come along.

Walter hemmed and hawed. Then he explained there might be gunfire and they didn't have any spare bulletproof vests. Thinking quickly, I asked Walter if we could come if we brought our own bulletproof vests.

More hemming and more hawing. I could imagine what was going on in Walter's mind. On the one hand, Janet and I had definitely contributed more to the case than everyone else put together. On the other hand, the consequences of our being injured or worse, killed, would be really bad for all concerned, but especially for Detective Chief Inspector Walter Tregethick. In the end, Walter relented. We arranged that he'd tell us by four o'clock whether there would be a raid that night. If so, we'd rendezvous at the Port Botany police station at eight.

After lunch, we acquired our bulletproof vests. As a former lawyer, I knew that it's illegal to possess body armor in Australia without prior authorization, but as a sometime successful financial planner I went with Janet to the warehouse of a grateful former client.

And I'm sure that you can work the rest out for yourself.

From there, Bruce drove Janet and me to Black's Hotel in Castlereagh Street for high tea in the main lounge. We were halfway through when Walter phoned to say that the raid was on. The scones they bake at Black's Hotel are the best in New South Wales, especially when topped with their homemade strawberry jam and clotted cream. Usually I take a minimal amount of the clotted cream but, with the raid in our near future, I decided to indulge for once. I was concerned that it might be a while before we had a chance to eat dinner.

Promptly at eight, we presented ourselves at Botany Bay police station, where we were introduced to the members of the raiding party. Then came the final briefing. Everyone else already knew almost all the details of the impending raid. However, that caused no difficulties for us, because Walter turned to Janet and me and unambiguously ordered us to stay put at the police station until the warehouse was wholly under police control.

We had no choice; we had to follow Walter's instructions and sit in the main room while the raiding party left the police station, heading for the warehouse some three blocks away. We heard gunshots, then more gunshots, then silence.

Fifteen minutes later Walter radioed the local area commander, telling her that we could proceed to the

warehouse but under police protection. After
checking that we were wearing our bulletproof vests,
two burly policemen drove us to the building. There
we found about twelve handcuffed men standing
outside; a troop of armed policemen guarded them
vigilantly. A few minutes later they herded the men
into two Black Maria vans and drove them away.

Walter now appeared at the door of the warehouse
and invited us to enter. The building was vast, with
racks reaching from floor to ceiling. There were cases
of wine on almost all the shelves. Some shelves were
packed full of wine, others had just two or three cases.
In addition to the area filled with racks there was a
small office; members of the drug squad were in the
process of thoroughly searching it, accompanied by a
sniffer dog and its handler. Just outside the office
door stood the owner of the company, Gioachino di
Campione, who was exhibiting precisely the right
amount of moral indignation. Walter just glared at
him.

Two hours later, the search was over. The police
had found nothing other than tens of thousands of
bottles of wine, almost all of them imported from
Italy. Gioachino di Campione was still exhibiting
exactly the correct amount of moral indignation, but
Walter was clean out of glares. In fact, Walter looked
utterly beaten.

Then Janet had an idea. She unobtrusively
measured the size of the warehouse, quietly pacing

out its length and its breadth. I think I was the only person who noticed what she was doing. If anyone else had seen her, which I doubt, they probably would've thought that Janet was just pacing up and down from sheer frustration.

Janet then asked Walter if she could go outside. Walter just nodded. Actually, by that time, if Janet had asked Walter if she could sing all 158 verses of *Ymnos eis tin Eleftherian*, the Greek national anthem, while dressed as an elderly moose, Walter would undoubtedly have agreed to that, too.

About three minutes later Janet came back inside, pointed to the wall opposite the front door of the warehouse and emphatically declared, "That's a false wall; there's a room behind there!" Gioachino di Campione stopped exhibiting anything and made a dash for the door. As he reached it, a police sergeant managed to catch him, cuff him, and march him back to Walter.

The owner's attempt to flee was enough to convince the police that Janet was right. They tried to find a door in the false wall but failed. In desperation, Walter contacted the police station again and asked for an axe. A large heavy policeman soon arrived bearing a large heavy axe. Three hefty blows revealed the secret room. Through the hole we could see that it contained all sorts of laboratory equipment.

Walter set up a police guard around the warehouse and ordered the rest of us to go home. Janet and I suddenly realized that, even though it was well after midnight, we hadn't yet eaten dinner. Ravenously hungry, we went to Harry's Café de Wheels, the gourmet pie cart located in Woolloomooloo. We each ate one of Harry's superlative meat pies and shared a custard tart for dessert. Then we shared another one. We slept well.

CHAPTER SEVEN

On our way to the office the next morning, my iPhone rang. It was Walter Tregethick.

"Tonight we're going to raid the house in Queen Maude Avenue, Willowbrook, the one where the wine bomb was supposed to be delivered. Please come to my office at five o'clock. And bring along your bulletproof vests, otherwise we can't take you with us."

I thanked him warmly. He hung up without saying another word.

Needing to fortify myself with lunch, I suggested to Janet that we eat at our favorite Vietnamese restaurant. Our driver was about halfway there when Walter rang again.

"I have some big news for you," he said. "Please put me on speakerphone; I want Janet to hear, too."

I pressed the appropriate button.

Walter then continued, "Even as we speak, the members of a team of forensic chemists are going through the hidden laboratory with a fine-tooth comb. Up to now they've made two interesting discoveries. They found a number of empty bottles of Castello Vecchio Chianti Classico, which they tell me is a truly outstanding Italian wine. The forensic chemists believe that the Italian members of the cocaine-smuggling gang dissolve their cocaine in pure alcohol, adding a water-soluble red dye to give the resulting liquid the color of chianti classico. They then bottle the resulting 'red wine' in dark green glass bottles that seem identical to the real thing. They cork the wine with corks bearing the correct lettering and add labels that seem indistinguishable from those of the authentic Castello Vecchio Chianti Classico. Lastly, on the top of the bottle they fasten a maroon capsule that's precisely the correct shade.

"It seems," he went on, "that the cocaine gang has access to bottle makers, printers, cork manufacturers, and everything else they need to make perfect replicas of bottles of Castello Vecchio Chianti Classico. When the 'red wine' arrives in the hidden laboratory in the warehouse at Port Botany, the alcohol and the red dye are extracted, leaving the white drug, which they then sell on the streets of Sydney. We also found cases of genuine Castello Vecchio Chianti Classico. That means that there must be some sort of mark on the outside of each case to inform the cocaine gang which cases contain bottles of excellent red wine and which contain bottles of cocaine dissolved in alcohol. Our working hypothesis is that the serial numbers on the outside of the case are what the gang uses to distinguish between wine and drugs, but we're not sure about that yet.

"The other interesting discovery consists of two tightly sealed metal cylinders that the forensic chemists believe contain triethylborane, as well as a cylinder of argon gas. They strongly suspect that the twelve wine bottles containing triethylborane were filled in the secret laboratory."

This was indeed "big news." By nightfall the whole case would probably be solved.

For the second time that day, I warmly thanked Walter. I replaced my iPhone in my pocket but quickly retrieved it again. A Vietnamese restaurant was inappropriate under the circumstances. I dialed La Cenerentola, one of Sydney's many excellent Italian restaurants, which happens to be located quite near to the Vietnamese restaurant to which we were headed. We eat at La Cenerentola at least once a week, which is why the restaurant is in my contact favorites.

"La Cenerentola, *buongiorno!*"

I recognized the voice of Massimo, the cellar master.

"*Buongiorno*, Massimo. Do you still have any of that sublime Castello Vecchio Chianti Classico in stock?" I asked.

Massimo recognized my voice in turn. "Yes of course, *Signor* Ogilvy, we have the 2006 vintage. And also, *Signore*, today Carmelo is making your favorite, Fegato di Pollo alla Prodica."

Carmelo, the chef at La Cenerentola, comes from a miniscule hamlet in Sicily called Prodica. Like Mullajumba, the town nearest to my childhood home, Prodica is too small to appear on most maps. Carmelo's secret recipe for chicken livers is beyond compare. Well, you know exactly what happened next. I instructed Bruce to head for La Cenerentola. There we ate a superlative lunch, starting with Carmelo's chicken livers sautéed in Marsala and herbs.

When he served us the 2006 Castello Vecchio Chianti Classico, Massimo went through the whole wine performance. He produced the bottle with a flourish or, rather, a restrained flourish; he didn't want to shake the wine in any way. When I nodded to confirm that this was indeed the bottle I'd ordered, he took it to a side table, produced an old-fashioned corkscrew and carefully drew out the cork, which he solemnly presented to me, saying, "*Il sughero, Signore.*"

I never know what to do when the sommelier presents the cork. In fact, nobody does. Some people sniff the cork the way a pig sniffs for truffles. Some inspect it carefully, with a look of anticipation on their faces as if they firmly expect all the secrets of the universe to be engraved on the cork. My technique is as follows: I solemnly accept the cork and equally solemnly lay it on the table next to my wine glass. Then I solemnly ignore it from then on.

Massimo sniffed the wine and poured a little into his tastevin, the shallow silver cup hanging around his neck on a silver chain. He sniffed the wine again, this time in his tastevin, tasted it, and delicately spat it out into the spittoon on his side table. Having checked the wine, he poured a little into my glass for me to taste.

I solemnly went through all the steps of my highly pretentious swirl-swirl-sniff-taste-savor-swallow act and pronounced the wine perfect. Massimo proceeded to pour two inches of wine into Janet's glass and then into mine, once again with a restrained flourish. For the record, the wine was truly marvelous. I was sorely tempted to order another bottle, but Janet wisely advised moderation.

By five o'clock we were ensconced in Walter's office, bulletproof vests in hand. By six o'clock we were in a room at the rear of a police station in the vicinity of Willowbrook. When the lookout radioed that the subject had arrived home, we put on our body armor and climbed into the back of Walter's car; for some reason, Walter was prepared to let us take part in the second raid.

A procession of five cars arrived at Queen Maude Avenue. A total of twelve policemen surrounded the house. Then Walter, Janet, and I approached the front door. Walter rang the bell. In less than twenty seconds the door opened. There stood Malvina du Plessis, the Roads and Maritime Services poster child for egregious service.

A methodical search of her home yielded about seven hundred grams of cocaine. There was no doubt that she was a member of the cocaine distribution ring while using her RMS position as excellent cover. After all, people supposedly take illegal drugs for pleasure, and pleasure is the very last thing anyone would think of on hearing the phrase *Roads and Maritime Services.*

Detective Chief Inspector Tregethick sat down with Malvina; Janet and I stood inconspicuously at the back of the room. He asked Malvina why the cocaine gang wanted to kill her. From the look on her face, it was obvious that Malvina had no idea what he meant. She said nothing.

Then Tregethick produced a copy of the delivery documentation from La Perouse Delivery Service for a case of wine, addressed to her at her home. He explained that what the cocaine gang had actually sent her was twelve bottles of liquid explosive. The chief inspector then reminded her of what had happened to Goran's Bottle Shop, only a few houses away. Malvina du Plessis turned white, but she still held her silence.

"Why did they want to kill you?" he asked her.

Malvina didn't say a word. And her face was totally expressionless.

"Malvina, we've rounded up about fifteen members of the gang, including Gioachino di Campione, but we're sure that there are more out there. What you're looking at is written proof that they've tried to kill you once, and I've no doubt that the remaining gang members will try again. If you want us to protect you, you'll have to tell us why they sent the wine bomb to you, even if it means incriminating yourself as a drug dealer. It's better to be alive in jail for a few years than dead and buried."

Malvina finally realized that, if she wanted to go on living, she'd better confess everything to Tregethick. She had no negotiating lever for a plea bargain; she had to talk to save her life.

Clearly, she was thinking hard. "I've been a middleman in the cocaine trade for about eighteen months. For the past three months, I've been skimming profits; I didn't share the full agreed percentage of my gains with Gioachino. No one said anything, no one asked me anything, and I assumed that I was getting away with it. It seems to me that the bomb was sent to my house not just to punish me but also to make very sure that, in the future, no one else would dare to cheat Gioachino di Campione.

"You're quite right, Chief Inspector," Malvina added. "Whoever takes over from Gioachino won't rest until I've been killed. And the next time they'll choose a method that couldn't possibly target the wrong person."

She said nothing more after that, not even at her trial.

We had one final interesting development in the case. Walter Tregethick and his team couldn't understand how the cocaine gang could produce such perfect replicas of Castello Vecchio Chianti Classico. After all, the glass bottles, the corks, the labels, and the capsules were absolutely indistinguishable from the real thing. After thinking long and hard, Walter belatedly realized why: They *were* the real thing.

That meant that the cocaine ring owned the Castello Vecchio vineyards, including its bottling plant. Ownership enabled them to produce genuine bottles of truly superb chianti classico, as well as externally identical bottles that contained a solution of cocaine in alcohol, colored to resemble the wine; any slight discrepancy in the shade of red would be masked by the dark green glass bottles. Tregethick contacted the Italian authorities and a raid of the Castello Vecchio winery proved that he was right. In particular, he was delighted that the Italian police found that the person running the enterprise was Claudio di Campione, Gioachino's brother, and they arrested him on the premises.

Martha and Geoffrey Wigram came to our office to thank us. Martha brought a rhubarb and apple pie she'd baked for us that was absolutely delicious. She clearly knew the right way to express her appreciation!

Other than expressing his heartfelt thanks when he came in and again when he left, Geoffrey hardly said a word. I'm not sure if he was still embarrassed that the police had arrested him and thrown him into prison, or if he's just naturally taciturn. Martha, on the other hand, more than made up for her husband. By then, she'd fully recovered from her ordeal and her bubbly personality was at its best.

We spent a pleasant hour going over what had happened. Almost all of what we discussed had already appeared in *The New South Wales Daily,* but rehashing the facts seemed to help the Wigrams return to their pre-explosion marital bliss. Consequently, Janet and I were only too delighted to go through all the details with them.

Later that day, Detective Chief Inspector Walter Tregethick phoned to tell us that, unfortunately, several members of the cocaine ring had escaped to Canada. The news of the raid had somehow spread almost immediately after the round-up at the warehouse in Port Botany. A number of gang members who hadn't been there rushed to Kingsford-Smith International Airport, and the next morning they all took the nonstop Canadian National Airline flight to Vancouver. Walter informed us that the reason they chose Canada is the lack of an extradition treaty between Canada and Australia. However, they'd overlooked the fact that Italy does have an extradition treaty with Canada. As a result of the evidence found in the Castello Vecchio raid, the Mounties apprehended all the gang members who'd fled to Vancouver. Walter hoped that they'd be extradited in due course to Italy, and either stand trial there or here in Australia after a second extradition.

Finally, for some reason, Malvina du Plessis never thanked us for saving her life. The base ingratitude of some people!

CHAPTER EIGHT

The case was over. We decided to celebrate in style, with lunch at La Cenerentola. I called the restaurant to make the reservation. Someone other than Massimo answered the phone and took down our details. I didn't recognize his voice. That was curious, because the staff at La Cenerentola hadn't changed for donkey's yonks, as we say in Australia.

Janet and I arrived promptly at half past twelve and were shown to a table for two in the small back room on the right. A waiter I'd never seen before presented the menus and the wine list. I assumed that he was the person who'd answered the phone and taken our reservation earlier in the day. He looked vaguely familiar, but then I decided that I'd never seen him before. There was no sign of Massimo.

I asked the waiter, "Where's Massimo?"

"I'm not sure, *Signore*," the waiter replied, somewhat evasively.

"Well, ask him to bring us a bottle of the 2000 Santa Augusta Brunello di Montalcino."

There was a longish pause that I didn't comprehend, and then the waiter left the table abruptly. We waited considerably longer than I would've expected. Then Massimo appeared, bearing the bottle of the Brunello di Montalcino that I'd ordered. He was curt to the point of unfriendliness. Massimo brandished the bottle—there was no restrained flourish—to show me the label. He took the bottle to his side table, pulled the cork with his corkscrew, unscrewed the cork from the corkscrew—and put it in his trouser pocket.

I had no idea what was going on. I'd expected Massimo to hand me the cork, with his usual, "*Il sughero, Signore.*" But this time, he'd put it in his pocket. I was utterly baffled.

He sniffed the wine, very gingerly. He didn't pour any into his tastevin, another surprise. Instead, with a shaking hand, he sloshed a quantity into my glass. Was Massimo drunk? Was that why he hadn't taken my wine order? I know that the almost limitless access to free wine that their occupation affords them turns many wine professionals into alcoholics, but I'd not seen the slightest trace of that in Massimo. I really like Massimo, and I was truly upset that he seemed to have started on the downward path to alcohol addiction.

I went through all the steps of my ostentatious swirl-swirl-sniff-taste-savor-swallow performance completely mechanically; my mind was on Massimo. I didn't consciously smell or taste anything. But something was wrong with the wine. A few seconds later, something was wrong with me. The room spun, my vision blurred, my ears pounded in my ears. I heard the word "ambulance" loudly repeated over and over many times as I passed out.

When I woke up, I was lying on a narrow iron bed with a thin horsehair mattress. I looked around. I was in a small windowless room, with nothing on the walls or the ceiling. The floor was cement, the walls cinderblock, the ceiling unfinished. A galvanized iron bucket stood next to the door. Other than the bucket and the bed, the room was empty. A dim light bulb was screwed into a socket in the ceiling but there was no light switch. The metal door had a fisheye peephole. I tried to open the door but, as I suspected, it was firmly locked. I banged on it. Nothing happened. I banged again and again. Eventually I heard a loud metallic click. The door swung open, and there stood the new waiter from La Cenerentola. He still wore his uniform. In his hand he held a pistol. He gesticulated with the handgun to indicate to me to move back onto the bed. Then he shut the door with his left hand.

"Where am I?" I asked, or rather croaked. Something seemed to be seriously wrong with my voice.

He ignored the question. "Good evening, *Signor* Ogilvy. Allow me to introduce myself. I am Ottorino di Campione, the brother of Claudio di Campione and

Gioachino di Campione. Thanks to your meddling, both my brothers are now facing life in prison: Claudio in Italy and Gioachino here in Australia."

"What am I doing here?" I somehow managed to utter.

"You are my hostage. You will be released when Claudio and Gioachino are released."

I hoped that this was just a bad dream.

"How did I get here?"

"We learned that you eat at least once a week at La Cenerentola. We informed the owner that I'd be masquerading as a waiter in his restaurant all day and every day until you arrived. He agreed because he had no choice; had he objected, we would've burned his restaurant to the ground. And we would've burned it with him inside.

"When I started working as a waiter at La Cenerentola," the gunman continued, "Massimo was most unwilling to cooperate with us, until we snatched his wife and four-year old son. Then he changed his tune, I can tell you. Today, when you ordered your wine, I told Massimo to bring me the bottle. I took a hypodermic syringe with a long, thin, sharp needle, filled it with what they call knockout drops, pushed the needle through the cork, and injected the contents into the bottle. I then told Massimo to serve it. He refused. Then I told him, in exquisite detail, exactly what we were going to do to his wife and son unless we had his fullest cooperation. Fortunately for them, he changed his mind.

"He opened the bottle for you without tasting it, for obvious reasons. And he didn't want to show you the cork, just in case you spotted the small hole that the hypodermic needle made at each end. Instead, he put it into his pocket. He poured you some wine, you took a large sip, and that was enough to knock you out.

"We had an ambulance waiting around the corner, or rather, we had a vehicle painted to look like an ambulance. We carried you out of the restaurant and into the 'ambulance' and brought you here."

"Where's 'here'?" I asked. "And what's happened to Janet?"

No reply.

After a pause, I tried again. "How long do you intend to keep me locked up in this room?"

This time the waiter answered me. "It all depends on your good friend, Detective Tregethick. We've told him to fly Claudio to Australia from Italy. Then, we will exchange you for Claudio and Gioachino. The Italian and Australian governments have already agreed to the swap. That means that you'll remain here as a hostage until the exchange takes place. In the meantime, I'll bring you some gourmet Italian food from La Cenerentola."

He turned the knob with his left hand while continuing to point the pistol at me and walked out.

He slammed the metal door, and the lock clicked. Two minutes later he was back with a bottle of water and half a loaf of stale bread. He placed the bottle on the floor at his feet and threw the bread onto the cement floor next to the bucket. He laughed hollowly and then left me alone.

Being imprisoned in the cell was bad enough, but the lack of food drove me to the point of insanity. Every few hours Ottorino refilled the water bottle, and once he emptied the bucket, but I received no more bread. Clearly, Ottorino was punishing me for having his brothers arrested.

My watch had been removed and the dim light burned continuously; it was therefore impossible for me to tell how much time had elapsed. I couldn't take my mind off my hunger. Even sleep was a problem, because I have the greatest difficulty sleeping on an empty stomach. Every second I spent in that cell seemed to be the longest and most unpleasant second in my whole life. I could do nothing but think about food and worry about Janet. Had she drunk any of the doctored wine? And where was she? Was she also a prisoner of Ottorino? And I knew that asking him any questions would be a waste of breath.

After what seemed like a month but turned out later to be just two and half days, the deadbolt released. There stood Ottorino, pistol in hand as always, and behind him stood two tall men. One man wore a pilot's cap, and I noticed a captain's four stripes on the left sleeve of his uniform. I couldn't observe much more of him, because Ottorino's body blocked my view. The other tall man wore a black knitted balaclava helmet over his head; all I could see were his eyes and mouth. He was holding a heavy canvas bag and a pair of handcuffs. He cuffed my hands behind my back and then fastened the bag over my head. I was able to breathe, but my vision was completely blocked and my hearing was considerably impaired.

A man grabbed each arm, and they marched me for a short distance. Then I had to climb fifteen stairs. After another shortish walk, they forced me to climb a ramp. My legs were suddenly knocked out from under me, and I found myself lying face down, spread-eagle on a piece of metal. They tied my legs to the metal surface with ropes, then they looped other ropes around my upper arms and fastened them to the metal, and finally they tightened all the ropes. Then the metal surface started to move.

I've just told you that the time in that cell seemed to be the worst experience in my whole life, but the cell was paradise compared to the hours that I spent tied to what turned out to be the cargo bed of an elderly Holden flatbed ute; they'd especially stolen the pickup truck for the purpose.

The drive lasted for hours, but eventually the ute stopped. I was untied, someone removed the canvas bag from my head, but the handcuffs remained in place. My limbs were stiff. Also, after many hours of hooded darkness, my eyes couldn't tolerate the light. Ottorino and his partners escorted me down a wide timber board; that was the "ramp" I'd previously encountered. I hadn't heard it moving about, so they must have fastened it to the cargo bed of the ute.

I looked around. It was late afternoon; the sun was about two hours away from the far horizon.

We were on a huge airfield in a state of almost total disrepair. About half a mile away were two dilapidated Nissen huts and, behind them, an old hangar. In many places, weeds sprouted through the concrete runway. I guessed that we were on a Royal Australian Air Force World War II training base located way back o' Bourke, as we say in Australia, that was abandoned after 1945.

For obvious reasons, Ottorino's assistant had removed his balaclava helmet during the long ride to the airfield. But he'd forgotten to replace it, and I was able to see the ten-inch long, thick white scar on the left side of his face. His jaw was square, so square that he looked like a caricature of Dick Tracy. His gray hair was shaved close to the scalp. But his intense black eyes were his most distinctive facial feature. They looked like the barrels of two revolvers. There was an actual revolver in his right hand. Like Ottorino's revolver, it was pointing directly at my heart.

We stood next to the ute for some minutes. On one side of the vehicle I saw an old canvas tarpaulin lying crumpled on the concrete airstrip. I assumed that they'd fastened the tarp over the cargo bed so that no one could see me tied down there while they drove to the airfield.

Then a plane appeared in the sky. I couldn't see a control tower anywhere; it must've rotted away with time. The only navigational aid was a tattered old windsock, yellow-white with age. The plane came closer, the pilot lowered the landing gear and fully extended the flaps, and the plane slowly approached the landing strip. It flew over our heads, landed, then turned and taxied towards our truck, stopping about seventy-five yards from us. The propellers slowed and finally came to a complete standstill. I observed that it was a twin turboprop military transport. The door opened. The stairs were lowered. And we waited.

After about five minutes, Ottorino turned to the man with the captain's stripes and said, "Check that the plane is in full working order. And search it thoroughly."

Ottorino's pilot walked slowly towards the plane, climbed the steps, and entered the cabin. After about fifteen minutes, he reappeared and walked back to Ottorino, Dick Tracy, and me. When he reached us, Ottorino asked, "Did you check the fuel?"

The pilot replied, "Of course I did."

"How would it be if the plane ran out of fuel on the way to our destination? Go back, look at the gauges and check that no one has tampered with them. It would just be like the New South Wales Police Force to make the gauges read 'Full' when the engines are really just breathing fumes. And search the plane again."

The pilot walked back to the plane, climbed the steps, and re-entered the cabin. He stayed away even longer this time. When the pilot finally returned, the sun was close to the western horizon. I love sunsets. For me, the mixture of reds, oranges, purples, and pinks can be the most glorious sight on earth. But that afternoon my mind was definitely not on the setting sun.

The pilot rejoined Ottorino, Dick Tracy, and me. Ottorino yelled, "Okay, come out!"

Detective Chief Inspector Walter Tregethick appeared. He had a pistol in his right hand; his left wrist was handcuffed to the right wrist of Gioachino di Campione whom I'd last seen at the warehouse in Port Botany. They started walking slowly down the narrow steps; the cuffs that linked the two of them impeded their progress. Eventually they reached the ground. They moved about ten yards in our direction and then halted.

Now Janet appeared at the door. I was so relieved to see her standing there that I nearly darted forward, but I remembered just in time that two revolvers were aimed at me and that any sudden movement on my part might well prove fatal.

Janet's body blocked my view of the face of the person handcuffed to her, but when they were partway down the steps, I could see the other man. He was a slimmer version of Gioachino di Campione; I assumed that this was Gioachino's brother Claudio. Surprisingly for someone cuffed to another person, Janet navigated the steps with ease, and soon she and Claudio were standing next to Walter and Gioachino. Janet also had a pistol in her right hand.

Some minutes later, the pilot of the aircraft appeared. He was wearing the uniform of a Royal Australian Air Force flight lieutenant. He joined Walter, Janet, and their two prisoners.

Next, Ottorino shouted, "Okay, circle to the right." Each group moved to their right in such a way that they kept the distance from the other group at a constant fifty yards. As a result, we each followed a semicircular path. Now the four of us were standing with the plane behind us, whereas Walter, Janet, the flight lieutenant, and the other two di Campione brothers were where we'd been standing next to the ute.

Ottorino ordered, "Approach to twenty yards." The four of us stayed where we were, while the other five walked slowly to within twenty yards of us. Ottorino kept his pistol pointed at me but when the other five came within shooting range, Dick Tracy shifted his aim from me to them.

The next command from Ottorino was, "Keys!" Janet, Walter, and Ottorino each produced a handcuff key and held it above their heads. On the command "Unlock!" the three pairs of handcuffs were opened. The three pairs clunked onto the concrete airstrip one after the other, and I slowly started to move my painfully stiff arms. Then there was a long pause.

Ottorino gave a signal to the tall man in the pilot's cap. He turned around, boarded the plane for the third time, and restarted the engines. When the propellers were rotating at full speed, he gave a thumbs-up signal through the side window of the cockpit to Ottorino who immediately bellowed, "Slow walk!" over the roar of the turbines. He prodded my back with his pistol, to get me started on my way. I could see that Gioachino and Claudio had already started walking towards me.

After ten yards I found myself walking between the two brothers—a weird experience. At last I reached Janet, Walter, and the flight lieutenant, who all stood stock-still and didn't even greet me; the two guns that were now trained on the four of us induced absolute silence, notwithstanding the guns that Janet and Walter were brandishing in the direction of the three brothers and Dick Tracy.

Gioachino and Claudio walked on past Ottorino, up the steps and into the cabin. Then Dick Tracy followed and stood in the doorway of the plane at the top of the steps, his revolver trained on us. Finally,

Ottorino climbed into the plane and stood next to Dick Tracy, also covering the four of us. As soon as the steps started to leave the ground, the pilot started to taxi. The door of the military aircraft remained open while our guns were within range of the plane, to enable Ottorino or Dick Tracy to return fire if Janet or Walter decided to try to take a pot shot. As the plane moved down the runway, the door was slammed shut.

Within thirty seconds, the plane was airborne. We watched it climb as we stood there in total silence. Then, as the turboprop reached a height of about three thousand feet above the ground, there was an explosion. A huge red and yellow fireball enveloped the aircraft. Pieces of glowing metal fell from the sky. And then there was silence.

"They specified that the fuel tanks had to be full to the very top," Walter said, in a satisfied tone of voice. "But they said nothing about a bomb in the lavatory."

I was rendered speechless with shock. When I finally could talk, my first words were, "But what about the pilot?"

"He was a member of the gang," Janet replied. "He took his chances and he lost his life."

"But who sanctioned the bomb? I didn't know that Australia or Italy went in for assassinations, even of drug lords."

Walter's silence was palpable.

Janet changed the subject. "How are we going to get back to civilization? Ottorino's pilot confiscated our phones before we left the plane."

I asked Walter, "Wasn't the plane under continuous radar surveillance? Can't they come and pick us up?"

Again I could feel his silence. And then I realized that the powers that be had taken steps to ensure that there would be no evidence of the flight ever having taken place. In the unlikely event of someone finding pieces of the wreckage of the turboprop out there in the middle of nowhere, the official line would be that they came from an old plane that had crashed during a World War II training exercise.

I tried another tack. "You could drive their ute to the nearest town and contact your colleagues from there." This time Walter reacted favorably to my suggestion. The four of us couldn't squeeze into the cab. Instead, Janet and the flight lieutenant climbed up the ramp onto the cargo bed, Walter drove, and I sat in the passenger seat. Always the gentleman, I'd wanted Janet to sit in the cab, but everyone overruled that in view of what I'd been through for the past three days.

Before Walter had a chance to start the ute, I asked him, "What's happened to Massimo, his wife, and his four-year-old son?"

"No dramas. They'll all be okay. Soon after you were kidnapped, his wife and son were released. The boy is fine, his wife is currently recovering in a convalescent home. We explained to Massimo that we know he acted under duress. He won't be charged for any criminal acts. He's most relieved, and he's helping us to the best of his ability, as is the owner of La Cenerentola, who's also starting to recover."

We drove along the landing strip until we reached a road. The sun was setting. "And now, left or right?" Walter asked. "I've absolutely no idea where we are. It would make life much, much easier if crooks took the trouble to steal a ute with a built-in GPS."

"Having fasted for goodness knows how many days," I said, "I don't need electronic devices. My stomach tells me that the nearest food is to the right." And how right I was. After about ninety minutes, we arrived at a small town consisting of about half a dozen houses, a café, a small wooden church that looked remarkably similar to the one in Mullajumba, and a one-roomed schoolhouse. Walter parked outside the café, which was on the point of closing.

Walter stated that he was a police officer, and asked to use the phone. At the same time, I told the café owner that I hadn't eaten for many days, and asked him to bring me everything on the menu and as quickly as possible. Janet and the flight lieutenant just stood there while the café owner tried to make sense of two people talking insistently at the same time, both using words like *urgently* and *quickly*.

Fortunately, the café owner was a former serviceman. Seeing a RAAF officer's uniform, he quickly grasped that he had to do something important, although the details escaped him until Janet told Walter and me to shut up to enable her to handle the situation with her usual aplomb.

While we waited for someone to come and pick us up, we ate. More precisely, Janet, Walter, and the flight lieutenant merely ate, while I made up for three days of fasting. When I was finally replete, I asked Walter about the bomb.

"You're secretive about what happened," I said. "I can understand that. But for obvious reasons, I'm intensely curious as to how the bomb was triggered."

"As you say, I can't tell you very much," Walter said, "but here's some of the story. In return for your release, the cocaine gang insisted that we fly Claudio di Campione from Italy to a military airport near Sydney and transport Gioachino to the same airport from the Goulburn Supermax Prison. When they arrived, we were supposed to take the two brothers to a Beechcraft Super King Air B200C turboprop plane waiting on the runway with its tanks full. Unfortunately, the only two B200Cs we could locate are in use by the Royal Flying Doctor Service, and both of them were out of service, undergoing major maintenance. When Ottorino contacted us again, we told him we were supplying a Beechcraft C-12 Huron, the military equivalent of the B200C. He was unhappy about that, but the plane's two thousand-mile range was enough for their purpose. Consequently, Ottorino agreed. That was why you saw a military plane and why we have a military pilot here with us.

"While we were taking Claudio on board the C-12, the Flight Sergeant who was in charge of refueling the plane smuggled the bomb into the lavatory through the outside hatch used to empty the septic tank. The trigger mechanism was a barometric sensor. Once the plane had landed, I armed the bomb by pushing a button on the side of my iPhone; our electronics experts built a small device into its casing. Ottorino's pilot searched us the second time he entered the plane. He actually turned on the iPhone, but it looked normal enough and he put it in his pocket with the other phones. Once the plane had climbed to three thousand feet above the ground, the bomb was triggered."

"But what if Ottorino had loaded all of us into the plane?" I asked.

Walter pulled a wry face. "That wasn't in the script he gave us for the handover. Just be grateful that he stuck to it."

I was about to ask him why they hadn't installed another button on the side of the iPhone for disarming the bomb, but I said nothing. It seems that an empty stomach for three days can instill tact!

About an hour later, the rumble of a helicopter grew louder. It landed on the dusty school playground, and the four of us clambered aboard. We arrived at Sydney Airport at about three in the morning. As we walked towards the terminal, I turned to Walter and said, "I'm really looking forward to a long, hot shower, and then to sleeping in my own bed tonight."

"Sorry, that's not going to happen," Walter said. "While you were seated in the café making up for seventy-two hours without food, I was on the phone to headquarters. We've got to get the two of you out of Australia as quickly as possible. The relevant departments of the British and Australian governments have given us permission to issue you both with Australian passports under false names. You'll sleep tonight—or rather, what's left of tonight—at the Lord Berkeley Hotel at the airport, under police guard. Janet, if you'll please let me have your keys to the penthouse, I'll pack a bag for you and one for Damon. And this afternoon I'll come to the hotel to give you your new passports. Tomorrow we'll take you straight from the hotel onto the flight of your choice out of Australia, bypassing the terminal for the sake of security."

"But why? What's going on?" I asked, and I could hear the note of confusion in my voice. "All three of the di Campione brothers are very dead indeed. With my own eyes I saw Gioachino, Claudio, and Ottorino get onto the C-12, and I saw the plane, loaded with fuel, explode in a ball of fire. No one could possibly have survived that explosion, let alone the fall from that height."

"No one did," Walter responded, "But twin brothers Arcangelo and Domenico di Campione are very much alive. The two youngest di Campiones are even more psychopathic than their older brothers—if that were possible—and both the Italian and the Australian police are certain that they'll do everything they can to kill you and Janet, no matter if they die in the attempt. For safety's sake, tomorrow you'll both leave Australia for overseas, and you'll stay overseas until Arcangelo and Domenico are both safely in custody."

The thought occurred to me that I should ask him to supply us with photographs of the murderous twins. But pictures wouldn't be much help if one of the twins held a gun to my head, so I didn't bother to ask. That proved to be a really bad mistake.

CHAPTER NINE

We enjoyed a late room-service breakfast. It wasn't quite up to the standard of some of the breakfasts we'd enjoyed in Paris, but after three days of total starvation followed by the meal at the café, it was more than adequate. I felt ready to face the future.

Then Janet and I sat down to discuss where in the world we wanted to flee until the police had captured Arcangelo and Domenico. New Zealand was too obvious; the twins would, in all likelihood, send gang members there to hunt us down. It goes without saying that Italy would be an exceedingly bad choice. I thought the United Kingdom would be a good idea, but then Janet pointed out that the government wouldn't allow a British citizen like her to enter the country on a false Australian passport. We batted countries back and forth but were unable to agree on anything. In fact, I disagreed with all my own suggestions as well as every country Janet put forward.

And then I had an idea. "What about Canada?" I suggested. "The remaining members of the cocaine gang fled there, but the authorities arrested them all and will soon deport them to Italy. That tells me that we should be safe there."

Janet thought about this for a moment. "Okay, let's give Canada a try. It has a really excellent air service, so if things start getting too hot in Canada, we can always fly to somewhere else in the world in a hurry. All we have to do is to stay alive until Arcangelo and Domenico are in custody. Then we can come back to Sydney."

That afternoon, Walter came to the hotel with our new passports and our suitcases. I'm not going to tell you the names on those passports, in case we need to use them again at some future time, but I will say this: Our new names were nothing like Damon Ogilvy and Janet Maitland.

Now that I come to think of it, actually it can do no harm for you to know our new names, for a reason that you'll soon learn. So, here goes. My new name was Jesse Presser, and it's a good thing I don't lisp. If you want to know Janet's new name, I think you should ask her.

The passports seemed to be genuine Australian passports, but many of the pages had immigration stamps from countries we'd never visited. Both documents were badly scuffed and definitely looked well-traveled. The photographs were extremely clever. They looked like us, but then again, they didn't look like us. I assumed that some clever computer nerd had started with genuine photographs but then doctored them in some way to ensure that the resulting photographs couldn't really be used to identify us. I know I'm not making much sense here, but I hope you get the idea.

Walter also provided us with credit cards and a driver's license for Janet in our new names. The photograph on the driver's license was a genuine RMS-issue black smudge; as always, there was no way anyone could possibly recognize her from that mug shot. My new credit card was unfortunately not an American Express Centurion card, but Walter assured us that the credit limits on our new cards were more than adequate for our needs. He also explained that the cards were linked to my bank account, and a computer would automatically transfer funds at the end of the month to pay the balance. That way our new location would stay secret.

"For obvious reasons," he said, "I can't give you a phone. If you need one overseas, I suggest you buy a 'burner' phone, one of those cheap, disposable, throw-away phones that drug dealers use. That way, no one will be able to trace you."

The three of us ate dinner together in our room. Janet and I drank abstemiously. It was an interesting evening, because it turned out that Walter's a teetotaler. Yes, I know, the phrase *Australian teetotaler* is an oxymoron, but there it is. We learned that the cases of wine that he'd previously ordered over the internet had been for his dinner guests. As a result, all three of us stayed stone-cold sober throughout an absolutely delicious room-service dinner.

At the end of the evening, we told Walter that we wanted to fly to Canada. He immediately endorsed our choice of country and said he'd make the necessary arrangements at once. He was as good as his word. The next morning, after breakfast in our room, we left the hotel through a back door and a police car took us straight to a Canadian National Airline plane bound for Vancouver. Walter came to the plane to take our passports to be stamped. He returned with them five minutes later, wished us bon voyage, and left.

***

There was only one other passenger in the first-class cabin of the Canadian National Airline flight. He and I got up to stretch our legs at about the same time, and we started chatting in the galley.

Gus Buccleuch looked and dressed like a grizzled prospector, but it turned out that he was the president and chief executive of a major oil prospecting company based in Calgary, the fourth largest city in Canada. Something Gus said reminded me of Barnett Mornay, my former client and quondam partner in the gold mine. Knowing that Barnett had made multiple fortunes in Texas oil in the past year, I asked Gus if he knew Barnett. Gus roared with laughter and said that the two of them had become cutthroat business rivals and bosom buddies. And any friend of Barnett's, Gus declared, was a friend of his.

Gus asked us if we were travelling on business or pleasure. I replied, "A bit of both." Of course, that statement was entirely false; we were travelling to avoid being murdered, and we weren't earning a penny in the process.

"I assume you're going to include the Calgary Stampede in your trip," Gus remarked.

I had no idea at all what he was talking about. "Is that like the running of the bulls in Pamplona?" I asked.

This time Gus laughed so hard that I thought he'd do himself a serious injury. "No," he finally said, "the Stampede is the world's largest rodeo; it's a competition with cattle-based events." Much to my surprise, he pronounced the word "*ro*-dee-oh." I love to watch TV cop shows and cop movies. In the ones filmed in Los Angeles, the actors sometimes mention Rodeo Drive in Beverley Hills, only they pronounce the word "Ro-*day*-oh." It hadn't occurred to me that the two words were pronounced differently. Then I realized that the super luxury stores on Rodeo Drive were about as far removed from cattle contests as ravens are from writing desks.

"What happens at the Stampede?" I asked.

"Well, there are a whole lot of events like steer wrestling, bull riding, and barrel racing. And then there's chuckwagon racing. The prize for the winners at Calgary is one million dollars, which means there's a lot of interest in the contest. A team of four horses pulls a chuckwagon and—"

"Hold it!" I interrupted. "What's a chuckwagon?"

"Well, when the prairies were being settled, a key part of the wagon train was the wagon that carried the food, the water barrel, a stove—that sort of thing. They say it was called a 'chuckwagon' because the name of the man who invented it was Charles someone-or-other. But who cares about that?

"Anyhow, as I was saying, a chuckwagon race is an event with four teams, each consisting of a driver and his team of four horses, plus two outriders on horseback. Each race begins with the outriders 'breaking camp' by tossing two tent poles and a barrel, representing the stove, into the back of the wagon. They then follow the wagon as the team pulls it in a figure-eight path around two larger barrels and then onto the racetrack. The first team across the finish line wins, but there are time penalties for things like not throwing the tent poles or the 'stove' properly into the wagon or for knocking over a barrel as the wagon circles it.

"You simply can't travel to Canada in July without going to Calgary to see at least one night of the

Stampede. I'm sure there's a law against it. And if there isn't a law, there definitely should be one. Or several.

"Come to think of it, Calgary is going to be packed to the gills. You're not going to be able to find a hotel room for a hundred miles, and all the tickets for the Stampede were sold months ago. But there's a way, of course. There always is."

Gus took two business cards out of his wallet. He wrote on the first card and handed it to me. "Give this to the manager of the Algonquin Hotel. I've written his name on the front."

I turned the card over. On the back Gus had written, "Pierre: Give them the best suite you got. Regards, Gus."

Then he handed me another card. "When you get to Stampede Park, show them this card. Tell them to take it to Pedro Marquez; I've written it down."

On the back of this card I saw the words, "Pedro: Give them my suite. Best, Gus."

I thanked him, and we returned to our seats.

***

When the plane landed in Vancouver, Janet and I sailed through immigration and customs. The immigration officer greeted us in a friendly way but didn't ask us any questions. She simply stamped our passports and handed them back. I've no idea whether that was because our false documents were extremely skillfully prepared or whether, when she scanned them, a message popped up on her screen instructing her to give us the VIP treatment.

We took our suitcases from the luggage carousel, walked to the departure hall, and used my new credit card to buy Canadian National Airline tickets for Calgary. As the friendly reservations agent returned my card to me, I realized that we had no Canadian money. I asked her to point us in the direction of the nearest ATM. We then acquired a supply of small change for tips by each buying a cup of coffee with a twenty dollar note. The coffee, by the way, was undrinkable by Australian standards.

A smooth ninety-minute flight brought us to Calgary International Airport, from where we took a taxi to the Algonquin Hotel. The doorman opened the taxi door and summoned a porter, who put our luggage onto his cart and indicated where the reception desk was. A man dressed in a smart black suit greeted us; the sign on the desk said "Jeff Malloy, Guest Services." I handed Gus's card to Jeff. Jeff bowed, and took the card to Pierre du Pont, the manager. Pierre burst out of his office dressed in a tailored suit, bespoke shirt, and handmade silk tie, and welcomed us effusively. He told us that we'd be staying in the Penthouse Suite; he didn't ask how long we intended to stay at his hotel.

I handed him my new passport and credit card, but he waved them away. "Sir," he said, "I don't need to see your passport, and there'll be no charge for your stay." I learned later that Gus was the sole owner of the huge luxury hotel.

When we opened the suitcases that Walter had packed for us, we came to the conclusion that, for some reason, Walter had assumed that we'd want to hide on a tropical island. Canada, on the other hand, has a relatively cold climate. Even in midsummer Calgary can be chilly, as we discovered when we exited the airport and headed for the taxi rank. Not surprisingly, we spent the afternoon buying a supply of warm clothes and larger suitcases in a huge mall not far from our hotel. We were most impressed by the helpfulness of the shop assistants, unlike most of their Australian counterparts. In addition, they seemed to know every detail of the products they were selling, which was a refreshing change.

We took a taxi to Stampede Park to arrive in time for the chuckwagon races, which were scheduled to start at eight. Gus's card proved to be as effective there as at the Algonquin Hotel. At the gate we asked for Pedro Marquez. A compact and energetic man in ornate western gear greeted us effusively and then escorted us to the Lazy S Executive Suite that Gus kept for his clients and guests. A uniformed attendant opened the door and showed us to a large table where he served us a gourmet three-course meal complete with Canadian wines, which we certainly enjoyed. We then repaired to our ergonomic swivel chairs on our private seat deck to watch the show.

The program began in true North American style with a parade of cowboys and cowgirls on horseback carrying flags and pennants. Next, a pretty young woman in a red and white dress sang the Canadian national anthem, "O Canada." I was surprised how enthusiastically the crowd joined in. You're probably thinking that they were trying to drown her out but you're wrong; she had a truly great voice and a most warm personality. Best of all, she didn't try to show off. On the contrary, she sang with sincerity from the heart.

Next the first chuckwagon race began and it was really exciting. The outriders tossed the tent poles and the "stoves" into the backs of the wagons and then followed the wagons around the figure-eight path marked by two barrels. The race came to an exciting climax as three of the four chuckwagons dueled for first place at the finish on the racetrack. Janet and I leapt to our feet and cheered.

After the race, we were about to go back inside for a drink and possibly a light snack when suddenly I had the feeling we were being watched from the seating area below and in front of us. Instead of following Janet into the executive suite I stayed in my seat and looked around. But no one seemed to be overtly staring at me. Nor did anyone turn their head aside as

I looked in their direction. Somewhat reassured, I went inside the suite.

"What held you up?" Janet asked.

"You won't believe this, but I think we're being watched."

"You're quite right, I won't believe it. Why should I believe it?"

"Janet, I'm telling you, two people were watching us immediately after the race."

"They saw two thin people in the executive suite area and wondered what we were doing in an area reserved for fat cats."

"Janet, please don't make jokes. I'm being serious. I think we're being followed."

"Right, let's go outside again and check."

We left the suite and returned to the private seat deck. We looked around carefully but neither of us noticed anyone watching us. "Damon, it's your overactive imagination," Janet said. In case you're wondering, she was always careful to call me "Jesse" when other people were within earshot.

"You may be right," I replied.

We watched the next race but somehow my heart just wasn't in it any more. Janet sensed how I was feeling, and by tacit mutual consent we took a taxi back to the Algonquin Hotel.

When we arrived at the Penthouse Suite, Janet asked me, "Damon, in your opinion, when we were on the seat deck at Stampede Park, did some man just turn around and idly look at the area behind him or did you get the feeling that we were actually being watched?"

"I definitely thought that two people were watching us. Do I have any proof? None at all. It was just a feeling I had."

"Tell me, would you feel happier if we left Calgary?"

"There were thousands and thousands of people at the Stampede. I'd be considerably happier to be in an area with a lot fewer people. That will make it much easier to determine if we're being followed."

"Fine. What do you suggest we do?"

"I noticed a travel agency in the hotel lobby," I said. "Let's go there tomorrow and see what they advise. One of my clients from my former life as a financial planner told me that the Canadian Rocky Mountains are extremely beautiful, but the word *mountains* implies climbing and camping and similar outdoor activities that I really enjoyed in my youth. These days, however, I tend to relish my creature comforts. Too many years of soft living, I guess. Let's get some advice from a travel professional and then decide what to do."

We snacked on the contents of the large of bowl of tropical fruit in the living room of our suite. Soon afterwards we went to our respective bedrooms.

In order to explain what happened next, I need to share with you a little more about myself. As I think I may already have told you, I grew up on a sheep farm in rural New South Wales. I received my primary education at home via the School of the Air. Distances in Australia are vast. As a result, the educational authorities used short-wave radio to teach children like me living in isolated areas; nowadays they use the internet, of course. My formal education consisted of one hour each day learning by radio with my teacher at the School of the Air. The rest of the morning my mother supervised me as I worked on the assignments that the school mailed to us. But once I reached high-school age, I had to go to a boarding school for children who live beyond the black stump, as we say in Australia; the school was "only" about three hundred miles from home. Then I was lucky enough to win a scholarship to study law at the University of Sydney, and for several years I rented a room in Darlinghurst, on the edge of the Sydney central business district.

In the second week of my final year of studies, a drunk driver killed my parents. One Sunday morning they were on their way to church in Mullajumba. A young man thought, wrongly, that he'd slept off the effects of the previous night's binge drinking, and he smashed into their car at high speed. After the funeral, my older brother and I sat down and decided that it would be best to sell the farm. We received a good price, but after paying off all the many debts, there was almost nothing left. I used my share to start my law practice in Katoomba. But a day doesn't go by without my thinking fondly of my parents, whose lives were cut tragically short in their early forties.

As a consequence of all these different experiences, especially having to leave home at the age of twelve, my coping skills are well developed. That's probably how I managed to survive the three days in captivity at the hands of Ottorino followed by the explosion at the airfield, seemingly with no ill effects. In fact, you may have noticed that after we finally arrived at the Lord Berkeley Hotel at Kingsford-Smith International Airport it never occurred to either Janet or Walter that a doctor should give me a thorough examination, probably because they both thought of me as a tough farm boy who could handle anything. And even the death threat from the di Campione twins seemed to me to be just one more of life's little problems.

But the minor incident of apparently being watched at the Calgary Stampede somehow proved to be the proverbial straw that broke the camel's back. As I climbed into bed, surge after surge of fear pulsed through my body. I'd never experienced anything even remotely similar. It was like sitting through a horror movie, only a hundred times more intense. I tried to tell myself this was just a reaction to what I'd recently lived through and that it would soon pass. But sheer terror forcibly expelled all rational thoughts from my brain. I lay in bed, quaking with fright. I was having a full-blown panic attack.

Eventually the feeling passed, and I managed to fall into an uneasy sleep. But from that moment on, the di Campione twins were never out of my thoughts. And I was no longer the fearless fellow from the farm.

CHAPTER TEN

Her hair was blonde, her eyes were blue, her face was pretty, her clothes were the latest fashion. The nametag on her chest read "Marcelle." Underneath was printed "Calgary Travel Shoppe."

I have a particular dislike of shops that call themselves shoppes. I consider it highly pretentious, and I'm relentlessly opposed to all forms of pretentiousness—in others. I'm sure you remember that my wine-tasting routine elevates pomposity and ostentation to previously unscaled heights. But that's the "farm boy makes good" component of my personality.

Back home in Mullajumba, beer was the sole alcoholic beverage; wine was a biblical liquid that we heard about in church on Sundays. But now that I'm able to afford to drink fine wines in fancy restaurants, I want the world to notice it. At the same time, I'm still a farm boy at heart, and that's why I detest pretentiousness of any kind in others. Contradictory?

Certainly. Hypocritical? Unquestionably. But what did you expect? I'm a human being like everyone else.

Anyhow, I found myself in a shoppe. I was about to suggest to Janet that we leave, but this was the only travel agency in the lobby of our hotel, and I just didn't have the energy to go elsewhere. Traveling one-third way around the world in one day does that to you, even when you fly first class. The impact was compounded by the experience I had gone through the previous night.

We sat down. Janet told Marcelle that Calgary was too large a city for our tastes and asked for suggestions for where we might travel.

"Well," Marcelle said, "Calgary has a population of about one million people. Edmonton, the capital of Alberta, is only two hundred miles to our north and has a population of only eight hundred and fifty thousand. Would that be more to your taste?"

I quickly realized that Marcelle wasn't the brightest bulb on the Christmas tree. However, other travel agents in Calgary might be even less inspiring. I therefore decided against walking out immediately. However, I'd give her two minutes and not one second more to come up with a sensible suggestion.

"We were thinking of something much smaller than that, but we want to stay in luxury hotels and eat in fine restaurants."

"Oh," Marcelle said, "Then you want to go to Banff, in the Canadian Rockies. Banff has fewer than ten thousand inhabitants, but it has a huge luxury hotel and lots and lots of fine restaurants. It also has golf courses and there are lots and lots of mountains to climb."

The size of Banff sounded reasonable to me, and the lots and lots of fine restaurants appealed greatly; but the rest of what she said was considerably less attractive. The idea of a huge luxury hotel was particularly uninviting. I was seriously concerned that Domenico and Arcangelo were somehow on our trail, and I was aware that a vast hotel with extensive public rooms is a killer's paradise.

"Are there any smaller luxury establishments?" I asked.

"What do you mean by 'establishments'?" Marcelle asked.

I tried to rephrase my question in monosyllables. "Are there any nice places to stay that are a lot smaller than the big hotel?"

"Well, there are plenty of bed and breakfasts," she responded.

In addition to shops that call themselves shoppes, I hate, loathe, and detest bed and breakfasts; and anyway, shouldn't the plural be *beds and breakfasts?* Why do I abhor them, you ask? No, this isn't another case of "farm boy makes good." One pet peeve is that beds and breakfasts are endowed with furniture that has been rejected by the local Salvation Army store— and furniture has to be in a pretty terrible state to be turned down by the Salvos. In particular, the beds are medieval instruments of torture, carefully designed to keep travelers awake all night. Then there are the china figurines and ornaments that cover every square inch of horizontal space, crowding out the notices like "Use the red towel to dry your hair and the green towel to dry your feet." In fact, there are notices everywhere, notices regarding the use of water, the use of electric lights, the use of air conditioning and heating. On the walls, the owners post lengthy catalogues of activities that may not be performed in the room under any circumstances, such as smoking, eating, and drinking.

But worst of all is the breakfast ritual. You're expected get up at some ungodly hour, sit at a large table with total strangers, and make polite conversation with people with whom you have absolutely nothing in common, other than the fact that you all had a sleepless night trying to find one comfortable position in an ancient bed with broken springs, in a room decorated with china gnomes and innumerable cardboard notices. Breakfast conversations at beds and breakfasts are not merely utterly dull, they are boring and banal, prosaic and predictable, trite and trivial. In short, just hearing the phrase *bed and breakfast* is enough to get my knickers in a knot, as we say in Australia. And please don't get me started on the food served in the morning in those establishments. In short, the worst aspects of beds and breakfasts are the beds and the breakfasts.

Marcelle couldn't have been completely stupid, because she noticed the look on my face when she dropped the b-and-b bomb. She quickly said, "My boyfriend and I stayed at a wonderful bed and breakfast in Banff. Tweedsmuir House is small, only three or four rooms. It's just a few years old and it was actually built as a bed and breakfast; it's not a converted prison or anything like that. And all the furniture is new and the beds are soooooo comfortable."

Well, this was something truly unique, a bed and breakfast with a comfortable bed. I didn't dare to tempt fate further and ask about the breakfasts. I knew with total certainly that I'd have to sit next to a seventy-year-old redheaded woman from Portland, Oregon, wearing bell-bottom jeans, a tie-dyed blouse, and a batik bandanna. I knew exactly what she'd ask me, "Where are you from? What are you doing today? Where did you go yesterday? Don't you think the scrambled eggs are delicious?" And because she'd be a really good and kind person, except for the fact that for the past fifty years she's worn the same clothes that she wore when she went to Woodstock in 1969, I'd have to be polite and answer her well-meaning questions in a friendly fashion while desperately suppressing an overwhelming urge to strangle her.

Now I had to make a life-changing decision: the bed and breakfast Marcelle recommended was small, and therefore it would be that much harder for the two death-dealing psychopaths to watch us than if we were in a vast hotel. Following us in and out of the bed and breakfast would also be a problem for them. Also, the beds were soooooo comfortable, which was soooooo unusual for a bed and breakfast. And it wasn't a converted prison, unlike almost all the other beds and breakfasts in which I've I stayed. But there was still the make-or-break issue of breakfast with the woman from Portland. At that moment in my life, an imaginary redheaded female seemed more important to me than the all-too-real murderous di Campione twins. Blind terror does that to you; it warps your mind.

I was trying to decide one way or the other when Janet proclaimed, "Fine, we'll stay at Tweedsmuir House. Now, how do we get to Banff?"

"I strongly suggest a seven-day conducted tour by bus, visiting all the sites in the area, including Lake Louise, Radium Hot Springs, Jasper, and—"

"Hold it, hold it," I said. I'd instantly realized that it would be too easy for the bad guys to follow us if we travelled around as part of a large group of people on a bus. "Just how many people will be on this bus tour?"

"Forty-four," Marcelle said.

"And will one of them be a seventy-year-old red-headed woman from Portland, Oregon, wearing bell-bottom jeans, a tie-dyed blouse, and a batik bandanna?" I asked. Raw fear made me say that aloud.

But before she could reply, I quickly added, "Never mind that, bus tours are out. Totally."

Marcelle wasn't the least bit disconcerted. "My second suggestion would be to rent a car. You can then drive wherever you wish around Banff National Park. It's an extremely beautiful part of the world. You can drive to Lake Louise, Radium Hot Springs, Jasper, and—"

"Just a minute. How great are the distances in this National Park?" I asked.

"Oh, everything is within easy driving distance. For example, if you want to drive to Jasper, it'll take only five or six hours. Of course, you'll want to stop at the Icefield Centre and take a snow coach to the Athabasca Glacier. And you'll stop all the time to take photographs, especially if you see bears. The whole drive from Banff to Jasper and back shouldn't take you more than fifteen or sixteen hours; you'll be back in Banff before you even know it."

I tried to interrupt Marcelle again to tell her to go on to the next alternative, but she had rendered me speechless. Unchecked, our travel agent continued to tell us about option number two.

"There's one drawback to renting a car, though. The car-rental places here in Calgary are totally disorganized, even the best ones. No matter what time you reserve your car, you can wait two or three hours at the car-rental depot to pick up your vehicle. One of my clients, after waiting five hours, had to take a taxi to Banff. The car-rental company paid the three-hundred-dollar fare, and they delivered the rental car to him the next morning in Banff."

"And what's option three?" Janet asked quickly, trying to forestall a truly tactless remark from me in the unlikely event that my powers of speech had miraculously returned.

"You can rent a luxury car and driver/guide. He can then drive you all over the National Park. For example, he can drive you to Lake Louise, he can drive you to Radium Hot Springs, he can drive you to Jasper, he can—"

"Yes, yes, we understand the concept," Janet said. "That sounds like a good idea. How many days should we spend in the Banff National Park?"

That question was a serious error.

Marcelle replied, "Well, you can spend one day driving to Lake Louise, one day driving to Radium Hot Springs, one day driving to Jasper, stopping at the Icefield Centre to take a snow coach to the Athabasca Glacier, one day—"

Janet once more made an attempt to interrupt the incessant flow of words.

"Should we spend a week in Banff, then?"

Marcelle stopped to think. There was blissful silence for a long while as she slowly counted on her manicured fingers. I could see her lips moving, and you know exactly what she was saying to herself. Finally, she pronounced her verdict: "Yes, that would be good."

Janet tried to bring the meeting to a quick close, "Please book us a week at the bed and breakfast, and we'll rent a car and driver/guide for a week. Here's my credit card."

But Marcelle was having none of it. Ignoring Janet's proffered plastic, she asked, "And after the week in Banff, I assume you'll take the two-day luxury Western Canada Sightseeing train trip to Vancouver, travelling Diamond Class?"

By this time, I was willing to do anything just to get out of the Calgary Travel Shoppe. Without asking her anything about the Western Canada Sightseeing train, I immediately said, "Of course." In my rush to escape, I didn't stop to think that being on a large train would be considerably more dangerous than on a forty-four-seater bus.

Unfortunately, agreeing to go on the train trip didn't do the trick. Marcelle still had yet another ace up her sleeve.

"And where will you be staying in Vancouver? I can strongly recommend the Postillion Hotel."

I thought quickly. Unless we could stop Marcelle, by brute force if necessary, we'd end up with reservations for every day of the rest of our lives. Hoping to avoid having to stoop to violence to stem the flow, I took out my phone, pretended to carefully peruse my diary, which for obvious reasons was totally blank, and said the first thing that came into my mind. "The day after that we have a ticket to fly from Vancouver to Dordrecht."

Dordrecht, where in the world was Dordrecht? Fortunately, it didn't matter.

"Fine," Marcelle said, "I'll reserve a two-bedroom suite for you in the Postillion Hotel for just the one night then. Will it be okay if I charge everything to this credit card? I'll deliver the vouchers to your suite in about an hour's time."

We thanked Marcelle, Janet took back her credit card, and we fled the shoppe.

"I don't want to be anywhere in this hotel when Marcelle brings the vouchers, let alone in our suite. Let's see the sights of Calgary," Janet declared.

We strolled to the door of the hotel. Regressing to my former profession of financial planner, I mentally added up all the commissions that Marcelle was about to earn from our trip to the Canadian Rockies and on to Vancouver. She wasn't the least bit stupid.

***

Outside the hotel a taxi was waiting. I was about to open the door for Janet when she grabbed my other arm. "Never take the first taxi," she cautioned. "Rather, walk in the direction in which the taxi is headed and hail a passing taxi coming from that area."

I was about to thank Janet for her advice when I suddenly realized what had just happened: Janet had tacitly admitted that we needed to take precautions against being followed. I was simultaneously delighted that she'd finally accepted my claim that we'd indeed been watched at the Calgary Stampede, and also worried out of my mind that the deadly di Campione duo had somehow got onto our trail and were breathing down the backs of our necks. The terror that I'd felt in bed the previous night was starting to return, though not quite as strongly this time.

Following Janet's instruction, we turned into Jasper Avenue and hailed a cab. Janet said to the driver: "We want to drive around for two hours to see the sights of Calgary. What do you suggest?"

The driver seemed nonplussed. He was obviously used to being told where to take his passengers, and being asked to suggest a destination was something new to him. After a pause, he replied, "Where d'you wanna go?"

Janet repeated, "Please show us the tourist sights of Calgary."

The driver was clearly confused. Janet realized that we weren't getting anywhere, in either sense of the phrase. She opened her bag, took out her coin purse, gave him a two-dollar coin, and we got out of the taxi.

"Let's go back to the hotel, ask the concierge what to see, and then we'll take a different taxi," Janet said.

Returning to the Algonquin Hotel was another seriously bad mistake. We entered the lobby and strolled towards the concierge desk, but Marcelle caught sight of us through the plate-glass window of her shoppe. She rushed out and buttonholed us. "I have the first two vouchers here," she explained. "As you can see, your driver/guide will call you from the lobby at nine o'clock tomorrow morning. And here's the voucher for Tweedsmuir House. I'm still waiting for confirmation from the Western Canada Sightseeing people and the Postillion Hotel in Vancouver, but I think that both will be fine. There are always two or three seats available in Diamond Class on the train." She handed me the two vouchers and sashayed back to her shoppe.

Janet looked as if she was about to explode. Turning to me, she growled, "The French playwright Georges Feydeau constructed his hilarious farces according to Feydeau's Rule, which states that if the plot demands that two characters must not meet under any circumstances whatsoever then they must be brought together on the stage as soon as possible. It seems to me that Calgary operates under Dingbat's Rule, which is similar, but applies to three people: you, me, and Marcelle. Damon, we have to get out of here before she reappears with the next voucher."

"But we don't know what the sights of Calgary are."

"I don't care." She hustled me out of the lobby. "I'd rather drive around the block for two hours until Marcelle's shoppe closes for lunch than bump into her again. One thing I do remember: The Olympic games took place here about twenty or twenty-five years ago. Let's go to where the games were held."

We returned to Jasper Street, hailed a taxi, and asked the driver to take us to the Olympic games area. "Do you want the Canada Olympic Park or the Olympic Hall of Fame and Museum?" he asked.

"Let's start at the Olympic Park," Janet said.

The drive took more than half an hour. Then we saw what looked like three ski jump towers on a tall hill in front of us, and I suddenly realized that Calgary had been the venue for the *Winter* Olympics.

The closer we got to the ski jump area, the more incongruous everything looked. The ramps weren't coated with snow and ice; it would've been quite impossible to ski down them. Also, the landing area was now a lush grassy hill.

Then I realized that only one of the three structures on the top of the hill was for ski jumping. The others were for different events, like luge and bobsleigh. Also, I was sure that there had to be an ice rink somewhere, but I wondered whether they kept it going in summer or whether in July a large pool of water replaces the huge Zamboni-smooth sheet.

We arrived at the park, and our driver pointed out some of the buildings to us, including the Olympic Hall of Fame and Museum. He stopped the car and suggested we explore for a few minutes. Janet and I walked to the ski run and wondered whether we should take up ski jumping; the sport looked like a lot of fun. Suddenly Janet spoke. "Don't turn around, but do you think we're being followed?"

In my current state of fear, I panicked, of course, but I somehow managed not to turn around. Looking straight ahead, I said, "I hadn't noticed anyone. Who's following us and how did they get onto our tracks?"

"Didn't you see that I kept looking behind us as the cabbie drove? I watched the cars in our vicinity, but I couldn't spot a tail. Also, I've been looking around all the time we've been here on this hill, and I didn't notice anyone. I agree that it's possible that the two people you saw yesterday at the Stampede were observing us out of idle curiosity and that they weren't tailing us. But let's keep vigilant."

We returned to the car. I asked our driver to take us to the ice rink. He laughed. "The ice rink isn't here, and today it's going to be a little difficult to visit it."

"Why isn't it here? Where is it? And why is it 'going to be a little difficult to visit it' today?"

The driver laughed again. "When they hold the Olympic games, there are so many kinds of sports that the events are spread out over a number of different venues. As you saw, here at the Olympic Park we had the bobsleigh, luge, and ski jumping events."

"I understand," I said. "But where was the figure skating held?"

"At the Saddledome. Now it's used for hockey." I realized he meant ice hockey, not the field hockey we play in Australia.

Then I wondered why the driver had said that we shouldn't visit it that day. Actually, initially I wasn't at all interested in the Olympic ice rink, but forbidden fruit tastes the sweetest, and the driver's remarks had made me exceedingly keen to see the Saddledome.

"Just why shouldn't we visit the Saddledome today?" I asked.

"Because it's bang in the middle of the Stampede Grounds, and I'm sure you two have noticed that that part of Calgary is particularly busy today. If you want to see the Saddledome, I suggest you wait until the Stampede is over."

There was silence while we digested his remarks. Then I turned to Janet and asked, "Do you think that Marcelle has gone to lunch yet?"

"With all my heart, I hope that's the case."

Not caring what the taxi driver might have made of that last exchange, we asked him to take us back to the Algonquin Hotel. All the way back, Janet kept looking behind us. The good news was that she nodded to indicate that all was well when we arrived back at the hotel; as far as Janet could tell, we weren't being followed. The even better news was that the Travel Shoppe was closed for lunch.

CHAPTER ELEVEN

We packed the next morning after we'd eaten our room-service breakfast. Promptly at nine, the phone rang. The hotel front-desk clerk told us that our driver was waiting. Janet asked him to send up a porter for our luggage, and we took the elevator down to the lobby.

I greatly admire punctuality in a driver. I also like to see a driver smartly dressed in the international uniform of drivers: white shirt, black tie, black suit, and black military-officer style cap with a black plastic peak. Our driver had already qualified time-wise, and far exceeded expectations uniform-wise: gleaming white shirt, freshly ironed; black suit that looked like it'd been picked up at the dry cleaner's only a few minutes before; and crisp black tie held in place with a silver tie clip. Her nametag said "Darleen," a name I associate with the American Deep South, and how right I was. She smiled a smile that filled every inch of the huge lobby of the Algonquin Hotel, looked me straight in the eye and said, "Howdy! Ah'm Darleen. Ah'm mighty pleased ta meetcha. Heidi do!"

Ottorino's assistant had looked like Dick Tracy. Conforming to the theme of characters in comic strips, Darleen looked a lot like Lil Abner's Daisy Mae. Below her cap was lots and lots of wavy blond hair. She was pretty, too. The key difference was that Daisy Mae was voluptuous, but not to put too fine a point on it, Darleen was definitely on the plump side.

The porter loaded our suitcases into the trunk of the black Lincoln Town Car, Darleen opened the rear door for us, and Janet and I entered. Darleen settled herself behind the wheel, turned towards us and, in a warm Southern drawl brimming with magnolias, bourbon, molasses, and pecan pie, asked "Where y'all fixin' to travel to today?"

Actually, that wasn't quite how she said it. For example, she didn't say "where," she said "way-yer." Or maybe there were three syllables, or even more. But Ah thank y'all might could unnerstan' wut she wuz sayin'. Gosh dang it, Ah'm sure y'all do.

Darleen is one of the nicest people I've ever met. She has a heart of solid gold. During the week that she drove us around the Canadian Rockies, she never once lost her radiant smile or her happy demeanor. She also never once lost her broad Southern accent. Most of the words I could work out, but on several occasions I had no idea at all what she was saying.

You'll be pleased to hear that I'm going to take pity on you. So, if'n the Lord's willin' and the crick don' rise, from now on I'll translate what Darleen said into English.

We asked Darleen to drive us to Banff, to Tweedsmuir House, so that we could check in and leave our luggage there. As we drove away from the Algonquin Hotel, the sky suddenly darkened. Darleen soon found an on-ramp to a major freeway and we barreled along Highway 1, the Trans-Canada Highway, which traverses over five thousand miles of Canada, from the Atlantic Ocean to the Pacific. We passed the Canada Olympic Park, with the huge ski jump standing out starkly on the top of the hill, overshadowing the buildings for the start of the luge and bobsleigh races. But Darleen suddenly had to slow down as the heavens opened and visibility reduced to a yard or two.

Fortunately, the drenching lasted for only a few minutes, but the heavy clouds remained. This was something of a mood depressant. There I was, about to spend a week in what many consider the most beautiful part of the world, concerned that rain and cloud would spoil the glorious vistas. And as my spirits drooped, fear of the revenge of the di Campione twins grew larger. I instinctively tried to look through the rear window of the Town Car, but the glass had misted up, and I could see nothing.

At the same time, I definitely didn't want to say to Darleen, *Please could you demist the rear window because Janet and I are concerned that, despite the precautions we've been taking, the psychopathic di Campione twins may be on our tail and they're determined to kill us.*

I decided not to say anything, but I became more and more frightened as we neared the Canadian Rockies.

The scenery changed from hills to mountains. Despite the fact that this was July, there was snow on many of the peaks and also on some of the higher north-facing slopes. The scenery was spectacular: tall mountains, rivers rushing along valley bottoms, unending forests, lakes, birds—including bald eagles, wild animals. The beauty was so intense it was like eating course after course of over-rich food.

The transition from wilderness to the town of Banff was quite sudden. One minute we were in the middle of mountains and rivers and fir trees, and the next we were in a charming town. The style of many of the buildings was reminiscent of Swiss alpine villages or, to be more precise, of the Swiss alpine villages I've seen in movies and TV shows; I've never been to Switzerland. A few blocks after entering the town we were in a shopping area, and two blocks farther Darleen stopped at Tweedsmuir House.

From the outside, it was all that Marcelle had promised. It was a modern building with a timber exterior. Colorful flowerbeds lined the perimeter, and an abundance of geraniums poured out of all the window boxes. Geraniums are my favorite flower, perhaps because my parents had geraniums in pots outside our farmhouse near Mullajumba, and any place with geraniums automatically ranks high on my list. The roof had gables, yes, but a respectable number of gables, a restrained number—unlike the building two doors down that seemed to have more gables than the total number of geraniums growing in Tweedsmuir House, if not the whole of Banff.

Darleen parked the car, we all got out, and Janet opened the door of the bed and breakfast for us. A short passageway led into a large paneled room with an inviting fireplace. I walked towards the fireplace. I noticed a wooden table on my right with a bowl of gleaming red apples and a large plate filled with huge home-baked cookies. The small sign said: "Homemade chocolate chip and macadamia nut cookies—please help yourself." The cookies looked absolutely delicious. I could see that they were baked to the perfect color, they seemed to have just the right texture, and they were brimming with large chocolate chips and macadamia nuts.

The three of us had our mouths filled with cookies when the owner appeared. Vicki McKenzie was no older than twenty-five, muscular, clearly supremely fit, and without an ounce of fat anywhere on her lithe body. Nevertheless, she was as friendly and as happy as a plump couch potato. She smiled approvingly as we munched her cookies—it later turned out that she'd baked them earlier that morning—and she had the good grace not to point out that we'd left the healthy apples untouched.

Vicki welcomed us to Tweedsmuir House and showed us around the establishment, which was singularly free of notices of any kind, other than the tiny sign that invited us to partake of those cookies. Downstairs was a large room. It contained the breakfast area, a substantial lounge area with the cozy fireplace I'd seen, and a large table groaning with bottles of spirits; guests were welcome to help themselves to an after-dinner drink. Leading from the lounge area was a nice-sized balcony, resplendent with geraniums. The rest of the downstairs comprised the kitchen, still smelling of the freshly baked cookies, and the McKenzies's own quarters.

It appeared that Percy McKenzie was off on a run to the top of a rocky hill somewhere but would be back within minutes. Soon the front door opened and another young healthy person breezed in. Percy was as muscular as his wife, as slim and fit as she was, and certainly as friendly and as happy. He welcomed us as warmly as Vicki had done, then excused himself. My understanding was that there was another hill in the area he wanted to sprint up and dash down in the hour before lunch.

Vicki led us upstairs to our rooms. On the way, she asked us to please keep the front door locked at all times. Banff is a tourist town, she said, and it was necessary to keep the front door locked to keep the curious out. This was strange because we'd found the door unlocked when we'd arrived. I was about to say something when Janet gave me a meaningful look. She knew what was coming, and she didn't want me to upset Vicki with one of my usual tactless remarks.

I was sorry that I'd maligned Marcelle, because after tasting Vicki's chocolate chip and macadamia nut cookies, there was no way I was going to stay anywhere else, even if Tweedsmuir House had been plastered wall-to-wall with peremptory notices in lieu of wallpaper.

I opened the door of my room and immediately tried out the bed. It was as superlative in its own way as the cookies had been; this was a supremely comfortable bed. Then I felt something under my right calf. I'd laid my right leg on a booklet of some kind. I picked it up and found it was a glossy brochure for the Western Canada Sightseeing train that we were taking to Vancouver in a week's time.

This surprised me because the McKenzies appeared to be actively advertising the train in return for a commission based on the fares they brought in. However, they certainly didn't seem to be like that. Quite the contrary, in fact. I decided to subtly probe the matter, but then I remembered that I'm pathologically incapable of subtlety, let alone tact.

Anyhow, while I was deciding what to do, I heard a knock. I opened the door, and there stood Vicki with my suitcase. This was another surprise. In beds and breakfasts, you carry up your own suitcase. And if your room is on the fifth floor and there's no elevator—and there never is in a bed and breakfast—you carry your suitcase up five flights of stairs when you arrive and down five flights when you leave.

But Tweedsmuir House was quite different; the hosts fetched and carried the luggage. I thanked Vicki for bringing my suitcase from the car. Then, trying my very best to be subtle, I held out the brochure and asked, "How did you know that we're travelling from here to Vancouver next week on the Western Canada Sightseeing train?"

Vicki looked thoroughly puzzled. "What do you mean?" she asked.

"Well," I said, "you left this brochure on my bed, and I wanted you to know that we're taking the train."

"What brochure?" Vicki asked.

"This brochure," I said. The dialogue was becoming truly stunning. When we return to Australia, I thought to myself, I'll definitely need to contact David Williamson, Australia's answer to Neil Simon, to co-author a hit play.

"What brochure is that?" Vicki asked. Now the dialogue was starting to positively scintillate.

"This brochure," I repeated. My previous line had been so perfect that I could find no way to improve on it. Not even David Williamson himself could've written the line more perfectly, and that's saying something.

"I've never seen it before," Vicki said. "What was it doing on your bed?"

"It was lying there."

"But I didn't put it there when I made your bed yesterday, and there were no guests in your room last night. How did the brochure get there?"

At this point, the dialogue was starting to get a little surreal. Perhaps my selecting David Williamson to co-author a play was a poor decision. Maybe, I thought, Luis Buñuel would be better. Then I remembered that Buñuel had died years ago. But then, when it comes to surrealism, the fact that the co-author of a screenplay died some thirty years before the screenplay is to be written poses no problem at all.

Returning to reality with the greatest difficulty, I started at the beginning. "Vicki," I said, "when I came into the room, I found this brochure for the Western Canada Sightseeing train lying on my bed."

"But I didn't put it there," Vicki replied.

"Maybe the maid did," I suggested.

"But we have no maid; Percy and I do all the work around the house."

That figured. The thought crossed my mind that they probably spring-cleaned any unoccupied rooms every morning at about three o'clock, after which they went for a lengthy run before breakfast.

I put forward another possibility. "Well, maybe Percy put it there."

"But why would he do that?" Vicki asked. "About half our guests arrive on the Western Canada Sightseeing train, which means that they wouldn't need the brochure. And almost all the others leave on the train, like you and Janet, having made their reservations long before coming to Banff. They wouldn't need the brochure either."

I needed to change the subject right away. I quickly asked, "Can you suggest a nice place for lunch?"

I probably should've delicately segued from the brochure to my next meal, but it was too late. The good news was that my prosecutorial cross-examination of Vicki had apparently not upset her.

"What sort of lunch do you want?" Vicki asked. "A sandwich and a cup of coffee?"

That wasn't what I fancied at all. Rather, I was hoping to sample the delights of Canadian cooking. The question was how to say that in a kind way; after the discussion regarding the brochure, I wanted to be scrupulously polite to her. Vicki is a really nice person and I wanted to be really nice myself.

"Not exactly," I said. "I was thinking of something a little more substantial. I've heard great things about Canadian food." Actually, that last statement was absolutely true. About seven minutes earlier, both Janet and Darleen had been most complimentary about those memorable cookies.

"Won't you please come downstairs?" Vicki asked. "Percy and I have prepared a binder with the menus of all the restaurants in Banff."

Now that sounded like the sort of reading matter I really enjoy. I accompanied Vicki down the flight of extra wide steps. No, they weren't wide to cater for extra-large people. When they built Tweedsmuir House, Percy and Vicki constructed extra wide stairs to make it easy for guests to carry their luggage up to their rooms on the upper floor. Having spent the extra money on the stairs to make their guests' lives easier, they then carried the guests' luggage up for them. Talk about being doubly considerate!

Near the foot of the stairs was a large wooden armoire. Vicki opened one of the top doors and gave me a thick binder filled with menus. I asked Vicki about various restaurants and I received another surprise. Notwithstanding her previous unstinting helpfulness, now she usually answered in monosyllables and her rare slightly longer answers essentially boiled down to "Look in the binder." Clearly she wasn't going to say anything negative about any restaurant. More significantly, she wasn't going to say anything positive either. That meant that my initial reaction to the Western Canada Sightseeing train brochure had been absolutely correct. The McKenzies were definitely not the sort of people to advertise on behalf of others, even if they weren't getting a commission. Vicki's stubborn taciturnity regarding the restaurants of Banff only heightened the mystery.

I heard Janet and Darleen chatting in the lounge area, and I took the binder to them. Janet said that the French-Canadian restaurant on page six looked interesting; she'd never tried that kind of ethnic food. We asked Darleen to join us and she agreed. The three of us shouted goodbye to Vicki who, by this time, was in her kitchen, hopefully replenishing her supply of cookies. We drove off to La Petite Pierrette. When our meal arrived, we wished that Vicki had been a little more communicative food-wise. A word in our ear regarding La Petite Pierrette would've been most welcome, a lot more welcome, in fact, than the food at that restaurant.

After lunch, we strolled down Banff Avenue, the main street of Banff. We passed an ice-cream parlor. More correctly, we didn't pass it. Instead, we stopped at the parlor and thoroughly enjoyed the homemade gelato. The gelato reminded me of Italy, and Italy reminded me of the di Campione twins. Yes, Italy usually reminds me of superlative food, fine wines that are beyond compare, friendly people, and scenery that I hope someday to experience in person. But under the circumstances, I was reminded of Arcangelo and Domenico. However, because Darleen was with us, I couldn't say anything about the terrible twins.

We continued walking up Banff Avenue. Our guide, Darleen, spoke up. "I want to show you a store that sells something I reckon you've never seen elsewhere."

Darleen led us into a shop and pointed to a large stuffed horned animal standing by the door. "That's a musk ox. Go on, stroke the inner layer of fur. It's softer than anything else I know. They call it *qiviut*. It's stronger than sheep's wool and eight times warmer; it has to be extremely warm because the musk ox lives in arctic regions. Qiviut is softer than cashmere. It's also ruinously expensive, because each musk ox produces less than three kilograms of qiviut per year."

We were admiring the quality of the men's and women's qiviut clothing in the shop when I heard a couple talking. The Aussie accent was unmistakable; they were definitely talking Strine. I went up to them and asked them where in Australia they lived. Paul and Henrietta said that they came from Darwin. Naturally, I asked them why people from the tropical Top End were interested in such warm clothing. They laughed and said they'd been drawn into the shop by the sight of the huge musk ox. I introduced Darleen and Janet, and pretty soon the five of us were seated in the Teal Hotel enjoying afternoon tea.

Henrietta and Paul were having a wonderful time. They'd purchased a three-week package from the Western Canada Sightseeing organization, including train travel from Vancouver to Banff, hotels in

Vancouver and the National Park, and train travel from Jasper back to Vancouver, as well as various bus tours around Vancouver and in the Park. I asked Henrietta about the Western Canada Sightseeing train, and she replied, "Have you heard about the strike and the lockout?"

I said no, and Janet also shook her head. Darleen said nothing; I assumed that she didn't want to become embroiled in a discussion about trade unions. Henrietta then explained that the service on the trains is superb. "Each coach has three chefs who cook your gourmet meals, and each coach has three waiters and a guide; they call them 'attendants.' Anyhow, the attendants have just gone on strike. What's happened is that, after months of negotiations about overtime and scheduling that led nowhere, the attendants' union served a strike notice and management gave the union lockout notice."

"When did this happen?" Janet asked.

"The day before we travelled from Vancouver to Banff," Henrietta replied with a laugh.

"And what happened? Was one of great train trips of the world ruined beyond repair?"

Janet asked.

"Not at all," Henrietta insisted. "Knowing that the strike was coming, the company conducted courses for replacement attendants. Yes, management did their very best to prepare replacement attendants for the job. But you can't achieve much in two days, and instruction should obviously be done on site in an actual train. However, the trains were en route to their destinations, and the managers were therefore forced to instruct the more than a hundred replacement attendants in a classroom. It was like training sailors on dry land.

"The good news is that the replacement attendants are all highly experienced in the hospitality industry. The better news is that they're really keen to make a success of their new jobs. As a result, they didn't walk, they ran. The bad news is that our trip was their first trip and they had no experience of the specific job they were now doing. For example, when Paul asked an attendant for a beer, the man ran to the front of the carriage. We saw him scuttling around looking for the beers—eventually he found some cans of a really nice Canadian lager in a fridge under a counter—but then he had to hunt for a glass. There were no glasses to be found, and he ran down the service stairs to the galley to get some. He came up again, slightly more slowly this time, because he was carrying a huge tray of glasses; there must have been sixty or more glasses in a plastic frame. He poured the beer into a glass, then ran back to Paul and gave him his beer.

"And that was the pattern for the whole two-day trip. Keenness and enthusiasm made up for a lack of slickness, to say the least. The guide had to read her remarks from a thick binder; there hadn't been time for her to memorize her lines. And she had almost no idea about the locations of the physical landmarks that were listed in the binder as the places at which she should start her spiel. Sometimes she described a town that we'd passed five minutes before, sometimes it was a major engineering feat that was coming up some fifteen minutes ahead. Yes, she was Canadian. And yes, she knew the area well. But she'd never been on a train from Vancouver to Banff. Despite the many inconveniences, the passengers in our coach were overwhelmingly happy with the service they received from our four attendants. I'm sure that, at the end of the trip, the tip envelopes were filled to overflowing."

While Janet and Henrietta were engaged in this conversation about the Western Canada Sightseeing train, I kept thinking about the brochure I'd found on my bed. I hadn't yet been able to discuss it with Janet because Darleen had been with us, and now Paul and Henrietta were there as well. I firmly believed Vicki when she said that she knew nothing about it, and I knew that Percy had been out climbing mountains. But I really wanted to know how the brochure had ended up on my bed. More importantly though, I had to find out *why* it had ended it up there.

Eventually the tea party came to an end. We exchanged email addresses with Henrietta, said goodbye to Paul, who'd hardly said a word all afternoon, and parted. We told Darleen we'd like to take it easy until dinnertime, so we asked her to drive us back to Tweedsmuir House and pick us up at seven for dinner.

Then I realized the mistake I'd made. We had with us a driver/guide who knew the area. But more importantly, much more importantly, Darleen loved eating; you only had to look at her to see that. Clearly, she was the person I should've consulted about restaurants, not our toothpick-thin host Vicki.

I quickly asked her, "Darleen, where should we eat tonight?"

And Darleen replied, "I'll make a reservation for you and Janet at the Alberta Grille. They have prime Alberta beef, game, fresh fish, and wonderful, wonderful desserts."

Halfway through that last sentence I immediately knew that I'd asked the right person. And when I heard those magic words *wonderful, wonderful desserts* I was actually grateful to Marcelle for arranging for Darleen to be our guide to Banff National Park and, equally importantly, to the gourmet restaurants there.

Darleen drove the five or six blocks to the bed and breakfast. Janet and I unlocked the door, walked in, strolled past the cookie plate—regrettably now bare—and sat in the lounge area. Vicki appeared like magic and asked if we'd like something to drink. We assured her we'd just finished a lavish tea at the Teal Hotel, and Vicki disappeared equally promptly. She was almost like a magician's assistant who materializes and dematerializes at the wave of a wand.

I looked around. We were definitely alone. I turned to Janet. "There's undoubtedly something funny going on." Keeping my voice low, I told her about the brochure I'd found on my bed.

Janet was clearly puzzled. But she wasn't concerned. "I'm sure there's an obvious explanation of some kind. In any event, whatever this is, it has nothing to do with the reason we're here, which is to lie low for a while until we hear from Walter that the police have taken the twins into custody. Just stop worrying and let's enjoy ourselves."

We went to our rooms, changed for dinner, and enjoyed ourselves big time. The Alberta Grille was everything that Darleen had promised, and more. In fact, every single thing we ate and drank was so outstanding that, when we left, we made a reservation for three for the next night; we decided to take Darleen along with us to thank her for her superb recommendation.

Rather than take a taxi for the short ride back to Tweedsmuir House, Janet and I decided to walk. It was summer but it was chilly, because Banff is situated at a height of nearly five thousand feet above sea level. Knowing that Banff is the community with the second highest elevation in Canada, we'd taken with us to dinner the overcoats we'd bought in Calgary. As it happened, the cold night air was refreshing. On the way back, we managed to convince ourselves that our short stroll would enable us to walk off the thousands of calories we'd consumed at the Alberta Grille.

We arrived at Tweedsmuir House, decided against a nightcap, and walked up the broad staircase. I wished Janet a good night and unlocked my door. And there on the bed was a copy of *This Week in Banff Magazine* open at a double-page advertisement for the Western Canada Sightseeing train.

CHAPTER TWELVE

I lay down but I couldn't sleep. The Western Canada Sightseeing mystery was rapidly turning into the Rocky Mountain Horror Picture Show, compounding my already sizeable fears. But then the sheer limitless comfort of that bed massaged the concerns out of my tortured, terrified brain, and I eventually fell into a deep slumber. In fact, it'd been a long time since I'd slept that soundly. The sound of Janet pounding on the door woke me at nine o'clock. She reminded me in a loud voice that we'd told Mrs. McKenzie that we wanted our breakfast at half past eight sharp.

Breakfast was a real treat: blueberry pancakes, or more accurately, huckleberry pancakes—huckleberries are essentially wild blueberries—served with whipped cream and maple syrup. I simply couldn't understand it. Vicki was clearly a gourmet cook specializing in high-calorie food, yet she and her husband looked half starved. It was a great mystery, comparable to the Western Canada Sightseeing mystery in its degree of weirdness. I was obsessed with both conundrums, even though neither was the least bit important in the greater scheme of things, which included the murderous di Campione twins.

We'd arranged with Darleen to pick us up at half past nine, but it was ten o'clock before we were underway. Darleen suggested a drive to Radium Hot Springs and we readily agreed. By this time, Darleen had established herself as an expert on all aspects of the Banff area.

After a wonderful day of touring through gorgeous scenery, we arrived back in Banff in time to change for dinner and to take Darleen to eat at the Alberta Grille. Janet repeatedly declared that the food and wine were just as good as the previous evening, perhaps even better. She constantly praised the braised elk and she raved about the chocolate crème brûlée.

But I couldn't enjoy my meal for three distinct reasons. To begin with, I was worrying *what* I might find on my bed when we returned to Tweedsmuir House after dinner. Then, I was worrying even more *how* the Western Canada Sightseeing material was getting onto my bed. Percy and Vicki were clearly out of the picture. That meant that someone was unlocking the front door, sneaking undetected into Tweedsmuir House, and then unlocking my door and leaving the material on my bed. Thirdly, I was worrying still more *why* the Western Canada

Sightseeing brochure and the advertisement had been left on my bed.

Of course, this was all much ado about nothing. As Janet had pointed out to me earlier, whatever was going on was peripheral to our real concern, which was to stay alive. The fact that someone had a pathological need to break into my room surreptitiously and leave Western Canada Sightseeing materials on my bed shouldn't have bothered me. After all, everything happened while I was out; it wasn't as if someone had sneaked in while I was sleeping. And if I wanted to worry about something serious, I had the di Campione twins at my disposal.

When the meal was finally over, Darleen dropped us off at Tweedsmuir House. I naturally became tenser and tenser as we neared the bed and breakfast, and when we arrived, I was ready to explode. Janet and I unlocked the front door and walked upstairs. With my heart pounding in my chest, I tried to unlock my door. I simply couldn't do it. I handed my key to Janet, who turned the key, opened the door, and turned on the light. There was nothing on my bed.

Janet returned my key to me without a word and went to her room.

***

Darleen had suggested the previous night that we should schedule a seven o'clock wake-up call to enable us to visit Lake Louise and Moraine Lake in Banff National Park in a single day, as well as Emerald Lake in the adjoining Yoho National Park. We reluctantly agreed to the early start. In fact, I started to whinge a bit about it, but almost immediately remembered that every single suggestion that Darleen had made up to now had turned to gold. Accordingly, before we went to bed, we'd left a note downstairs for the McKenzies asking them to wake us at seven and requesting breakfast thirty minutes later.

A light tapping on my door at seven woke me from a deep refreshing slumber. I'd slept unbelievably soundly because the Western Canada Sightseeing paper plague was over and I could enjoy our holiday, or at least enjoy it as much as I could with the di Campione twin-edged sword of Damocles hanging over our heads.

Janet and I arrived at the table promptly at half past seven. I was delighted to find that Vicki had prepared a full Australian breakfast made from the freshest, finest ingredients. It was absolutely superb. But for some strange reason that I simply couldn't work out, she insisted that she'd made a full *Canadian* breakfast made from the freshest, finest ingredients.

You can set your watch by Darleen. Promptly at eight o'clock she appeared, smiling as broadly as ever. And we set off for Lake Louise along the scenic Bow Valley Parkway. An hour later we found ourselves at the village of Lake Louise and then at Lake Louise itself. Darleen parked the Lincoln Town Car in one of the huge parking lots. A short walk through the trees brought us to the water.

Lake Louise has been described as the pearl of the Canadian Rockies, and it certainly is a gem. Much to my surprise, the water wasn't blue; instead, it was a milky turquoise. In fact, the glaciers surrounding the lake are the reason for the color of the water. It seems that as a glacier inches its way down a mountain the ice grinds the bedrock. This glacial erosion generates fine particles of rock called rock flour. As the glacier melts, the rock flour is carried down the mountain in rushing streams and eventually becomes suspended in rivers and lakes. In fact, almost everywhere we went, the water in the rivers and lakes was a cloudy turquoise.

We took a short walk along the shore, then turned around and retraced our steps to the car. The area was crowded with tourists, many of whom were dressed in hiking gear. One woman struggling to carry a huge rucksack on her back wore a metal bell about two inches in diameter mounted on the upper of each of her hiking boots. Darleen explained that the tinkling is intended to drive bears away. Looking around the crowded foreshore of the lake, Janet commented drily that the bells certainly seemed to be working, because there were definitely no bears in sight.

The presence of crowds raised the hairs on the back of my neck again. Yes, the Western Canada

Sightseeing paper chase was over and, yes, there was no possibility whatsoever that the di Campione twins had the slightest idea where we were. Nevertheless, hundreds of people milled about, and malefactors could be somewhere in the crowd. For example, the two people who'd been watching us at the Calgary Stampede might well be standing nearby as we gazed at the endless beauty of the lake. I looked around. Two men stood about ten yards to the left of us. They were about twenty-five but had no particular physical characteristics, other than their unusual height. What also made them stand out was the undeniable fact that they were identical twins. They didn't look familiar in any way, and they stared out over the lake. Consequently, I didn't take any further notice of them, but I was somewhat relieved when Darleen suggested we move on to Moraine Lake.

Soon we were on our way south through unspoiled forest, river, and mountain scenery. I was reminded of the hackneyed phrase "where every prospect pleases." Then I recalled the whole line—it's from Heber's hymn, *From Greenland's Icy Mountains*—which reads: "Where every prospect pleases, and only man is vile." That last part made me think di Campione thoughts again. However, as we neared Moraine Lake, the glorious landscape pushed everything from my mind except the unmatched panorama.

The view from the pile of huge boulders forming the moraine is called "The Twenty Dollar View" because it appeared on the back of the 1969 Canadian twenty-dollar banknote. The Canadian dollar must've increased in value considerably since then, because what we saw from that moraine was undoubtedly a billion-dollar view: ten majestic snow-capped mountain peaks, beautiful Moraine Lake itself, and deep green pine forests.

We scrambled down from the moraine and walked towards the lodge and restaurant nestled in a conifer forest. And there I noticed the really tall identical twins I'd seen at Lake Louise maybe half an hour earlier. I nudged Janet. "Those twins were at Lake Louise." Janet just gave me a withering glance.

We walked back to the car and settled down for the drive to Yoho National Park. Before we stopped for lunch, we parked at the train tunnels of Kicking Horse Pass. Darleen suggested that we start by walking over to the display that shows why and how the two spiral tunnels were constructed. Standing at the first diagram were the two identical, tall, young men I'd seen at Lake Louise and at Moraine Lake.

"Look over there. Those are the twins we saw twice before," I hissed at Janet, trying to keep my voice down to ensure that Darleen, who was some distance behind us, wouldn't hear me.

"They got here first," she hissed back.

"That's because they knew we'd stop here," I replied in kind.

At this point Darleen joined us and we had to stop imitating a pair of angry adders. There was no way for Janet and me to talk privately. We had to resort to gesticulations while we walked behind Darleen. Janet rolled her eyes to indicate that I was being ridiculous. And I could see her point; the three of us and the two of them were following a standard tourist route that hundreds of thousands of visitors to Banff National Park follow each year. In response, I tried to nonverbally convey panic, anger, and fear, in that order. As usual, I failed miserably on all three counts, and Janet had the greatest difficulty suppressing her laughter.

The last scheduled stop was Emerald Lake. Only a few visitors stood with us on the jetty overlooking the water's edge, and none of them even remotely resembled the tall twins I'd seen three times earlier that day. Back in the car, I had to admit to myself, albeit reluctantly, that Janet must've been right; they were just two tourists who were following the same well-travelled route that we were.

As we neared Banff, Darleen asked us if we wanted to visit Jasper. I told her what Marcelle had told us. Darleen laughed. "No sane person drives to Jasper and back the same day. If you want to go—and I strongly recommend the trip—I'll arrange accommodation for you in Jasper overnight and we'll return the next day. You need to know that Jasper doesn't have luxury accommodation, but there's a motor lodge located in the woods just south of the town that's really nice. And I can suggest an excellent restaurant for dinner. It's typical Alberta food: juicy steaks, fresh fish, and well-prepared game."

That convinced me, but for some reason Janet wavered. Clever Darleen clinched the deal by telling her, "And I'm sure we'll see bears on the road to Jasper."

When we reached Tweedsmuir House, Janet and I decided to sample Vicki's cookie du jour. We were munching away on an oatmeal cookie—good, actually extremely good, but fractionally less than in the same league as her prize-winning chocolate chip and macadamia nut cookie—when a thought struck me. "Janet," I asked, "just how old do you think the di Campione twins are?"

From the lack of irritation in her voice, I could tell that Janet had also been worrying about the twins. "Gioachino di Campione, the Sydney drug lord, must've been about forty-five, maybe fifty. You also saw Claudio di Campione at the disused airport. He looked in his middle-to-late forties. Ottorino di Campione, the waiter turned kidnapper, was at least forty, maybe forty-five, but no more than that. Why?"

"Could the youngest brothers, the twins Arcangelo and Domenico di Campione, be about twenty-five?"

Janet saw where this was leading. "Are you suggesting that Tweedledum and Tweedledee are in fact the deadly duo? Get real! Yes, they look like one another; that's because they're identical twins. But they look nothing like Gioachino, Claudio, or Ottorino. No way, José. Just forget about it."

I tried to argue with her, but Janet refused to listen. "Here's the clincher. If those two guys were Arcangelo and Domenico, neither of us would be alive and sitting here in Tweedsmuir House, eating Vicki's oatmeal cookies."

And there the matter rested. For a while.

CHAPTER THIRTEEN

For the second morning in a row, Vicki McKenzie woke us at seven o'clock. After selling us the trip to Jasper, Darleen had gently broken the news that another early start was in store for us. She also strongly recommended that, when we packed a bag for the night, we should take with us our warmest clothes. Neither "suggestion" was particularly welcome. Years of luxurious living had taken the farm out of the farm boy, and tending the sheep before dawn on a freezing cold winter morning in the foothills of the Curtain Range was now just a blurred memory from a former life. Traveling to Jasper certainly didn't seem to be the kind of trip that the Damon Ogilvy of today would enjoy very much.

After another of Vicki's wonderful breakfasts, Darleen drove us to Highway 93, the Icefields Parkway, which leads straight to Jasper. The road ran parallel to the beautiful Bow River, laden with rock flour. Limitless forests of lodgepole pine and other conifers covered the lower reaches of the mountains. And the sun shone in the blue sky. Life was good.

The weather suddenly turned nasty. The rain came in torrents relieved only by the occasional snow flurry—in July. We continued slowly through the rain and arrived at the Icefield Centre around noon. This was a huge lodge containing restaurants, hotel rooms, and the starting point for tours of the Athabasca Glacier, one of the eight glaciers situated across the road from the Centre.

In view of the pelting rain, Darleen parked the car as close to the Icefield Centre as she could. She suggested we put on our warmest clothes. Then we walked through the rain to the Icefield Centre, where Darleen bought snowcoach tickets for Janet and me.

We stood outside under shelter in the waiting area, watching the rain pour. To our amazement, the rain abruptly ceased as suddenly as it had started; this boded well for our trip to the glacier. After about fifteen minutes, a bus drew up and the two of us climbed aboard, together with about fifty excited Francophone tourists. The bus drove us across the road and up a hill to a waiting snowcoach, essentially a six-wheel-drive bus with six huge low-pressure tires. We alighted from the bus and climbed into the snowcoach, which slowly inched its way down one ice slope and up a much longer ice slope. After a few minutes we found ourselves on the Athabasca Glacier. The driver opened the door of the snowcoach and let down the stairs, and we all trooped onto the ice.

Now we understood why Darleen had told us to dress warmly. It was bitterly cold. The wind at ground level at the Icefield Centre was chilly, but the gusts that buffeted us on the mountain while we were walking on the glacier were brutal.

We had to walk slowly to avoid slipping on the wet, packed ice. In front of us was a vertical ice face about a yard high. The ice face separated the area that was open to tourists from a virgin ice sheet that stretched far into the distance. Water dripped down the vertical ice face and flowed into a stream that ran along the base. I unthinkingly put my hand into the stream, which was unarguably at thirty-two degrees Fahrenheit. Trying to warm my hand by putting it in my pocket, I clambered back onto the snowcoach. Janet and I had been on the ice for only about ten minutes, but I for one thought that I'd never be warm again. When all the passengers were aboard, the driver slowly drove us back to the snowcoach depot. There, the otherwise slick operation broke down for some reason, and we had to wait out in the open with a frigid wind blowing over the ice until a bus filled with the next load of tourists on their way to the waiting snowcoach finally arrived to drive us back to the Icefield Centre. The last two passengers who climbed out of the bus were the towering twins.

It was freezing cold on the wind-swept glacier. It was even colder waiting for the bus. But when I saw the twins again, my blood turned to ice in my veins. I looked at Janet. All she said was, "So?"

The bus drove us back to the Icefield Centre and a buffet lunch that looked superlative. But the food turned to ashes in my mouth—what little I could eat of it.

After lunch Darleen drove for a long while and finally turned into the parking area at Athabasca Falls. The falls are beyond outstanding, not because they are high—the drop is only eighty feet—but because of the sheer volume of water. We spent more than half an hour wandering around the area. I tried to focus on the spectacular sights, but I found myself continually scanning the site for the twins. Tourists came and went, usually in twos but sometimes in larger groups, but no identical twins appeared. I hoped that we'd seen the last of them, but I feared the worst.

Our last scheduled stop before dinner was the Hesperides Lodge, where we were to spend the night. But we had to make an unscheduled halt en route. Just before we reached Jasper, we saw cars parked on the side of the road. Darleen immediately realized what was going on. She stomped on the brake pedal and shouted, "Bear!"

A young woman behind the steering wheel of the car that was parked in front of us got out, camera in hand. She came up to our car, and said, "It's a black bear and her cub, over there." She pointed towards a clump of trees on the other side of the road. A bear is always dangerous, but a mother bear with her cub is potentially lethal. Notwithstanding this, the driver in front of us crossed the road, camera in hand. I was concerned about the traffic on Highway 93. If the mother bear had charged her, the young woman wouldn't have had an escape route back across the road unless at that time there was a gap in the passing cars. The degree of utter stupidity that some people can demonstrate to get a photograph of a bear and her cub is quite amazing.

I was pleased that the cub disappeared into the bushes extremely quickly, which lowered the danger level. The mother bear ambled about for a minute or two, then followed her cub and vanished from our sight.

Darleen turned to Janet. "There, didn't I tell you there were bears on the road to Jasper?"

Janet just smiled contentedly.

The bear-spotting excitement over, the car in front of us pulled out and drove away. Darleen was about to follow it when a medium-sized white car passed us, slammed on its brakes, and slid backwards into the now vacant space in front of us. Darleen, a careful driver, waited until the white car was fully stationary before she pulled out. As she drove past the parked car in front of us, I could clearly see the tall identical twins in the front seats. I nudged Janet, who just rolled her eyes. I was cold all over again.

The bear sighting had occurred only a mile or two from our hotel for the night. The Hesperides Lodge turned out to be delightful, with wooden cabins constructed out of thick logs. I, however, was unable to appreciate the comforts of the hotel, the beauty of the forest in which it was located, or the glorious restaurant in downtown Jasper that Darleen chose for us that night; all I could think about for the rest of the day was the twins.

Janet was no help. I went to her cabin before dinner to discuss the situation, but she was having none of it.

"There are millions and millions of identical twins all over the world," she said. "Some are short, and some are tall. And some of them are currently in Banff National Park. Some of them are on a two-day trip from Banff to Jasper and back to Banff the next day, and everyone on that trip, twins or not, stops at the Icefield Centre, and everyone stops to see bears. You were shocked to see them on their way to the glacier and on the side of the road where we saw the bear and her cub. I, on the contrary, was most surprised *not* to see them at the Athabasca Falls. And I wouldn't have been paralyzed with fear if I'd seen them checking in at the lodge just after we did. Nor will I be overcome with terror if it turns out that they've decided to eat their dinner at the same place where we're going to tonight. They're just tourists visiting the same things we're visiting because we're also tourists."

"But they're twins!"

"Yes, they are. But they aren't the di Campione twins."

"But they're twins!" I repeated, forlornly.

"Yes, you're right. They definitely are twins. And Canada is a free country, and twins are free to visit Canada and go to the Banff National Park and visit all the sights. Although there are an almost infinite number of spectacular views that are beyond compare in their endless loveliness, there are only a small number of specific sights, like the Athabasca Glacier or Lake Louise. The laws of probability dictate that visitors to the Park are likely to bump into one another repeatedly."

"But they're twins!"

"Even twins have to obey the laws of probability." She reached into her handbag. "Here's an elastic band." She handed it to me. "Take it and pull yourself together!"

I was clearly wasting my time. I stumbled out of her cabin and sat in mine until Darleen came to call us for dinner.

***

The first stop the next morning on our way back to Banff was a repeat visit to the Athabasca Falls. It had rained during the night, and consequently the Athabasca River was even more swollen with water and the falls were even more spectacularly powerful. No twins showed up, which was a great relief to me.

Our second stop was unscheduled. Yes, you've guessed it; Darleen found another bear for Janet. More precisely, Darleen saw a car stopped on the side of a meadow full of wild flowers, and correctly deduced the reason. We all hoped that it was a grizzly bear, but grizzlies are rare, and in the middle of the meadow was another black bear.

For about twenty minutes, the bear ate dandelions and Janet stared fixedly at the bear. Eventually, Darleen and I realized, unless something was said or done, Janet would watch the bear until every last dandelion had been eaten. The bear was large, but the field of dandelions was considerably larger, and there was a very real risk that it might be several weeks before the bear moved out of the field. I surreptitiously nodded to Darleen, who slowly eased the car onto Highway 93. Janet said nothing. And I couldn't see the twins in any of the other cars that were parked for bear-watching purposes.

An hour later, I saw a sign reading "Peyton Lake— Bow Summit." Darleen turned off the highway and parked the car. We started walking.

The path to Bow Summit began horizontally. The inclination started to increase, slowly to start with, but soon the trail became quite steep. The numerous alpine wildflowers on both sides of the path were a pleasant surprise, especially the western anemones.

But as beautiful as the flora was, nothing could prepare us for what we saw as we reached the large wooden viewing platform at the top of the path.

In the huge valley below us lay a long, somewhat narrow lake, surrounded by forests of conifers. But what took my breath away—or rather, what was left of my breath after I'd climbed up all the way to Bow Summit—was the color of the water. Yes, by this time I knew all about rock flour, and I'd seen numerous glacial lakes of various hues. But the turquoise blue of Peyton Lake was quite different. This wasn't the milky turquoise green of Lake Louise but rather an intense shade of blue. We stood there for some minutes, saying nothing, just marveling.

Then we started down the mountain. As always, the walk down was harder than the climb up had been, but I arrived at the parking area in reasonable shape—until I saw the identical twins walking towards us. Then I all but fainted from the shock.

The rest of the day was a blur. Janet was visibly disgusted by my reaction. The twins were clearly the wrong age to be the di Campiones and they hadn't tried to kill us. On the contrary, they'd completely ignored us every time we'd encountered them. We hadn't heard them speaking, which meant that we didn't know if they were Italophone, but they certainly didn't physically resemble the many other people of Italian origin whom I'd met in Australia. Nevertheless, my totally irrational reaction on seeing them was as if Arcangelo and Domenico were standing right in front of us, their handguns aimed unwaveringly at Janet and me.

Janet told me later that we went to get lunch at a café at Bow Lake immediately after we saw the twins. All they had left were sandwiches, and I ate one sandwich consisting of stale bread and dried out tuna, which tells you what kind of state I was in. After that, I was told, we walked outside the building to see beautiful Bow Lake, but the rain suddenly started again. Janet had to order me to come back under shelter; apparently, I just stood there, getting wetter and wetter. And then I simply sat silently in the black Lincoln Town Car while Darleen drove us back to Tweedsmuir House in Banff.

Worse was to come.

***

The next morning, I sat up in bed, stretched, yawned, and then noticed the Western Canada Sightseeing postcard on my bed. It was only with the greatest self-control that I stopped myself from screaming aloud. While I was sleeping, someone had unlocked my door, tiptoed in, and put a postcard on my bed.

I dressed as quickly as I could and, holding the postcard in my hand, rushed to Janet's room. She looked at the color photograph of the train against the backdrop of snow-capped peaks, and I could see that she immediately realized what it meant. But then she thought for a minute.

"Are you quite sure it wasn't there last night?" she asked. "You were in no fit state to notice anything when we came back from dinner in Banff. You ate mechanically and you didn't say a word all evening. In fact, you probably don't remember this, but I ordered for you and I had to prod you to eat your food and drink your wine. And you barely touched your dessert. So how can you be sure that the postcard wasn't there when we returned from dinner?"

There was nothing I could say. Janet was right, of course. She usually is. She stays cool and rational, no matter what. Rudyard Kipling put it perfectly in the opening lines of his poem "If —":

> *If you can keep your head when all about you*
> *Are losing theirs and blaming it on you*

Well, Janet keeps her head at all times. Rather than panicking, as I was doing big-time at that moment, she calmly turned the postcard over. Scrawled across the back in hasty block letters was the message:

WE'RE LOOKING FORWARD TO SEEING YOU AGAIN ON THE TRAIN. BON VOYAGE!

It was unsigned.

"Do we take this to the police?" I asked Janet.

"No, we go and have a good breakfast downstairs and then we discuss this. We have plenty of time; we asked Darleen to pick us up at ten o'clock to take us to the Banff Gondola ride to the top of Sulphur Mountain."

I shook my head feebly in protest. Janet took absolutely no notice, and we went down to breakfast. I was frightened, and I was desperate to solve the Western Canada Sightseeing mystery. Janet was relaxed, phlegmatic, and clearly hungry. Vicki had made buckwheat pancakes with turkey sausages, and there was plenty of warm maple syrup. As usual, the coffee was excellent. I think it was the coffee that brought back my courage, which up till then had been sadly lacking. About halfway through the meal I suddenly realized how badly I was behaving and how terribly stupid I was being. I turned to Janet and declared, "We're going to crack this, no matter what!"

Janet just smiled.

After the meal, we moved into the lounge area and settled ourselves in comfortable armchairs. "Repeating the question that I asked you before breakfast," I said, "do we take this to the police?"

"Would you be prepared to sign a sworn affidavit that the postcard wasn't there when you came in last night? I think not. That means that all that will happen is that the Banff Mounties will ask us if we want to lay criminal charges against our hosts for: (a) leaving a brochure on your bed before we arrived at

Tweedsmuir House; (b) leaving a free magazine on your bed while you were out; and (c) leaving a postcard on your bed while you were at dinner. And then they'll lock us up for wasting their time."

I could see that Janet was right.

Then she continued: "Furthermore, I doubt that Vicki and Percy will be too happy after the police have interviewed them. We'd have to find somewhere else to stay until our train leaves. And now there's no question that we have to take that train, no matter what. We can't possibly ignore the message on that postcard."

"But how did the person who left it on my bed know that we're going to be on the train?" I asked. "We made the booking with Marcelle in the morning, and when we arrived in Banff the next morning the brochure was already lying there. Someone living in Banff must be responsible for all this. There simply wasn't enough time for anyone else to pull that stunt."

Janet just grunted.

I went on. "He left a copy of *This Week in Banff Magazine* on my bed while we were at dinner. And he put the postcard on my bed while I slept, although I'm grudgingly willing to concede that he might've left it there while we were at dinner last night. Again that points to a local."

"Not necessarily," Janet replied. "What if, as soon as we left her shoppe, Marcelle contacted someone in Calgary? He or she could've driven to Banff, arriving more than half a day before we did. That would give him or her ample time to organize the brochure before we arrived. Marcelle could even have phoned a contact in Vancouver, who then flew to Calgary and drove here. A person in Edmonton could also have managed it; from there to Banff is only a four-hour car drive. And having arrived here, he or she could've stayed for a few more days somewhere in or near Banff to orchestrate the other two stunts."

"Why do you keep saying 'he or she'?" I asked. "Do you seriously think a woman could be behind this?"

"It's certainly possible. After all, suppose that someone actually sneaked quietly into your room last night without waking you. Isn't it more likely that the perpetrator was a woman?"

Once again I had to agree with Janet.

"And look at the postcard. The writer has used block letters in an effort to disguise his or her handwriting. If the writer is indeed a woman, she'd probably go to some lengths to hide that fact. In my opinion, not only is it possible that the person behind all this is a woman, I think it's likely."

"Okay, you've convinced me. But there's still one huge problem with all this: Why is someone leaving Western Canada Sightseeing materials on my bed?"

And, try as we might, neither of us could come up with any explanation at all, let alone a reasonably plausible one.

"How about asking Vicki or Percy?" Janet said.

"What would be the point? The last time I asked Vicki, she denied knowing anything about it, and I just upset her. And Percy never seems to be around."

Janet stood up. "Well, if we can't explain it there's clearly no point in going to the police, is there? Let's go upstairs and get our things. We're about to go up a mountain in a cable car."

CHAPTER FOURTEEN

D arleen drove us past the Banff Springs
Hotel and the Upper Hot Springs to the
Banff Gondola. Unfortunately, I don't have
a head for heights, and I certainly wasn't looking
forward to the eight-minute ride to the top of Sulphur
Mountain. Darleen told us that the upper terminal is
at a height of about eight thousand feet, but I just
couldn't see the point of going that high in the sky.

Darleen bought the tickets, and the three of us
entered the lower terminal. There was no queue. As
we reached the entrance, a gondola large enough for
four people arrived. A young attendant ushered the
three of us aboard and locked the door. Maybe it was
because the gondola all but skimmed the treetops, but
the ride to the summit wasn't too frightening for me.
In fact, I quite enjoyed it. We reached the summit, and
the three of us climbed out.

The altitude and the fact that nothing blocked the
freezing wind made the air bitterly cold. But the view
was stupendous. To the north we could see Banff

below us in all its glory, including a beautiful golf course situated on one side of the Bow River. To the south was the town of Canmore, also on the Bow River, which gushed its way to Calgary. To the east and the west towered mountains and more mountains, and forests dominated the landscape everywhere we looked.

Then we saw a wooden boardwalk leading across a saddle to the next peak. "It's only 380 steps to the top of Sanson's Peak, and on the summit you can see where there used to be a laboratory for studying cosmic rays," Darleen said.

I assumed that she'd made that remark for information purposes only, because there was no way that I was going to walk up three hundred and eighty steps to see the world's leading observatory for studying anything at all, let alone an empty building that once housed a laboratory. But that was before I saw the tall twins coming through the door leading from the upper terminal.

At that point I didn't know what to do. My initial reaction was to run, but that meant one of only two options. We could go onto the boardwalk, but that was a dead-end route. Alternatively, we could follow one of the many trails that started at the top of the mountain, leading who knew where into the surrounding peaks. Then I realized that, as before, the twins were totally ignoring us.

The best thing to do would be to ignore them. Consequently, when I'd finished admiring the glorious view, I stepped inside the upper terminal without even glancing at the terrible twosome. The three of us then stood in line for a gondola to take us back down to the lower terminal.

The trip down was a little worse for me than the trip up, but that was easy to solve: I simply closed my eyes until I felt a bump. The problem was that the bump wasn't because we'd arrived back at the lower terminal. Instead, the Banff Gondola had come to a halt. I looked behind me and saw about fifteen stationary gondolas. I looked in front at another fifteen or so. In other words, we were stuck halfway up Sulphur Mountain or, if you prefer, halfway down. And talking about "down," I looked down. We were stuck at one of the few places where the wires are considerably higher than treetop level. In fact, we were so high above the ground that, unless the power was restored, a helicopter would be the only way that the emergency services could ever rescue us.

At the upper terminal we'd read about the two stand-by motors—one diesel, one electric—and the electric power generator. It didn't state anywhere that total stoppages were impossible or even highly unlikely, but that was the impression I'd received. Why had the system come to a sudden total halt?

Naturally, I immediately concluded that the twins were responsible for the problem. After all, with multiple motors and a generator to supply power if the electricity supply were interrupted, that clearly was the only possible explanation. The fact that our gondola had been brought to a halt so far off the ground was absolute proof that the twins were involved.

At this point in my thinking, two things happened. I realized that, unless there was a way to somehow cut the one-and-a-half-inch thick steel cable, which even in my feverish imagination was a highly unlikely possibility, we were totally safe where we were. If the tall twins were in fact trying to kill us, this wasn't a particularly effective way to try to go about it. Then, the gondolas started moving again and we soon arrived safe and sound at the lower terminal. There, they told us that a brief interruption in the power supply had occurred, but the electricity came back within a few seconds, even before the engineers could start the standby generator and bring it online. Those "few seconds" had seemed like hours to me.

When Darleen dropped us at Tweedsmuir House after lunch, neither Janet nor I commented on the incident. I assumed that Janet kept silent because nothing particularly remarkable had happened. I said nothing for obvious reasons. By now, I'd worked out that I was suffering from posttraumatic stress disorder. For the umpteenth time, I wished that it would clear up once and for all.

***

We'd been on the go morning, noon, and night for six days and we definitely needed some down time before the train trip. After breakfast the next morning, we told Darleen we were going to take things very easy. We'd eat at restaurants near Tweedsmuir House. Perhaps we'd walk the six blocks to downtown Banff, and then again perhaps we wouldn't. But whatever we decided to do or not do, we wouldn't require Darleen's services that day. Then we realized that the following day we were taking the Western Canada Sightseeing train to Vancouver, and all we'd need was a ride to the station at half past seven in the morning. A cab would do the trick.

Accordingly, Darleen arranged with a reliable taxi driver to be at the bed and breakfast at the appointed time the following morning. I'd paid Marcelle in advance for the week for which we'd engaged Darleen, but I gave our wonderful guide a hefty tip, and thanked her profusely for everything she'd done for us.

The day that Janet and I spent together in Banff wasn't pleasant. On the one hand, we had all our creature comforts: books we'd bought at a most excellent bookstore in Banff, cozy padded armchairs in the lounge area of Tweedsmuir House, and a truly scrumptious lunch and an outstanding dinner at restaurants a block or two away. Our reading was interrupted every so often by Vicki McKenzie bearing refreshments, including her incomparable cookies. When she arrived with a tray brimming with food and drink, Janet and I would put down our books, eat and drink, and converse in a desultory manner.

This chatting was the problem. Obviously, we both wanted to talk about the towering twins, but we were extremely reluctant to start that conversation. We also wished to discuss the Western Canada Sightseeing material that someone had placed on my bed. However, that topic was equally taboo. Janet knew how concerned I was about both issues and wanted to reassure me that we had no need for worry about either subject. At the same time, she was well aware that, in the course of a conversation, I might raise some new aspect that we'd previously not considered. Following that line of thought might then result in making the whole situation seem a lot worse than it actually was. Consequently, Janet kept quiet for fear of inadvertently adding fuel to the flame. As for me, I was barely keeping my PTSD-linked nervousness under control, and I didn't dare say anything in case it increased my anxiety beyond breaking point.

Somehow, we got through that day. We were scrupulously polite to each other. But you could've cut the tension with a butter knife. In retrospect, we should probably have asked Darleen to drive us around all day anywhere she chose, just to keep our minds off the two taboo topics.

The next morning, we hurriedly ate the alpine buffet Vicki provided: cold meats, cold cheeses, and freshly baked croissants, washed down with her incomparable coffee. Percy was out climbing mountains somewhere.

The taxi was waiting outside seven minutes early—that's always a good sign. The driver was a taciturn elderly man who'd dressed for the summer's day by wrapping himself up in a heavy overcoat and donning a scarf, gloves, and a red and blue knitted woolen cap. Unlike everyone else we'd met in Banff, he at best grudgingly grunted responses to our friendly morning greetings and inquiries after his health. I hoped that he'd warm up later in the day, in both senses.

He drove us to the station where we had to cross a picket line of striking Western Canada Sightseeing attendants. Strikes are all too common in Australia, which meant this was certainly not the first picket line I'd ever seen. But this was definitely the first time I'd encountered smiling, friendly, pleasant picketers. I had to conclude that either this was the Canadian way of striking or else the Western Canada Sightseeing organization hires only people who are perpetually cheerful.

We checked in our suitcases at the Western Canada Sightseeing desk at the station and then sat down in the waiting room until the train arrived from Calgary. A drizzle started. We hoped that it wouldn't prevent our feasting our eyes on the incomparable scenery that we knew we'd encounter en route to Vancouver.

The train arrived, pulled by two powerful locomotives. We walked to our carriage in the light rain. The attendants had rolled out red carpets in front of the Diamond Class carriages, and flags flanked the runners. To help the passengers board, a small step had been placed in front of the doorway. Furthermore, one attendant took our hand luggage while another stood ready on our other side to help us up, should such assistance prove necessary. This was the incomparably high standard of service when the trip started, and this remained the standard all through the train ride.

We stepped into the carriage. To our right was a sliding glass door leading to an open viewing platform. To our left was the dining saloon. In front of us was a spiral staircase. We climbed the staircase and found ourselves in a dome coach. The seating accommodated about seventy passengers. At the front of the coach, a large serving area held a bowl of fruit. Alcohol was freely available at no charge.

The train slowly drew out of Banff Station. On our left, a white wolf stood on a grassy knoll, staring interestedly at the train. The drizzle stopped and, even though the sun didn't come out until later, the sky brightened visibly. And our rail journey through Banff National Park commenced.

The train trip was nothing short of astounding. Even though we'd driven on numerous roads in the area, everything looked better from the train: the mountains seemed taller, the lakes appeared deeper, the trees greener, and the rivers wider and faster.

Adding to the magic, of course, was the food. At the start of the trip, various managers gave us orientation talks. Janet and I pricked up our ears when food was discussed. We learned that the dining saloon, with thirty-six seats, could cater for only half of the passengers in our carriage at any one time. As a result, the travelers would have to eat in two sessions. It came as no surprise to us that, when the first group of passengers were invited downstairs for breakfast, those of us still seated upstairs were served tea and scones; the Western Canada Sightseeing organization doesn't allow its guests to go hungry for long.

As soon as we'd eaten our pre-breakfast snack, we went down the spiral staircase to the open viewing platform at the rear of our carriage. It was nice to be in the open air, face-to-face with nature. We exchanged pleasantries with fellow guests, two of whom then walked through a gate at the back of the platform to the next carriage. We realized that this was how the managers traversed the train from one end to the other. After about ten minutes on the platform, we returned to our seats in the dome car.

Soon it was our turn to go down for breakfast. We were presented with a menu that included omelets, Eggs Benedict made with Montreal smoked meat, and buttermilk pancakes. Fresh croissants were served while we were waiting for the chefs to prepare our scrambled eggs with smoked steelhead salmon, topped with kelp caviar and lemon chive crème fraîche.

After our second cups of coffee, we got up from our seats in the dining saloon and started walking towards the spiral staircase. The door to the viewing platform was in front of us. Through the glass I could see the tall twins. I nudged Janet. Her faced stayed impassive, she said nothing, but when we'd returned to our seats, she wiped her forehead with a tissue.

"What are they doing here?" I asked.

"They're not in our carriage. They must've crossed to the viewing platform from another carriage."

"But why would they do that?"

Janet was silent. Then she said exactly what I was thinking. "They stood there in order to be certain that we'd see them when we returned to our seats after breakfast. Let's talk about this when we get to Kamloops."

I've just realized that I forgot to tell you something else that you need to know. The Western Canada Sightseeing train runs only during the day. The passengers sleep at hotels at Kamloops the end of the first day, with their accommodation there organized by the ever-efficient Western Canada Sightseeing organization. When the train reaches Kamloops station, buses swoop onto the platform and stop at the relevant carriage. Passengers step from their train carriage onto their bus, and the bus takes them to their hotel, where they spend the night. The next morning the buses pick up their passengers and transport them back to the station.

Diamond Class passengers find their luggage waiting for them in their hotel rooms, and yes, every suitcase somehow seems to end up in the correct room. The next morning the passengers leave their luggage in their hotel rooms when they check out, and their luggage equally bafflingly ends up waiting for them at the Vancouver station when the train arrives there at the end of the two-day trip. The tall twins and the materials on my bed were nothing compared to the mysteries of the luggage elves of Western Canada Sightseeing organization!

That evening in the Kamloops hotel, we discussed the twins. But after half an hour of intense analysis we could do no better than our conclusion earlier that day when we saw them: the reason they'd stood on the viewing platform was to guarantee that we'd see them when we returned to our seats after breakfast. We also realized that this had been their game the entire week. All they wanted to do was to ensure that we'd repeatedly see them. But why they were doing that utterly baffled us.

CHAPTER FIFTEEN

The next morning our bus arrived at our hotel promptly at half past seven, and we soon found ourselves back in our comfortable reclining seats in our carriage. Our ever-helpful attendants were again attentive from the word go. Then I noticed something had changed. A new attendant had replaced one of the previous day's attendants. His substitute was in an ill-fitting uniform. Furthermore, he seemed totally at sea as he walked up and down the dome coach.

Then I worked out what must have happened. The original replacement attendant must have fallen ill during the night, which meant that a last-minute substitute had to be found. What with the strike and the lockout, experienced back-up attendants weren't waiting in Kamloops to fill in for such an emergency, and they'd had to press into service a substitute replacement—yes, you know exactly what I mean. He obviously couldn't have had a uniform, which meant that he'd have to wear the original replacement's uniform, presumably hurriedly dry cleaned and pressed. But despite all the efforts of the organization, the uniform didn't fit properly. Anyhow, that wasn't my problem; I was sure that everything would be sorted out when we arrived in Vancouver. And if the substitute replacement attendant wasn't quite as slick as the original replacement attendant, well, we'd manage somehow.

Those passengers who, like us, had been second-session diners the previous day now ate in the first session, which meant that Janet and I enjoyed a delicious early breakfast. As we left the dining saloon and headed for the spiral staircase, we surreptitiously glanced at the open-air viewing platform. No twins to be seen.

We reached our seats in the dome car and settled down for the day's travel. Because the scenery was pleasant but by no means as stunning as on the first day, I started a crossword puzzle and Janet took out a book. An hour or two passed, during which time the guide drew our attention to some bald eagles perched on telephone poles. Then the second session passengers returned from their breakfasts. A few minutes later Janet left her seat. I assumed she was going to the restroom, and I continued with my crossword puzzle.

Hardly had I read the next clue when the substitute replacement attendant approached me. Previously, he hadn't interacted with me in any way, but now he came up to me and said in an accent that I couldn't place, "Your companion would like you to join her for tea in the dining car."

He courteously stood back as I got out of my seat, then he led the way downstairs and into the dining saloon. I found no sign of Janet, but two teacups and saucers had been placed on the window side of a table for four, and a teapot, milk jug, and sugar bowl were laid out between the two cups. He escorted me to the table and indicated that I was to sit on the far end of the banquette, facing the engine, that is, with my back to the entrance to the saloon. I slid in, sitting directly opposite one of the cups and saucers.

To my undisguised surprise, the attendant slid in next to me. Before I could say anything, he drew a medium-sized hypodermic syringe out of an inside pocket of his jacket. In one fluid motion, he quickly removed the plastic shield covering the point of the needle and held the needle against my upper arm. He then put his other hand on the teapot, a clever move that ensured that, in the unlikely event of someone entering the dining saloon between meal times, at first glance it would look as if he was pouring tea for me.

"One shout out of you and I will plunge the needle into your arm and you will be dead. The doctors will say you died of a heart attack. And you'd better hope that no one comes into the dining saloon, because I will kill you immediately if they do."

I was absolutely shocked. I could hardly speak. The best I could manage was to croak out, "Why?"

"Thanks to your meddling, two of our finest comrades are facing life in prison."

Much to my surprise, I was able to solve the puzzle immediately. "You took part in the Srebrenica genocide," I said.

His reaction stunned me further, if that were possible. "It wasn't genocide! We killed only men and boys, not women or girls. That means it couldn't be genocide—genocide means killing a whole people."

I wasn't going to argue with the Bosnian Serb's revisionist interpretation of the term *genocide*. But I wanted to know the facts. "How did you find us?" I asked.

"Easy. You ordered a room-service breakfast at the hotel at Sydney Airport just before you left for Canada. The room-service waiter at the hotel was on the lookout because we'd made sure that all our comrades in Sydney knew about you. When he saw the two cops standing on guard outside your rooms, he put two and two together. And we easily obtained your new names from the Canadian National Airline passenger list; there were only three first-class passengers. When you got to Vancouver, we assumed that you'd take the Western Canada Sightseeing train from Vancouver to Banff. The wife of one of our comrades is a reservations clerk with the Western Canada Sightseeing organization. We told her to scan the passenger lists every hour or two. Much to her surprise, your name turned up on a Banff to

Vancouver reservation. It's standard practice to record where the passenger is staying in Banff in order to be able to communicate with them in case of a change of plan or a delay. As a result, we knew all about Tweedsmuir House. The comrades contacted me in Calgary, I loaded some Western Canada Sightseeing train material into my car, and I drove to Banff.

"When I got to Tweedsmuir House, Vicki was out but I asked Percy McKenzie to 'play a practical joke' on you. He refused point blank. In order to get his full cooperation, I told him in the greatest detail what I'd do to Vicki if he didn't cooperate and what I'd do to him and Vicki if he went to the police. He's a brave man, but I managed to terrify him. He then did everything I asked. And it was equally easy to persuade that other attendant to call in sick. He's a coward; I didn't have to tell him even a fraction of what I told Percy McKenzie."

"But why did you instruct Percy to leave the brochure and the postcard on my bed?" For some reason, I overlooked the copy of *This Week in Banff Magazine.*

"We wanted to be 100 percent certain that you'd be on the train to enable me to kill you here. The Canadian police in the cities are highly efficient, but the country Mounties are hicks. When they find your body, I'll tell them you had a heart attack, and that will be that. And now I'm going to kill you."

He raised the syringe in order to plunge it firmly into my upper arm—and Janet hit him hard on the head with a bottle of nonvintage British Columbian champagne or, more correctly, sparkling wine. The Bosnian Serb collapsed on the table, his head breaking the cup and saucer in front of me. Bubbly poured from the broken bottle over his unconscious body.

I later learned that when Janet returned to her seat and saw that I wasn't there she quickly realized that she hadn't seen me outside the restroom or on the viewing platform. So she went to investigate. As she entered the dining saloon, she saw the attendant sitting next to me. She grabbed the bottle from the display stand near the entrance to the saloon and tiptoed up to us. Once she'd overheard what was going on, one hard blow from the bottle was sufficient to save my life.

What followed was like a Keystone Cops movie, only considerably more chaotic. On hearing the noise in the dining saloon, two chefs rushed in. One brandished a butcher's knife, the other a large cleaver. They saw the attendant lying unconscious on the table, blood pouring from the wound on his head, while Janet stood over him with a broken bottle in her hand. They immediately assumed, correctly, that Janet had viciously attacked the attendant, but they didn't appreciate the circumstances of the assault. Understandably, they called for help from their colleague, and all three chefs quickly trussed Janet up.

Two attendants who rushed to assist them participated in the binding. Janet didn't resist in any way, and wisely said nothing.

To cut a long story short, when the train arrived at the next station, which was situated precisely in the middle of nowhere, two country Mounties were waiting on the platform to arrest Janet. They came into the dining car with guns drawn. They removed the heavy string the chefs had tied around Janet, and they cuffed her hands behind her back. Then they took a look at the body of the recumbent attendant and confirmed by radio that the ambulance the train manager had summoned was indeed needed.

We waited in silence for about fifteen minutes until the ambulance arrived and two emergency medical technicians entered the carriage. They carefully loaded the Bosnian Serb "attendant" onto a stretcher and carried him to the waiting ambulance.

I thought that, by this time, nothing more could surprise me, but the Mounties managed it. They looked at one another, nodded, and proceeded to arrest and handcuff me as a material witness; I *think* that was what they said. Unlike Janet, who'd stayed silent, I started shouting, "He tried to kill me, get the syringe!"

They ignored me, and marched Janet and me to their car, which was parked on the platform. They loaded us into the back seat. I kept screaming, "He tried to kill me, get the syringe!" but to no avail.

As they were about to drive off, the policeman in the passenger seat suddenly said, "Hold it!" to his colleague. He turned to me and asked, "Did you say something about a syringe?"

I briefly explained what had happened. There was silence for a while. Then the cop in the passenger seat said to his colleague. "Watch them carefully. I'm going to look for the syringe, if there is one."

More silence reigned as Janet and I sat there uncomfortably with cuffed hands. Eventually the Mountie returned with a plastic evidence bag containing the syringe. He opened the car door, sat down, fastened his seatbelt, and they drove off without a word. Strong silent types may be one thing, but those two were taking the concept to ridiculous extremes.

Soon we arrived at a rural police station. The policemen took us out of the car and marched us to separate cells. We couldn't communicate with one another; unlike the cells you see in some movies, these had solid walls and doors. My cell contained a bed, a commode without a seat, and a washbasin with a tap. And that was it. At least they'd removed my handcuffs, and I hoped that they'd done the same for Janet.

***

A couple of hours passed. Eventually the cell door opened, and the Mountie who'd found the syringe escorted me to the main room of the police station. Two men in plainclothes stood there. I wondered if they were senior detectives who knew all about what had happened in Srebrenica. If not, Janet and I were in for a long stay in jail. The men introduced themselves by their last names, Smith and Jones— clearly not their real names. They invited me to sit down.

Mr. Smith said to me, "Can you show me some identification?"

I took out my passport and handed it to him. He scrutinized it the way immigration officials do, except that he didn't have the computer they use. He looked at me, looked at the passport photograph, then closed the passport and put it down. But something made him think for a minute. He looked up idly at one corner of the room, paused again, then picked up the passport once more, scrutinized it even more carefully this time, looked at my face feature-by-feature, then asked, in a slow, level voice, "Mr. Presser, where did you get this passport?"

I quickly decided that this was no time to be clever and immediately replied, "Detective Chief Inspector Walter Tregethick, New South Wales Police Force, gave it to me."

He wrote this down. "It's about half past one here now. What time is it in Sydney?"

I thought for a moment or two. "About half past six tomorrow morning."

"Fair enough. You don't happen to have his phone number on you, do you?"

Once a financial planner, always a financial planner, which means that memorizing numbers is automatic for me. I gave Smith the number and told him the country code. He wrote it all down.

Mr. Smith took out a cell phone and started pushing buttons. Thanks to modern communications technology, a few seconds later he was talking to Walter. More precisely, to judge from what he was saying, Smith was talking, and Walter was trying to wake from a deep sleep with a cell phone in his hand out of which a voice with a pronounced Canadian accent was emanating.

It took Walter longer than I would've expected to wake up, but once he did, I deduced that he was all business. Smith's conversation became clipped and rapid. Finally, Smith said to Walter, "Fine, I'll call you back."

He put down his cell phone and turned to me, "Mr. Ogilvy," Mr. Smith said, calling me by my real name, "Please tell me what happened on the train."

"I'd have to go back a bit to put the story in perspective. How much do you know about what happened in Sydney?"

"Enough, I think, at least for now. Would you please start from when you arrived in Canada?"

I told him the story in detail. When it came to reporting what the attendant had said to me, I added a hypothesis of my own. "Percy McKenzie was never around; he was always said to be running up hills or climbing mountains. He impressed me as being absolutely honest, and my experience is that the more honest the man, the less convincing a liar he makes. My guess is that he introduced himself to me when we arrived but disappeared immediately afterwards to ensure that he could never be around to answer questions about the brochure, the copy of *This Week in Banff Magazine*, or the postcard; he must've known what a poor prevaricator he is."

"Are you saying he left his wife alone with that killer around?"

"No, I'm not saying that at all. If you ask him, I think he'll tell you that he protected Vicki by not telling her anything at all about the Bosnian Serb murderer or the material from the Western Canada Sightseeing organization. But when he told her that he was going out to climb mountains, my guess is that he quietly returned and hid in one of the unused bedrooms. Tweedsmuir House has four bedrooms for guests but only two were in use during our stay. I think that he stayed in one of the other two bedrooms, carefully watching from a window in case the killer returned."

When I finished talking, I asked him about Janet. Of course, I didn't know what name to use, her real name or the name on her false passport. So I simply said, "Will you please release my friend now?"

"Of course," Smith said. "We'll need a detailed statement from her, too, and if her story corroborates yours, the two of you will be free to go."

A few minutes later, the policeman appeared with Janet. I was asked to wait in another room to allow them to interview Janet independently. As I left for the station commander's office, I heard Smith phoning Walter again. I suppose Smith wanted to know the real name of "my friend."

I had to wait about thirty minutes. Then I was called back into the main room. Janet, Smith, and Jones were sitting there. Their body language told me that all three of them were relaxed.

Smith told us that we were free to leave but that we'd have to stay in Canada until the contents of the syringe had been analyzed. Jones suggested that they should get an interim report from the laboratory. That was the first time I'd heard him speak.

Smith pushed more buttons, had a brief conversation with someone, then turned to me. "The lab hasn't issued its final report yet, but one thing is certain: if you'd been injected with the contents of that syringe, you'd have died in a few seconds. Also, the preliminary finding is that superficially it would've looked as if you'd died from a heart attack. What this means is that we'll probably charge the Srebrenica killer from the train with attempted murder, and then after he's served his sentence, we'll deport him to Croatia to face trial for murder. The Croatian police will be delighted that we've found another member of Drugovi—that's the Serbo-Croatian word for *comrades*. Drugovi is the name of the organization that the people who committed the Srebrenica atrocity set up to shelter one another. It's like ODESSA was for former SS officers."

He nodded to indicate that the interview was at an end. I was about to say goodbye to Messrs. Smith and Jones when a thought struck me. "Where are we, and how do we get to Vancouver from here?"

Smith laughed. "You're in Connickville, about two hours by road from Vancouver. We drove here from Vancouver to interview you, and now that we know all we need to know, we'd be delighted to give you a ride back. Where are you staying in Vancouver, and how many suitcases do you each have?"

I told him. He immediately gave instructions to one of the policemen to contact the Western Canada Sightseeing organization to tell them to deliver our suitcases to the Postillion Hotel. Then he and Jones escorted us to their car, and we left for Vancouver.

It was a strange trip. Smith and Jones had extracted all the information they needed from us, but they were totally unwilling to impart anything at all about themselves. After a few utterly fruitless attempts at conversation, we sat in silence at the back of the car until Smith dropped us at the Postillion

Hotel. Needless to say, our luggage was waiting there for us; we'd expected no less from the Western Canada Sightseeing organization, of course.

We checked in and changed for dinner. When we asked the concierge to recommend a place to eat, she suggested a Chinese seafood restaurant on the waterfront. The food was every bit as good as she'd promised, and our table by the window offered a wonderful view of Vancouver Harbour by night. Once we'd eaten our fill—and we hadn't eaten since breakfast because for some strange reason they didn't serve us a gourmet lunch in the Connickville jail—we started discussing the case.

"Are we permanently on the Srebrenica killers' hit list?" I asked.

"Possibly. Possibly not," Janet said. "On the one hand, as a result of our activities three of their comrades have been taken, and they obviously aren't too favorably disposed towards us. On the other hand, there can't be too many of them left who aren't in jail, and they probably are starting to realize that it's highly inadvisable for them to tangle with us. My guess is that they'll leave us alone from now on. In fact, I'm sure they will because the forthcoming trials are going to renew the world's interest in what happened in Srebrenica. Everyone who was involved there is going to have to lie low for a long time. I suspect that Drugovi will just disappear; it's going to be too dangerous for its members to communicate with one another. After all, there are going to be police enquiries in Sydney, Vancouver, and Calgary. It's highly likely that if there are any more murderers out there the authorities will discover them."

I responded, "I agree," and I really meant it. At that moment I truly believed that we were finally safe from the comrades.

It was a wonderful evening after one of the worst days of my life, and I didn't want to spoil it by raising the subject of the tall twins.

CHAPTER SIXTEEN

After breakfast the next morning on the balcony of our suite at the Postillion Hotel, I told Janet that we needed to have a serious discussion about our future. "What'll we do next?" I asked. "Where do we have to go in order to be safe? The Drugovi crowd knows who we really are, and the twins do as well. And what do they want anyway?"

"We've talked about the twins ad nauseam, and we're no closer to uncovering the truth than when we started. It's time to call in professional help."

"By which you mean—?"

"I mean Mr. Smith and Mr. Jones."

"But we don't even know their real names. How do you propose to contact them?"

Janet picked up the phone and pressed zero. When the hotel operator came on the line, Janet said, "Please get me the police station in Connickville."

I assume that the operator had never heard of Connickville because Janet had to spell the name of the hamlet located fifty miles south of Woop Woop, as we say in Australia. After a considerable wait, the operator must have finally found the number, because Janet started speaking.

"I don't know if you remember me, but I was one of the two people you arrested yesterday on the Western Canada Sightseeing train and kept locked up for a couple of hours in your cells."

I had the greatest difficulty keeping a straight face; Janet's implication was that the local constabulary made a regular habit of apprehending groups of travelers on the train. After a pause while the Mountie responded to Janet's opening gambit, Janet continued.

"Oh, good, you do remember me. And do you also remember the two men who came from Vancouver, Mr. Smith and Mr. Jones? . . . Good, you remember them, too. Could you please do me a big favor? I need to talk to Mr. Smith as a matter of real urgency. I'm at the Postillion Hotel in Vancouver, Room 1301. Would you ask Mr. Smith to call me just as soon as he can?" Janet gave him the telephone number and then hung up.

We had to wait no longer than five minutes. Then the phone rang. Janet answered and said, "Mr. Smith, Damon and I would like to meet with you to discuss two men who we think were following us in Banff National Park and were also on our train. We didn't mention them yesterday because they didn't seem to be involved with Drugovi. But now we're not that

sure . . . Fine, see you then. We're in Room 1301."
And that was that.

"Smith is on his way," Janet reported. "He says he'll be here in about fifteen minutes. I'll bet that he brings Jones along with him."

The Vancouver traffic must've been as heavy as in Sydney because Smith arrived nearly thirty minutes later. And, as Janet had correctly predicted, Jones was with him. We invited them to sit down. They refused our offer of refreshments, and we got straight down to business.

"For about a week we've been followed by two extremely tall men, age about twenty-five years, no other particular distinguishing features other than they appear to be identical twins," Janet began. "Damon saw them at Lake Louise. We both saw them at Moraine Lake, at the spiral tunnel lookout at Kicking Horse Pass, at the Icefields Centre, on Highway 93 just a mile or two to the south of Jasper, at the Bow Mountain parking area for Peyton Lake, and at the upper gondola terminal on Sulphur Mountain. And finally, although they were in a different carriage on the Western Canada Sightseeing train, on one occasion we both saw them on the open-air viewing platform of our carriage. They ignored us at all times. In fact, they acted as if we weren't even there.

"The reason we're concerned about the twins," Janet continued, "is that we've been informed by

Detective Chief Inspector Tregethick that a pair of psychopathic twins have sworn to kill us."

"Ah, yes," Mr. Smith said, "that would be the di Campione twins."

I was utterly flabbergasted. "How on earth did you know that?" I spluttered.

Smith was as communicative as he'd been the previous day. He said nothing and his face gave away even less. But Janet worked it out.

"Damon, Mr. Smith surely phoned Walter again when he returned to his office after dropping us off here yesterday. And Walter must've told him that we're in Canada to try to stay alive until they can take Arcangelo and Domenico di Campione into custody. And I'm going to stick my neck out here, but I wonder if we haven't been under discreet police protection ever since we arrived at the hotel. Also, if we hadn't called him in this morning, I wouldn't have been surprised if Mr. Smith had visited us soon and suggested that we leave Canada."

Again Smith was silent, but the ends of his mouth rose about one hundredth of an inch as he tried to suppress a smile. Jones kept a poker face. He'd said nothing since he walked in, and it would've astonished me if he said anything at all.

"Describe the tall twins as accurately as you can," Smith ordered.

I left it to Janet, who gave a report in the best traditions of the Greater Manchester Police. Jones wrote down everything she said. Smith then asked me if I had anything to add. However, Janet had given a corker of a description, so all I had to do was just shake my head.

"I assume that they were on the Western Canada Sightseeing train yesterday as well," Smith said. "If they're still in Vancouver, it shouldn't be too hard for us to track them down. If we can't find them in twenty-four hours, we'll ask you to help us to put together a facial composite."

Smith must've seen my puzzlement because he added, "Like an Identikit picture, only nowadays the whole process is computerized."

Mr. Smith continued, "There are two reasons why we need to talk to the twins. First, they may be connected to Drugovi in some way. They're too young to have been at Srebrenica themselves, but they could've been recruited to assist the 'comrades.' If that's the case, the twins may be able to help us locate additional members of Major Falcon's unit. We'll deport them all to Bosnia to face trial.

"But it seems unlikely that the twins are connected to the 'comrades' in any way," he went on. "The brochure, the magazine, and the postcard were put on your bed to make sure that you'd be on the train. But why would the twins appear yet again on the open-air platform after you were already on the train? Most mysterious.

"Also, the 'comrades' wanted you on the train so they could kill you there, but the actions of the twins could've frightened you off and you might've returned to Calgary Airport and flown out of Canada. It's impossible to be certain at this time, but I think it's unlikely that the tall twins are connected to Drugovi in any way. Nevertheless, I need to talk to them to be sure.

"The second and more important reason why I want to talk to the twins is that it seems probable that they're connected to the di Campione twins. Yes, we've deported to Italy all the di Campione gang members who, immediately after the raid on the warehouse in Sydney, flew from Sydney to Vancouver. But the reason that they fled here in the first place could be that the gang has members in Canada who might've helped them. In other words, if we can lay our hands on the tall twins, we may get some useful information about any remaining members of the di Campione cocaine gang who are still in Canada."

"Isn't there a third possibility?" I asked. "Couldn't the twins just be innocent tourists with whom we coincidentally crossed paths a few times?"

Smith stared at me intensely for about five seconds. Then he asked, "You don't really believe that, do you?"

No one said anything for quite a while.

Smith cleared his throat. "The Drugovi people had no trouble finding you in Canada, your new passports notwithstanding. If I'm right about the twins, that means that the di Campione gang knows where you are, too. How did you book this room?"

"We went to a travel agent in Calgary. She booked our accommodation in Banff and our driver/guide and our Western Canada Sightseeing train trip and this hotel. Which means—"

"Which means," Smith interrupted, "that anyone who's interested in your movements knows precisely where in Vancouver you're staying. We're going to smuggle you out of here and take you to a safe house. You'll stay there until we've resolved the question of the twins. Then we'll get you out of Canada as discreetly as we can. Where would you like to go?"

I thought for a moment. "Our initial choice, Canada, hasn't turned out too well. Where do you suggest we go?"

"If I'm right," Smith said, "and the tall twins are working for the di Campione twins, then I think you should go to France."

"Why France?" Janet inquired.

"France has its own cocaine distribution channels that are independent of those of the di Campione crowd, to such an extent that it can prove fatal for cocaine gang members from the one country to even visit the other country on vacation, let alone try to do drug business of any kind there. But let's see what the twins have to say before coming to a final decision. In the meantime, neither of you is to leave this room until you hear from me." And Smith and Jones left.

Janet and I discussed Smith's suggestion. Neither of us was wildly enthusiastic about it, but France seemed as good a destination as any.

***

After our room-service lunch of sandwiches and fruit, the phone rang. It was Smith. "Vacate your room immediately. Go the elevator. My people are waiting for you there. Don't bring anything—we'll get your stuff afterwards." That was the end of the conversation.

I shouted to Janet, "We're leaving right now. Head for the lift." I opened the door of the suite. The corridor was empty, save for two men in dark suits who were standing next to the bank of lifts. As we neared them, they hustled us into a waiting lift, which then shot down to the basement. I was terrified again.

The lift door opened, and we found ourselves in a brightly lit loading area. To our right sat an opened crate filled with bananas. Beyond that, about forty cases of wine towered against a wall. For obvious reasons the cases of wine made me even more terrified.

To our left stood a delivery van belonging to a food purveyor. Every square inch of the exterior of the van was festooned with paintings of meat, fish, game, pies, salads, vegetables, and fruit. In fact, whoever was responsible for decorating the van with advertising material had managed to cram more edibles onto that vehicle than even a seventeenth-century Flemish still-life painter could possibly have managed. It was hard to discern the name of the company because the cornucopia of food items even encroached on the letters, rendering much of the writing illegible.

The back doors of the van hung open. Someone had placed portable steps there to assist Janet and me to clamber aboard. The two men in dark suits rushed us from the lift to the van and, once we'd climbed in, told us to lie down on the floor, which was thickly padded with mattresses. As we lay down, the doors slammed, the driver gunned the engine, and we were off.

The back of the van lacked windows, but two lights in the roof provided barely adequate illumination. Squatting in one of the far corners was a soldier in camouflage uniform. In her arms she cradled a large, powerful-looking semi-automatic weapon; I hoped that she wouldn't have to use it.

She smiled. "Welcome to our van!" she said. "We're on our way to an empty warehouse. The driver will enter through the front doors of the warehouse and park the van inside. Then he'll strip off the decorations, which are magnetically attached; my partner had great fun painting them some months ago. And about twenty seconds later, a plain black van will drive out of the back of the warehouse, on the way to the place where you'll be staying. I'm sorry, I can't tell you where it is, but it's about a forty-five-minute drive from the warehouse. Please let me know if there's anything I can do to make you more comfortable." And she smiled again. Despite her friendly demeanor she actively discouraged conversation. First Smith and Jones wanted no talking, and now this soldier.

Soon the van came to a halt. Doors slammed, and muffled voices shouted instructions. Then the van was on the move again. As our escort had promised, about three quarters of an hour later the van stopped. Someone opened the back doors, and we found ourselves in what looked like the garage of a private home. It held the usual disarray of a suburban garage: tools cluttered on top of a wooden bench, wood off-cuts on the floor, and replacement light bulbs on a shelf next to two large boxes of Christmas decorations. In their haste to rush us out of the hotel, the two men in dark suits had left the steps behind in the basement, but our driver found a box in the garage that he could use in its place. The soldier escorted us from the garage up a flight of stairs. At the top of the stairs was a suburban kitchen with a dining nook. A few magnets decorated the fridge, but they didn't fasten children's artwork to the door. A calendar hung on the wall, showcasing a picture of three yellow Labrador puppies looking cute. The one false note was that the blinds were closed, even though it was the middle of the day.

The rest of the house also looked in every way like a typical suburban dwelling, with two exceptions. As in the kitchen, all the curtains and blinds were drawn, and they remained that way throughout our stay. Also, the home lacked personal items. The whole place was as sterile as a hospital operating theatre.

"Sit down in the den. Make yourselves at home," the soldier urged us. "Please feel free to help yourselves to food and drink." She hadn't told us her name, but I'm sure that, following the example of Smith and Jones, she would've supplied a false one. Her camouflage uniform had no badges of rank or identifying material of any kind.

As you know, I watch far too many crime shows on TV. As a result, I knew for certain that every room in the house was bugged, and "they" were probably observing us too. By now, Janet and I knew one another extremely well indeed, and we were therefore able to subtly signal to each other that we were under observation. More precisely, Janet signaled in a subtle manner, whereas I made my usual clumsy attempts at miming. If the hidden observers were watching me at the time, I'm sure they would've zoomed in on me and then replayed the recording over and over to discover what I was trying to convey to Janet. I doubt if even Marcel Marceau himself could've worked it out.

There was a bookshelf in the den. Janet chose a book and buried her nose in it while I watched daytime television. But I soon got sick of the gameshow reruns of, the mind-numbing soap operas, and the endless talk TV. Bored out of my mind, I read a book on the history of radio, which surprisingly enough turned out to be quite fascinating.

We stopped reading only to help ourselves to food from the well-stocked kitchen. Neither of us felt much like cooking, so dinner was sandwiches and fruit once more.

After our meal, I picked up the book again and was completely immersed in it when Smith and Jones arrived without prior warning, bringing all our luggage from the hotel. Smith looked amused, Jones had his usual poker face.

"We had no trouble locating the tall twins," Smith said. "We found their names on the train passenger list. Given that they were the only people on the train with the same last names and male first names, it wasn't too difficult to discover that they are Jethro and Jett Culbertson, out-of-work actors. A key aspect in understanding what happened is that the twins aren't particularly intelligent. In fact, they're both as thick as two planks.

"From what they've told us," Smith continued, "we've been able to piece together the complete story, which we've fleshed out with information from the twins' agent and a Banff policeman. It seems that some man has been phoning theatrical agents in Vancouver asking about tall identical twins. When this person contacted the Culbertson twins' agent, he immediately suggested Jethro and Jett.

"The agent was told to instruct the Culbertsons to go to a film studio in North Vancouver. When they arrived there, before they could approach the receptionist they were intercepted in the lobby by a thin, blond woman wearing horn-rimmed spectacles who took them to a nearby café for coffee. There she gave each of them an envelope containing four thousand dollars in cash. She instructed them to fly to Calgary right away, rent a car, and drive to a certain house in Banff. She handed them Canadian Automobile Association maps of Calgary and Alberta. The map of Alberta had an inset map of Banff. A large 'X' marked the location of the house they were to go to in Banff, and she'd also written the address in the margin in purple ink. Then she got up and left them.

"The twins were nonplussed, but the money seemed real enough. Accordingly, they flew to Calgary, waited for hours for the rental car they'd reserved, then drove to Banff. They had the greatest difficulty finding the house; it turned out that the 'X' on the map was in the wrong place and the address that they'd been given was on the outskirts, beyond the city limits. They wasted more than an hour driving repeatedly around various areas of the town. In the end, they asked for help from a policeman who told us that he'd been about to stop them anyway because seeing the same car pass him six or seven times in succession had aroused his suspicions.

"They eventually arrived at the address the blond woman had written on the map. A man with a Groucho Marx moustache opened the door. He spoke with a heavy Italian accent. Both twins insisted that his accent is genuine and, no matter what we tried, we couldn't shake their certainty regarding that point.

"The man said that his name was Sam and that he was a movie director. He told them that he was making a blockbuster detective movie set in Banff National Park, and that they were being considered for the starring roles. They would play twin detectives on the trail of two terrorists. Sam asked them if they could convincingly play those roles. Of course they assured him that they could.

"Sam then said that he'd give them a test. If they passed the test, they'd get the starring roles. An extremely large sum of money was mentioned. As I already told you, the Culbertsons aren't very bright, and the megadollars Sam said that they'd receive for starring in his movie helped to wipe away any suspicions that they might've had that Sam was making all this up.

"The test was simple: They'd stay in a furnished apartment that Sam had rented across the road from Tweedsmuir House, and they'd follow the two of you. They were given a detailed map of the Park. Sam had marked all the main attractions and explained how easy it would be for them to tail you. The beauty of his scheme was that there are very few roads in Banff National Park and equally few major tourist attractions. If they managed to correctly guess which attraction you were going to visit next, they could arrive there either before you or after you, and then 'accidentally' meet you. For example, if they saw you driving in the direction of Moraine Lake, they could stay well behind your black Town Car, totally out of sight, knowing that it was all but certain that your destination was Moraine Lake. After all, the road that ends at Moraine Lake goes there and nowhere else. Once they were sure that your car was parked and that you were walking toward the lake, they could park their car and follow the path to the water, where they'd undoubtedly see you.

"They were given strict instructions to be observed by you, but under no circumstances were they to communicate with you in any way whatsoever. Sam assured them that he had cinematographers hidden in the bushes at the various places you might visit and that they would film the Culbertson twins as they carried out their test. Sam explained that you two were competing for their roles and that *your* test was to try to spot the Culbertsons following you. As a result, if the twins wanted the lucrative leads in the movie, they had to meet you as often as possible but never be seen actually following you.

"The Culbertsons bought this cock-and-bull story hook, line, and sinker. They had been out of work for quite a while; they're none too bright—and that's putting it charitably; they'd both just received a large sum of money, in cash no less; and this seemed to be their big break. Not surprisingly, they threw everything they had into Sam's test. They stayed up late at night studying their map and reading guidebooks. They were lucky enough to meet you seven times in the Park. They reported to Sam by telephone each evening, and he was most enthusiastic about every aspect of their performance. He said that the films his hidden cinematographers had taken were outstanding and that there was no question that they had the roles—provided they could successfully pass one final test.

"You both know what that final test was. Sam told them to let you see them on the open-air platform of your Western Canada Sightseeing train carriage, again without communicating with you in any manner at all. And they succeeded in this, too. When the train arrived in Vancouver, they went home to their apartment and waited to be contacted by Sam bearing their contract. We found them there, and they told us everything. After all, they had nothing to hide. We have a description of Sam, we know exactly where the house in Banff is, and we also have other leads we can follow, such as records of the telephone calls to the various theatrical agents and those that the Culbertson twins made to Sam."

After a pause, Janet spoke. "What you're saying is that all we know for certain is that some man contacted a number of theatrical agents. There's also a woman involved, the blond with the horn-rimmed spectacles who gave the twins the money in a café. Then there's Sam, the 'film director' with a Groucho Marx moustache, which may or may not be false, and a heavy Italian accent, which possibly is genuine. We also know that Sam and the woman have quite a lot of money. The twins were given a total of eight thousand dollars in cash. Sam had to pay rent for his house in Banff and for the twins' furnished apartment across the road from us. The rail tickets weren't cheap either. I take it you haven't traced Sam yet?"

For once Jones spoke. "We think that he left the country when you two left Banff. His job was done, which meant that there was no point in his staying on in Canada. Furthermore, it was possible that Jethro and Jett might mess things up on the train, given that they are sadly lacking in brain cells. It wouldn't be too pleasant for Sam if the police arrived and started asking penetrating questions. Actually, we have a witness who claims that a man without a moustache who somewhat resembled Sam and talked with a foreign accent sat next to him on a flight from Calgary to Frankfurt. We've discovered that the passenger in question was travelling on an Italian passport." And Jones lapsed back into his customary silence.

"I think I know why Sam paid the tall twins to keep crossing our path," Janet said. "The di Campiones haven't yet found a way to get into Canada to kill us, but in the meantime, they want us to be constantly aware of the fact that they're coming after us. They sent the Culbertsons to punish us for the deaths of their brothers by keeping us in a state of constant fear until they can get here to murder us."

"But wouldn't the continual presence of Jethro and Jett tend to keep us on our guard?" I asked.

"That wouldn't occur to the di Campiones," she said. "The twins are psychopathic killers, and people like that consider themselves to be all-powerful and invincible. They intend to take revenge for the deaths of their three older brothers, and nothing we say or do can deter them."

Smith said nothing and Jones once more behaved like the star of a silent movie.

Janet resumed speaking. "But one thing is clear. The Drugovi people were able to track us, and Sam's associates were also able to find us. That means that Arcangelo and Domenico know where we are. And as soon as they get here, they'll kill us. We need to leave Canada and hide somewhere else, and this time we'll have to be considerably more successful in concealing our tracks. Mr. Smith, what do you suggest?"

"I phoned your Detective Chief Inspector before we came here in order to ask for his advice. He's arranged for a fresh set of Australian passports and associated documentation to be sent to me as soon as possible, and we'll then deliver the material to you here. In the meantime, you two will be safe in this house. My people will see to that."

We still didn't know who Smith's people were. We suspected that he and Jones were high up in the Canadian Security Intelligence Service, but it was quite possible that they worked for some even more secret agency. Obviously, we had no way of finding out anything about them.

Smith continued, "Earlier today I suggested that you fly to France. I still think that that's the safest country for you. If you agree to go, I'll start working on finding a way to get you there as unobtrusively as possible."

Clearly, Smith wanted us out of Canada just as soon as our new identity documents arrived. He went on: "Would you like to go to France?"

Janet looked quizzically at me, and I inclined my head a fraction. She was thinking hard. Then she told Smith that we'd follow his advice and go there.

Smith nodded. Jones did nothing. Then they both stood up and left. We never saw either of them again.

CHAPTER SEVENTEEN

The three days that we spent in the safe house passed slowly but not too unpleasantly. We found healthy, plain food in the kitchen; we had a supply of books to read, some more interesting than others; and we could always watch television. Some of the time a discreet minder was with us in the house, saying as little as possible and never answering any of our questions. The rest of the time we were alone but, as I explained earlier, we were certain that we were being overheard and probably being watched as well.

You're probably wondering about the surveillance. Well, all the time we were there I was wondering about that, too. After all, it was clear beyond all doubt that we were totally innocent parties with respect to both the Bosnian Serbs and the cocaine gang. But because we were being overheard, I couldn't ask Janet why we were being overheard!

Some days later, when we were in France, I asked her about it. Janet said that she thought Smith and

Jones were actively involved in the two investigations because both cases had security implications for Canada. We'd already held back information from them in the Connickville police station. Of course, the reason that we didn't tell them about the twins at that time was because we thought that Jethro and Jett were irrelevant to our primary goal, which was to get out of jail as soon as possible. Nevertheless, as Janet explained, that omission on our part was a black mark against us.

"Smith and Jones suspected that we had additional information regarding the two cases that we hadn't shared with them," she said. "It didn't matter whether they felt that we were deliberately holding something back, or whether they thought that we'd merely overlooked some fact. Their objective was to obtain maximal information about both Drugovi and the cocaine smugglers, and their hope was that we'd let slip some morsel of information that would help them with one of their two cases."

On the evening of the third day, the soldier who'd been with us in the back of the van arrived at the house. She handed over a large, sealed brown envelope from Walter. But neither Janet nor I had the slightest doubt that Smith and Jones had unsealed the package, carefully photographed the contents, and then resealed the envelope before passing it on to us.

Inside were our new passports and credit cards, and a driver's license for Janet. But this time there were additional items, including Australian National Health Service cards for both of us and an NRMA card for Janet. The National Health Service cards were useless outside Australia, but I suppose that Inspector Tregethick gave them to us to add to the overall deception. As for the NRMA card, the National Roads and Motorists' Association has a reciprocal agreement with automobile associations in many other countries, such as AAA in the United States. We assumed that it was given to Janet in case our car broke down somewhere or if we needed top-quality driving maps.

Once we'd examined our new documentation, the soldier asked us to give her all our old papers for shredding and pulping. We emptied our pockets and handed over our previous sets of false documents. Obviously, we didn't want to be found with two sets of papers in two different names. The soldier placed our papers in a zippered pocket on the front of her camouflage shirt. Janet told me later that under no circumstances would the Canadians destroy our old documentation. On the contrary, good sets of paperwork are always kept because they can be used as a basis for forging papers for others in the future.

We carefully memorized our new names and tried hard to forget our previous false monikers. As I'm sure you know, it's much harder to try to actively forget something than to learn something new. As a result, *Jesse Presser* kept surfacing in my brain every time I practiced saying my latest name.

A few minutes later the soldier looked at her watch and asked us to please pack our suitcases because we were leaving in ten minutes. We went to our bedrooms to pack, then carried our suitcases down to the garage. There the plain black van was waiting, its back doors open. This time, however, the portable steps were in place. We climbed in, where the soldier was waiting for us with her weapon slung over her shoulder. The driver handed our suitcases up to her, then closed the doors. The soldier put down the luggage, fastened them to one wall of the van with straps, then unslung her weapon and held it at the ready. As before, I hoped that this was just a precaution.

"We're going to a military airbase. The trip shouldn't take more than an hour," she said. She smiled and then lapsed into her habitual silence.

Her time estimate was again accurate. The van stopped, and someone opened the back doors. We stepped out of the van and looked around. As she'd told us, we were on a military airbase. Even though it was now night, around us I could see a variety of military planes, including two fighter aircraft in a brightly lit hangar to the far left. The soldier handed our suitcases to a waiting serviceman, a sergeant in the Royal Canadian Air Force, who carried them as he escorted us to a large four-engine turboprop plane and up its passenger boarding stairs.

"Welcome to our newest Lockheed Martin C-130J Super Hercules," he said. "Please step inside and take a seat. I suggest you walk all the way back and sit in the rear, where the engine noise is less. I'm Sergeant Fergusson, your loadmaster. This may not be the most comfortable or the fastest plane you've ever flown in, but it'll get you to your destination. Please fasten your seatbelts. Have a good flight!"

He stowed our suitcases in a large locker and left us. He went straight to the plane door and shut it. The engines started. Then the plane taxied and took off. We had no idea where we were or where we were heading, nor did it seem likely that anyone would tell us.

I turned to Janet. "To date, we've met only two Canadian soldiers. Both are friendly, but utterly uncommunicative; once again I've no idea where we're going."

"What soldiers?" Janet asked.

"You know, the woman in the van and Sergeant Fergusson, the loadmaster on this plane."

"How do you know they're soldiers?" Janet asked.

"Are you trying to be funny? Can't you see they're wearing uniforms?"

"And what exactly does that prove?" Janet asked. "If I put on operating theatre scrubs and a mask, would that make me a plastic surgeon like my parents?"

And I suddenly realized that ever since we'd met Smith and Jones we'd been living in an alternate universe, one in which things were not necessarily what they seemed to be. I swiftly appreciated that reality was no longer a function of our five senses. Instead, Smith, Jones, and their people actively warped reality into what they wanted us to think was real. My newly acquired nervousness redoubled. I didn't know where I was, I didn't know where I was headed, and I couldn't even remember my current name.

During the flight, the loadmaster twice brought around coffee and biscuits—that's what we call cookies in Australia—but he mysteriously disappeared the rest of the time. After we'd been in the air for about three hours, he came to our seats. "Please fasten your seatbelts. We're landing in about fifteen minutes. Mr. Smith has told me to tell you that, for the next leg of your trip, you are senior executives of Canadian Express Logistics: it's a Canadian air courier service, like FedEx or UPS. You'll be flying on a CEL freight plane from here to Paris.

"Mr. Smith strongly recommends that you keep conversation on the plane to France to a bare minimum. The person who was supposed to be the loadmaster on the CEL plane broke his ankle, and we haven't been able to vet his replacement for the simple reason that we don't yet know who he'll be. Be careful to treat all personnel on board as possible agents for the other side. When you get to Paris, one of our people will meet you there. Good luck!"

We had no idea what the local time was because we didn't know in which time zone we were, but looking out the window of the plane we could see that the sky was dark. As we came in to land, I could see planes from a variety of carriers standing at the gates of a terminal building; we'd arrived at a commercial airport. The plane landed, but we didn't taxi to the terminal. Instead, the pilot took the plane to the cargo area. Our plane eventually came to a standstill, we undid our seatbelts, and "Sergeant Fergusson" fetched our suitcases and led us down the stairs to the taxiway.

He escorted us to a Canadian Express Logistics plane about two hundred yards away. At first glance, it looked like a typical Boeing 747, but something about the airplane seemed different. Then I realized that, because it was a cargo plane, it had almost no windows along the length of the huge aircraft. Sergeant Fergusson led us up the stairs, where a uniformed attendant met us. He showed us to a row of seats in a small cabin behind the cockpit. Then he stowed our suitcases in the baggage area behind us.

"Hi, I'm Claude," he said with a heavy Québécois accent. "I'm the loadmaster on this plane. I'm extremely glad to have some company because it's going to be a long flight from here to Paris. Is there anything I can bring you before take-off? We don't have any alcohol on board, of course, but I can fix you some soft drinks or snacks. And I'm about to brew some fresh coffee. Would either of you like a cup?"

Janet quickly realized that someone who was "extremely glad to have some company" was going to want to talk for the next ten or eleven hours. She fixed the loadmaster with a steely glare. "Son," she said, putting on what I think was a Texas accent, "it's the [expletive deleted] middle of the [expletive deleted] night. I sleep in the [expletive deleted] middle of the [expletive deleted] night and my colleague here does the same. You can bring us some [expletive deleted] pillows and [expletive deleted] blankets, and you can wake us when we get to Paris. Geddit?"

"Yes, *madame*. Certainly, *madame*," Claude replied hastily. He quickly brought us blankets and pillows, then dimmed the cabin lights. We kept our eyes shut for the whole trip. I, for one, had difficulty sleeping. But I quickly realized that Smith had given us a second chance to lose our enemies, and I wasn't going to blow that opportunity by accidentally letting slip to our loquacious loadmaster something that could help put the terrible twins on our trail. Consequently, both of us either slept or pretended to sleep the whole way to Paris. Asking for food or drink would've laid us open to chatty Claude's ceaseless conversation.

Eventually Claude woke us. *"Bonjour madame, bonjour monsieur,"* he said. "I'm afraid we have a problem. Paris airport is covered in fog. We've been instructed to land in Lyons instead. We'll be landing in about twenty minutes. Would you please be kind enough to fasten your seatbelts?"

And having said his piece, Claude quickly disappeared into the cargo area behind our cabin. It was clear that, far from wanting to "have some company," Claude was now eager to stay as far from Janet as possible. I winked at Janet, and we closed our eyes again until the plane landed. We slid up the window shutters to find that it was the middle of the day and we'd landed at a major commercial airport. When the plane came to a complete halt, we unfastened our seatbelts and thanked Claude, who retrieved our suitcases and carried them down the stairs for us.

"And where shall I take these?" he asked.

We had a problem, a huge problem. We'd been told that "one of our people" would meet us in Paris—but this was Lyons.

I thought quickly. "Please take us to an immigration official to enable us to get the formalities out of the way right now."

***

Claude asked a passing cargo handler something in French. The cargo handler pointed half-heartedly in the vague direction of a one-story building, and Claude led us to an office. Behind a desk sat a disinterested functionary. We handed him our latest false passports. He pulled them through his scanner in the usual way, but he hardly glanced at our travel documents as he paged through each passport in turn to find an empty page to stamp. Seconds later he pointed to a doorway behind him.

We thanked Claude, took our suitcases, and left the building. We found ourselves on a wide pathway. About two hundred yards ahead of us was a wooden hut with a high wire fence on either side topped with barbed wire. Beyond the hut was a wide road that ran parallel to the wire fence.

"That looks like some sort of customs post," I said. "Let's head that way. It should take us out of the airport."

The customs officer, as apathetic as his immigration colleague, simply waved us through the door on the other side of the hut to the footpath. He didn't even want to see our passports, let alone examine the contents of our suitcases. I suppose that two people lugging suitcases in the summer afternoon sun of Lyons were unlikely to be illegal immigrants or smugglers of any kind, but the total lack of interest on the part of the two officials seemed like a gross dereliction of duty to me. On the other hand, we were extremely grateful for the absolute absence of scrutiny on their part, because we might've had difficulty explaining why we'd arrived on a Canadian Express Logistics cargo plane, bearing Australian passports, but without any documentation that would show that we were employed by CEL, or had even the remotest connection with that corporation.

The traffic on the main road that lay beyond the customs post was rushing past at high speed. We didn't see any taxis. And even if we saw a vacant cab, we had no Euros with which to pay the fare, but hopefully we could use our new credit cards. But where would we go, anyway? Neither of us had ever been to Lyons before, and our French was limited to reading menus. Worst of all, we had no plan of action. Actually, worst of all was that we hadn't consumed anything other than coffee and biscuits for the past fifteen hours, but when your life is at stake, steak isn't an important part of your life.

"Janet, first things first," I said. "We're at an airport. There must be rental cars here. The problem is that we don't know where they are, and we can't go back to the customs official to ask him that or anything else because we don't want to make him suspicious. That means that we need to walk to the nearest car rental place. Which way should we go? Right or left?"

"Right," Janet said.

After walking longer than I would've liked, we encountered a man in uniform. I asked him in English where the car rental area was. Fortunately, he understood and pointed to a bus stop nearby. This posed a problem. A taxi might take a credit card, a bus never. But then we saw a map fastened to the pole that showed that the bus route ran from the terminal to the car rental center and various short-term and long-term parking lots. We realized, with some relief, that this was probably some sort of internal airport shuttle bus that took passengers at no charge. After looking more closely at the map, Janet pointed out that the car rental area was located no more than a hundred yards to the left of the customs post. Thanks to her intuition or, rather, a complete lack thereof, we'd walked in precisely the wrong direction.

We stood sweating in the hot sun. After about ten minutes a bus approached, and we got on. The bus continued in the direction in which we'd been walking. As a result, we traversed almost the entire area of the airport before the driver eventually deposited us at the car rental locale. On the other hand, this gave a chance to sit and think in air-conditioned comfort.

We had no maps of any kind. We needed to rent a car with a GPS because we didn't have phones. I vaguely remembered that Lyons was a large city and an old city, and navigation even with a map was likely to be hard. I learned afterwards, having paged through

This Week in Lyons Magazine, that Lyons was founded over two thousand years ago and is the second largest city in France with nearly two million inhabitants. The GPS turned out to be a godsend.

Then the thought struck me that we needed to have accommodation of some sort. I muttered to Janet, "Are we going to stay in a hotel or an apartment?"

"Let's talk in the car," she mumbled back.

We alighted from the bus at the car rental area. We went to Lyon-Car, and having showed her passport and driver's license, Janet was able to rent a medium-sized car with automatic transmission, air conditioning, and a GPS. She later told me that none of those three items are standard in Europe, so I considered us lucky.

We put our suitcases in the trunk. Janet sat behind the wheel, I sat in the passenger seat. She started the engine, turned on the air conditioning, and we put together a semblance of a plan.

"We can't ask someone to recommend a hotel, because that would give the bad guys an opening," Janet said. "We need to find a hotel by ourselves. But we don't have a guidebook. In fact, we know nothing about Lyons."

"Let's use the GPS to take us to the railway station. There must be hotels there."

"I don't think that would be a good idea," Janet said. "Hotels at railway stations tend to be seedy at best. If we want to avoid the bad guys, a fancy downtown hotel would probably be better."

"Okay, but how do we find a fancy downtown hotel without asking anyone else?"

"The GPS should give a list of hotels. If we see a name that looks familiar, we'll drive there. If it turns out to be a dud, we can always drive to another one."

"Fine by me," I said. "Let's turn on the GPS."

That was problem number two. The GPS had been set to display and speak French. Everything was in French, including the on-screen instructions for changing the language to English. I looked in the glove box for a manual. Triumphantly I showed it to Janet, who pointed out that the manual was in French, too. *Sacrebleu!*

Janet went back to the Lyon-Car office. She came back with a helpful clerk who pressed a few buttons and, *voilà*, the GPS communicated with us in English.

When the clerk was back in his office, we selected "Points of Interest" and then "Hotels." The problem was that the GPS displayed a list of hotels in increasing distance from the airport, and the airport seemed to be a long way from downtown. That approach didn't work.

"Okay, let's use the GPS to get us to the city hall," I suggested. "When we arrive there, we'll ask the GPS to provide a list of downtown hotels."

Plan B almost worked. We set the GPS to take us to the city hall. It put us on a freeway, and then told us to get off at Exit 12. When we got to Exit 12, we found that it was closed. Janet continued driving.

"What now?"

"It's recalculating. It'll find another route for us."

The good news is that it quickly found another route. The bad news is that the route that it found is the one that Lyonnais taxi drivers use when they want to charge strangers to their city an outrageous sum by driving them around and around in circles. Eventually, we drove over a bridge and saw a gigantic park on our left. Then we saw a sign that read "Convention Centre." The convention center seemed large, too. Then we saw a second sign. This one stated "Convention Centre Hotel."

"Turn left here!"

"Why? We're nowhere near downtown, according to the GPS."

"Turn! I'll explain."

Janet obediently turned into the hotel parking lot, found a parking place, and stopped the car. "Well?" she asked. And it was clear from the tone of her voice that she was waiting for a really good explanation.

"If the di Campione twins are looking for us, would they look for us at a convention center hotel?"

Janet was struck silent. Then she said, "That's truly brilliant! The only people who stay at a convention center hotel are people who are attending a convention, and no one would dream that we'd be attending a convention while we're on the run."

Then she thought again. "But how comfortable can a convention center hotel be?"

"I don't care. We need a safe hotel, and a convention center hotel in Lyons is about as safe as we can find." For someone who has learned to love luxury as much as I do now, putting safely before comfort should convince you as to just how scared I was. In fact, the after-effects of those two and half days in Ottorino's cellar were getting even more intense as the days passed.

Janet and I walked into the hotel and asked for two rooms, preferably adjacent. We registered—yes, I remembered my current name just in time—and went up in the elevator. The elevator was oddly shaped: surprisingly narrow, but deep. Also, the back wall was glass, and as the elevator rose, we had a great view of the beautiful park next to the convention center.

Much to our delight, the rooms were well appointed and comfortable. Best of all, room service was available, which meant that we could stay out of the public eye and eat in safety.

We quickly made up for not having eaten for nearly eighteen hours. Two waiters arrived at Janet's room with a dinner cart piled high with food. They seemed somewhat taken aback when they were informed that all this food was just for the two of us, but we didn't care. We tucked into an outstanding meal. It seemed that conventioneers in France eat and drink well.

CHAPTER EIGHTEEN

After a good night's sleep and a delicious breakfast served in my room, Janet and I held a council of war. We needed to decide how to live our lives until the police had taken the di Campione twins into custody.

I opened the conversation by saying, "Who knows that we're in France? Nobody. We were taken from the Vancouver safe house to a military base in a sealed van. We flew from there in a military plane to a commercial airport, but we deplaned in the cargo area and we walked, in the middle of the night, from the military plane to a cargo plane. The only person on the cargo plane who saw us was Claude, our loadmaster, and he firmly believes that we're senior CEL executives, thanks to the utterly charming way you spoke to him.

"Then we landed in Lyons and went through immigration on false passports. There's no way that anyone can connect us with those passports unless the higher echelons in the police and security services in

Australia and Canada have been penetrated by the Mafia; and if that's happened, we're dead as doornails, no matter what we do.

"And now we're sitting in a convention center hotel in Lyons, France. No one knows who we really are. The only way that the di Campiones can find us is if someone who knows us sees us and reports us to the terrifying twins. And that's a highly unlikely possibility."

Now it was Janet's turn. "No, there's another way they can find us. Interpol frequently sends out worldwide bulletins to inform police in every country about a suspected criminal. Suppose that the Mafia has put out its own worldwide bulletin for us. If their bulletin includes good photographs of us, we could be in trouble."

She went on, "I know that the cocaine gang is on the run in Italy and Australia, and in Canada, too. I also know that it's unlikely that there are members of an Italian cocaine gang in France, but what about a low-ranking drug runner who lives in a small town in Italy? If such a person were to come to France for whatever reason, the locals would almost certainly not recognize him as a member of an Italian cocaine gang. But if he saw us, he'd undoubtedly report it to his boss. The news would quickly travel up the command structure until it reached the di Campiones."

I interrupted her. "What you're saying is that the only way we can be 100 percent sure of staying alive is to remain here in our rooms until the murderous di Campione twins are in custody."

"Do you really think that if we sit in this room we'll be absolutely safe?" Janet asked. "What if one of the room-service waiters tells a friend about the man and the woman who spend all day, every day in their rooms in the convention center hotel? And what if the friend tells her friend? Eventually, someone in the gang will hear about us. No, I'm afraid that there's no way we can be 100 percent sure of staying alive. I think we should take calculated risks. For a start, we need to stop having our meals here. We need to eat in different places to be sure that we don't attract attention. During the day, we can drive into the country and eat our midday meal wherever we find ourselves at lunchtime. And we can make dinner reservations under different names each time; that might help a bit."

I thought long and hard about what Janet had said. I considered alternative strategies and then discarded them one by one as being inferior to Janet's proposal. Finally, I responded, "Fine, I agree. We'll do it your way."

"If we're going to get out, we're going to need a map. In fact, we're going to need a map of Lyons, and another one of the region around here. I'll call down to the concierge and ask where we can buy maps."

She listened for a minute, then put down the phone and turned to me. "This convention center is part of a huge new area called Cité Internationale—I suppose that's French for International City. Anyhow, our hotel is one component of the whole development, and right behind the hotel is a mall that contains the convention center itself and also shops and banks and restaurants and everything. And there's a bookshop where we can buy maps."

We went down to the lobby, exited through the rear door, and saw in front us the huge park we'd spotted from the car and from the elevator. There was a sign that read "Parc de la Tête d'Or." I thought about this for a moment or two. The *Parc* bit had to mean "Park." I knew that *Tête* means head. You see, Tête de Moine is a wonderful French cheese, and I'd been told that it means "monk's head." As for the *d'Or* piece, one of the finest French wine regions is *Côte d'Or* or "Golden Hillside." That's where the greatest Burgundy wines come from, like Gevrey-Chambertin, Meursault, and Nuits-Saint-Georges. Putting it all together, *Parc de la Tête d'Or* must mean "Park of the Golden Head." When you're a foodie, I thought, you can translate almost anything!

To our right was the mall. We walked until we found a bookstore, and there I used my new credit card to purchase the Michelin maps we had to have. I also bought a guidebook for Lyons. As we strolled back towards the hotel, we realized that we didn't have any Euros. But then we saw an ATM, and I used my credit card to get the cash we needed. Armed with everything we required for the moment, we returned to my room to study our maps and the guidebook.

"Are there any halfway decent restaurants in Lyons?" Janet asked.

"Probably not. This is just a huge provincial town. I expect it's just workingmen's cafés and fast food here. But I'll look in the guidebook just to make sure."

I opened the book, consulted the index, turned to the relevant page, and read aloud the following sentence: "For centuries Lyons has been acknowledged as the gastronomic capital of France."

Janet broke into a broad grin and her Texas accent. "Pardner, we've hit pay dirt!"

I read further: "'Lyons has over a thousand restaurants. In and around Lyon there are three Michelin three-star restaurants.' Janet, we've died and gone to heaven."

"Watch it," Janet cautioned, speedily wiping the smile off her dial, as we say in Australia. "I don't want to hear any more talk about dying. Eating, yes. Drinking, yes. Dying, definitely not. And talking about drinking, what's the wine around here like?"

"According to this guide, there are two major wine-growing regions close to here. Beaujolais is to the north of Lyons, and to the south is Côtes du Rhône, which this book says means 'the hillsides of the Rhone,' the river on which Lyons is situated. We now know that the food in this town is fantastic, and the wine in this town is equally fantastic. All we have to do is to live long enough to enjoy them."

***

Our life in Lyons was sheer and incomparable bliss. We ate and we drank, then we ate and we drank some more. And we staged a repeat performance the next day and the day after that. And we took long walks in the beautiful park next to our hotel to work off all that food and wine.

The food was unparalleled. The only regret I had was that we couldn't visit any particular restaurant more than once for fear of being noticed. This restriction nearly broke my heart after we visited Maison Ponti, Hippolyte Ponti's three-star restaurant in Lyons, one day and drove to Roanne to eat at Le Relais de la Chapelle Rouge, another three-star restaurant, the following day. I tried to convince Janet that there was no point in trying to stay alive if we couldn't eat repeatedly in three-star restaurants, but Janet was adamant. She persuaded me not to return to either establishment by faithfully promising that we would come back to Lyons after the terrible twins were safely in custody.

After a few days in Lyons, I suddenly woke up to the realization that there was no way that we would know when the police had found the di Campiones. Walter and Mr. Smith presumably knew that our plane had landed in Lyons, and they both knew the names on our false passports. But they had no way of contacting us to tell us the good news, if and when the big day came.

I said to Janet, "You know, it's quite possible that the police arrested the di Campiones days ago, and here we are sitting in Lyons because no one knows how to communicate with us."

Janet thought for a minute, and then she came up with a solution. "Let's go and buy a burner phone with a prepaid SIM card, as Detective Chief Inspector Walter Tregethick suggested just before we left Sydney. Then we'll use it to phone Walter. That way, he'll know our number."

Off we went and bought a throw-away telephone in the mall behind our hotel. I phoned Walter at half past seven, Sydney time. He was delighted to hear my voice. He began by saying that he wouldn't ask where we were, and I heartily endorsed that. I briefly told him why we were phoning, and he promised to let us know the moment he knew anything. I hung up after only thirty seconds, just in case someone was trying to trace the call. A stupid, unnecessary precaution, I know, but after what had happened on the train, I took many stupid, unnecessary precautions.

We visited all the tourist sites in and around Lyons. Then we visited them all again. But there were two we visited repeatedly. One was Vieux Lyon (Old Lyons), a district of the city constructed during the

Renaissance. The old buildings were fascinating, especially some of the more sumptuous houses. But best of all were the *traboules*, passageways constructed from one street to the next that pass through buildings and their courtyards. From the *traboules* we spied spiral staircases and gaped at graven galleries.

The other site we visited over and over again was the huge park next to our hotel, Parc de la Tête d'Or. The first time we wandered in, we found ourselves in a vast area of trees, lawns, and colorful flowerbeds. Then we spied a large lake with two wooded islands. At the far end of the lake were boathouses with boats for rent, and teenagers rowing on the water. We walked back on the other side of the lake and encountered youngsters riding horses, and then an extensive miniature railway. The carriages of the train were packed with children, who seemed to be having the time of their lives.

The second time we visited the park, we unexpectedly found ourselves at a zoo specializing in African animals. On another occasion we found ourselves at the entrance of a deserted velodrome. Each time we returned, we discovered some new feature.

But despite the many pleasures of Vieux Lyon and the Parc de la Tête d'Or, after four weeks we were both bored, utterly bored. Walter hadn't phoned, so we knew that the twins were still at large. But I was desperate to hear good news, and I used our burner phone to call him.

When he realized who it was, he said, "Sorry, no news. I promise I'll phone you if I hear anything." And that was the end of the call. A thick impenetrable fog of depression enveloped me. It seemed we'd have to spend the rest of our lives in Lyons, eating and drinking the finest food and wine imaginable but bored beyond belief.

Then Janet had an idea. "Do you see any reason why we shouldn't travel around France? What we've been doing is precisely that, but we've returned to our hotel every evening. Surely, we'd be equally safe if we travelled around the country. I think we should stay clear of Paris; you never know whom we might bump into there. But if we stay in the smaller towns, we should be as safe as we are here."

On the one hand, Janet's idea cheered me up considerably. On the other hand, although I'd grown to love travel for its own sake, by now I hated traveling in order to stay alive. Overall however, moving from place to place would be preferable to spending day after day in our hotel in Lyons. So we checked out of our home for the past month and headed south to Valence.

As far as I'm concerned, Valence is a truly boring town with two saving graces. Valence is where Napoleon Bonaparte was initially posted as a second lieutenant—he was only sixteen years old at the time.

The house in which he was quartered is now a bistro. Also, the finest restaurant in France—and therefore in the whole world and probably in the entire universe—is there. For some reason, the Lagousse family established themselves in Valence. The third-generation chef, Françoise Lagousse, keeps winning the award for the best chef in France. After we ate in her restaurant, L'Auberge de Lagousse, we understood why. I've never eaten food as wonderful as that in my entire life, even in other three-star restaurants. Course followed course, each distinctive in every way from its predecessor. When we walked out of the restaurant late that evening, I knew just how Lucifer felt after he was cast out of heaven. I'm not going to tell you what we ate; the pain of leaving L'Auberge de Lagousse with no possibility of return for the rest of our lives—at least until the twins were incarcerated—was just too great. If you're interested in her food, you can visit her website. Just leave me out of it for now.

Françoise Lagousse has built a five-star hotel to house her three-star restaurant. While we were staying there we took a walk through the town. We passed a travel agency. In the window was a poster advertising barge trips on the River Rhone. I think that I've already mentioned to you that Lyons is built on the Rhone. The river flows south from there, passing through Valence to Avignon, Arles, and on to the Mediterranean Sea.

Now, for Janet and me at that time, barge travel was as dangerous as bus travel and train travel, and I don't have to tell you again what happened to me on the Western Canada Sightseeing train. But the idea of travelling down the Rhone in a barge by day, mooring the barge at a different village each evening, seemed most attractive. We went to have a cup of coffee and a shared pastry in a nearby café, where I told my idea to Janet. She came up with an excellent solution.

"Let's go to the travel agency and ask about a small barge. We'll need a captain to run the boat, a cook to provide breakfasts and lunches, a maid to clean the barge and serve our meals, and a guide."

"Sure, but what about the problem of the other passengers?" I asked.

"What you have to do is pay for all the accommodation. Then the barge is ours. We can go where we like, see what we like, eat what we like for breakfast and lunch, eat dinner where we like, and the only security risk will be the captain, the chef, the maid, and the guide. In other words, rent yourself a barge and we'll travel our way down the Rhone."

We paid for our refreshments and walked back to the travel agent. Fortunately, the proprietor spoke excellent English and understood exactly what we wanted. But he was scandalized by the very idea.

"*Monsieur*," he said, "what a waste of money! Why pay for all the accommodation when all you need is two cabins?"

"What is the smallest barge you have?" I asked.

"We have one with four cabins that is available for two weeks, as you requested. The members of the crew are as you specified: the captain, the chef, the maid, and the guide. But I refuse to let you have all four cabins. It's a sheer waste of your money."

I thought for a moment. "What if I invite some Australian friends to join us? They'll reimburse me in full for their share of the cost of the trip, of course."

"In that case, *monsieur*, I will make all the necessary arrangements."

We left the travel agent. I could see that Janet was about to burst into laughter, but she managed to control herself until we were around the corner. Then she exploded into guffaws.

"A friend of mine claims that some French people are parsimonious, but they're stingy with their own money, not with other people's. What kind of living can he make if he refuses to let people spend their money the way they want to, even if it is extravagant?" Her peals of laughter continued as we made our way back to the hotel.

***

The next day, we returned the rental car to the Lyon-Car agency at Valence train station and took a taxi to the dock where the barge was moored, waiting for us to board. On the way, I suddenly realized that I'd overlooked something.

"Janet," I said, "I forgot to specify that the guide must speak English. How are we going to communicate with him or her? And it would certainly help if we could talk to the captain and the chef as well."

It turned out that, as always, I was worrying unnecessarily. When we arrived at the boat, the members of the crew were waiting on the wharf to greet us: Albert, the captain; Mathilde, the chef; Ghislaine, the maid; and Jean-Loup, the guide. All four spoke perfect English. When I complimented Albert on his English, he replied that the owner of the barge insists that all the members of the crew speak good English, because the majority of their clients are British or American.

The crew were a physically ill-matched quartet. Albert was short, much shorter than I am. Mathilde, in contrast, was tall and thin. She had the torso of a male adolescent: no breasts, no hips. Despite being exposed to food all day as chef, not an ounce of fat clung to her body. I wondered if her extreme thinness was glandular in origin or whether she was anorexic. Her face, like her body, was elongated and she had a long, thin straight nose. Ghislaine, our maid, looked just like the maid in every French farce—enough said. Finally, Jean-Loup was of average height, but he was bulky—and it was all muscle. He looked like a typical paratroops officer in the war movies I like to watch on late-night television. In fact, I once asked our guide if he'd been a paratrooper. He murmured, "Something like that," and changed the subject quickly. He did it politely but in such a way that made it unambiguously clear that he wouldn't be at all happy if I had the temerity to raise the subject again.

Albert escorted us aboard the *Marie Curie*. She was a former working vessel, converted into a luxury hotel barge. The gangway led to the forward deck. From there, double glass doors opened into the salon, which held fully stocked bar and several comfortable couches and armchairs. The door behind the salon led to a landing from where a staircase gave access to the lower deck with the four promised cabins. On the other side of the landing was the dining room, containing a highly polished wooden table and eight comfortable chairs. For obvious reasons, the kitchen was located behind the dining room. A passage from the kitchen led to the crew's quarters, which occupied the rear third of the barge. Above the salon were the bridge and the sun deck.

Life on board was wonderful. Mathilde would get up early, take her bicycle from where it was stored on the upper deck and ride into the nearest town or village. There she'd buy fresh croissants for our breakfast and the freshest local foods for our lunch. She'd also buy local cheeses. The barge housed an extensive wine cellar, but if Mathilde felt that we should try a local wine, then she bought that, too. Mathilde returned to the boat in time to make our breakfast.

Lunch was a leisurely affair. Mathilde loved to show off her skill as a cordon bleu chef, and we loved to eat the wonderful dishes she prepared for us each day. And in the evening, Albert would moor the ship at a riverside village, and we'd walk into town and see the sights. We'd stop at one café for an apéritif, usually a glass of Muscat de Beaumes de Venise from the southern Rhone valley. Then we'd walk around a bit more and perhaps go to another café for another glass. After that, we'd have dinner at a restaurant Mathilde had suggested. And we'd end the evening with coffee and liqueurs or cognac at yet another local establishment.

During the day, Jean-Loup organized a variety of excursions. Albert would moor the barge, and there at the dockside a taxi would be waiting to drive Janet and me to a point of interest, with Jean-Loup as our guide. Sometimes he took us to a carefully restored historic town or a quaint village. Sometimes our destination was a winery where we had the opportunity to talk to the winemaker and taste his products. Once we visited a nougat factory, once a factory where they made perfumes and cosmetics from lavender blossoms. My greatest regret is that we never once visited a chocolate factory!

I sometimes wondered if Jean-Loup and Mathilde were in competition with one another to see who could impress us the most. For example, one day Jean-Loup took us to a truffle farm. We saw the truffle farmer's dogs in action, locating and digging up truffles in a wooded area. Then we sampled the truffles—delicious! Before we left the farm, Jean-Loup bought some truffles and took them back to the barge, as if to say to Mathilde, *Okay, let's see what* you *can do with these!*

Mathilde, of course, rose to the challenge. For breakfast the next morning she served a truffle and wild mushroom omelet that I'll never forget. And for lunch the day after that, one of her dishes was a grilled filet mignon with a truffle sauce that was equally unforgettable. I'm delighted to report that Janet and I were the happy beneficiaries of this friendly rivalry.

All went well for about ten days. Then Jean-Loup announced that that evening we'd arrive in Avignon. Up to now, we'd visited villages and the occasional small town. But Avignon is a city, and this concerned me because of the number of people. Anyone might be looking for us and betray us to the di Campione twins.

As often happened, Janet took the opposite view. "We stuck out like sore thumbs in those little one-horse towns we visited. In Avignon we'll blend into the populace."

"That's possible," I said, "but a member of the Italian cocaine gang would also blend into the populace in a city like Avignon."

Janet conceded that I had a point, but insisted that, as usual, I was worrying unnecessarily. Nevertheless, we had dinner at a restaurant close to the wharf where Albert had docked the *Marie Curie*. And after dinner, we walked straight back to the barge for liqueurs from the bar and strong coffee brewed by Mathilde.

The next morning Jean-Loup took us to see the sights of Avignon, beginning with the gigantic food market. I thought I knew a lot about meat, fish, vegetables, and fruit, but the food market had item after item that I'd never seen before. Then we spent about an hour in the fascinating Papal Palace, the largest Gothic palace in Europe.

After lunch, Janet and I wandered through the streets of the old town. We found some interesting shops. I bought a tie and also a sweater, what we call a jumper. We both bought ice cream. Everything was going well until we saw a young woman pushing a double pram with identical twins in it. Yes, they were adorable little girls, no more than three years old. But they were identical twins. I nudged Janet and said, urgently, "Let's return to the barge."

As dinnertime neared, I got more and more tense. But Janet was right. We were safe in Avignon. Accordingly, we stuck to our previous routine: two different cafés for apéritifs, then dinner at a restaurant recommended by Mathilde, followed by brandy and coffee at a nearby café.

CHAPTER NINETEEN

We were both a little drunk when we left the café. I'd had one marc too many, and Janet had overindulged on the proprietor's excellent calvados. As we neared the barge, I noticed a seven-seater SUV parked on the wharf next to the *Marie Curie*. Furthermore, all the lights on the main deck of the barge were on, which was unusual for that hour of the night. We walked unsteadily up the gangway and onto the forward deck, and stepped into the salon. All four members of the crew were sitting there, together with two police officers. As we walked in, everyone rose to their feet.

Jean-Loup spoke. "The police have come aboard to check everyone's papers. Would you please show them your passports?"

I replied, "Mine is in my cabin, and I think that Janet's is, too."

Jean-Loup translated what I'd said into French for the benefit of the two policemen. They said something in French to Jean-Loup, who told us, "The police officers will accompany you to your cabins to get your passports."

I strolled through the door at the end of the salon and started to walk down the stairs, closely followed by one policeman. Janet and the other policeman followed. There was no way I could talk to Janet. We entered our respective cabins accompanied by our police escorts. I eventually found my passport and handed it to the policeman. Taking it in his right hand, he said, "*Merci*," and indicated with his free hand that I was to go back upstairs.

When we got back to the salon, Janet and the other policeman were already there. The two policemen pored over our passports and then said something in French to Jean-Loup. After a short back-and-forth, Jean-Loup translated. "The policemen say that you don't have the correct visa stamped in your passports. You'll need to accompany them to police headquarters in Avignon, where the matter will be sorted out. I will accompany you, in case the police there don't speak English either."

Jean-Loup turned to the policemen and said something in French, presumably that he was coming along with us. A loud, excited, lengthy argument followed; I didn't understand a single word.

Finally, Jean-Loup explained to Janet and me, "They refused to take me along. They said there wasn't room in the car. But I pointed out that they drive a seven-seater SUV, and there are only the five of us. They eventually agreed, but with the greatest reluctance."

Janet and I walked off the barge, each of us closely followed by one policeman, and Jean-Loup brought up the rear. We entered the police car. I was told to sit behind the driver in the middle row of seats, with Jean-Loup on my right; Janet lolled on the back seat. One police officer drove, while his companion sat next to him in front.

As we drove past the high stone walls of the old city, a thought crossed my mind. I've seen plenty of cop shows and movies on TV, but I've never seen a uniformed policeman driving an unmarked seven-seater SUV, not even in a French cop movie. Then I looked through the gap between the front seats at the policeman in the passenger seat. He looked scruffy. Yes, plainclothes men always look scruffy on TV, but not uniformed police. Also, his hair was long. Then I looked at the back of the head of the driver—his hair was long, too. Something was wrong.

We drove the length of the city walls, then continued into the suburbs, and finally we reached the open countryside. The car came to a T-junction. The sign pointing to the left said "Avignon." The driver turned right.

I started shouting, "Avignon is the other way. They're not policemen, they're kidnapping us."

The "policeman" in the passenger seat didn't understand English, but I'm pretty sure he got the gist of what I'd shouted. He drew an ugly-looking pistol from his holster, and pointed it directly at me, his arm in the gap between the two front seats. The pistol was less than a foot away from my head.

Jean-Loup suddenly shouted something loudly in French. Afterwards I learned that he'd screamed, "Look out!" As the passenger turned his head to scan the road in front of the car, he took his eyes off me for just a second. And in that one second, Jean-Loup pounced. He grabbed the pistol with his left hand and thrust it upwards towards the roof of the SUV, and with his right hand he delivered a downward karate blow to the passenger's right forearm that broke both the radius and the ulna—I heard two distinct cracks, followed by wails of agony. The passenger involuntarily let go of his grip on the pistol.

An instant after Jean-Loup used his right hand to disable the passenger, his left hand swiftly rotated the pistol he was now holding through ninety degrees, moved his left arm forward, and pressed the pistol firmly into the back of the driver's head. "*Arrêt!*" Jean-Loup shouted.

The driver obeyed. He slammed on the brakes, then allowed the car to roll slowly onto the grassy verge on the side of the road. He had no choice. His partner's gun was sticking into his head and his partner was totally out of action for a good while; two bones protruded from his right forearm. Jean-Loup told the driver to keep his hands on the steering wheel; at least, that's what I thought he said.

The car was now stationary. Jean-Loup turned to me. "Slide open the door, get out of the car, then open the driver's door. I want you to lean across the driver, open his holster, take out his gun, and give it to me. Don't worry, he can feel my gun in the back of his head, he's not going to try anything."

I did as Jean-Loup ordered. There was now a large pistol in my hand.

"Excellent," Jean-Loup said. "As you can see, I'm now behind the driver, where you were sitting. Janet is going to move to where I was sitting, and she'll open the sliding door on that side. Walk around the car and pass your gun to Janet through the doorway."

I handed Janet the gun. As a former police officer, she knew exactly what to do with it. She and Jean-Loup made a great team.

"Thank you. Now go back to the driver and make sure he has no other gun," Jean-Loup instructed me.

I'd never frisked anyone before, but I knew exactly how it was done, at least on TV and in the movies. I assured my two companions that the driver was now unarmed.

"Can you now frisk the passenger?" Jean-Loup asked. "He's writhing in agony, but we need to know he's unarmed too, just in case he has another gun and the driver grabs it."

Frisking the passenger was a lot harder, for obvious reasons. But eventually I reported to Jean-Loup that the passenger was clean, too. From innumerable cop shows, I knew that I'd used the correct technical term.

"Excellent. Now Janet will get out of the car, you'll climb in and sit in the back row of seats, where Janet was sitting before. Janet will then get back in."

Janet and I carried out this maneuver safely. There was no danger, though, because both "policemen" were completely disarmed—one was in total agony and the other had a gun pressed firmly into the back of his head.

Jean-Loup now used his cell phone to call the police. The conversation was lengthy because Jean-Loup wasn't certain precisely where we were, but eventually he ended the call. "The police are on their way, the real police I mean. Now, while we're waiting, please tell me why they wanted to kidnap you."

I was about to say, *They wanted to take us to their boss, who would've shot us both.*

But just in time I realized that Jean-Loup might share that information with the police, and who knows what might've then ensued. Instead, I said, "I'm a rich man. They kidnapped me to get the ransom."

Jean-Loup had the good grace not to ask why they took Janet as well. He must've realized that Janet was my employee, and taking two kidnap victims only made things more difficult for the kidnappers, especially if one of the victims is a former police officer. But he held his peace.

***

Jean-Loup had ordered the driver to turn the car's emergency flashers on, and that helped the police find us about ten minutes later. Emergency medical technicians loaded the SUV passenger into the ambulance that had accompanied the two police cars. Then the police took Janet and me in one police car to Avignon police headquarters, and Jean-Loup and the SUV driver went in the other. We never saw either of the two phony police officers again.

The rest of that night was a bureaucratic nightmare. Commissioner Delacroix of the Avignon police began by asking us for our passports, and I replied that the imposters had taken them. I nearly added that the fake policemen had taken our fake passports, but wisely suppressed any attempt at a witticism. The Commissioner phoned the hospital, but the nurse who answered couldn't locate our documents. Then I remembered that one of the "policemen" had put our passports in the pocket of his uniform jacket. Another phone call to the hospital led to the discovery that the staff had cut the uniform jacket off the badly injured bogus policeman when he arrived at the emergency department, but no one there seemed to know where they'd put it. Finally, a nurse found the missing garment. A policeman then drove to the hospital to fetch our passports and bring them to the Avignon police headquarters.

While all this was going on, Commissioner Delacroix interrogated us, together with two members of the DCRI, the French intelligence agency equivalent to the FBI or MI5. They called themselves Dubois and Petit, the French equivalent of Smith and Jones. The bad news was that no one in Avignon police headquarters seemed to be able to speak any English. The good news was that, all through that endless night, Jean-Loup interpreted for us. Having him there in the room made things considerably easier for us.

However, Dubois and Petit weren't as polite as Jean-Loup had been. They demanded to know why the kidnappers had snatched both of us. I suggested that they could get more ransom for two people than for just one. My story seemed to satisfy them, but you never know with security police.

The best news of all was that Dubois and Petit left the police station before our passports finally arrived from the hospital. As a result, they didn't find out that we were travelling with false papers. If they'd known that, it would've opened a whole new can of worms, and the three of us would probably still be sitting in that police station today.

At about half past five in the morning the police finally let us go. They instructed us in no uncertain terms, however, that the barge was to stay put, and we were to continue to live on it until the two phony policemen had made a statement. The unspoken implication was that their statements had better corroborate what Janet and I had said, or else. In the meantime, there would be a 24/7 police guard on the wharf where the *Marie Curie* was moored, just in case someone tried another kidnapping attempt.

They loaded us into a police car and drove us to the barge, which turned out to be located less than a mile from Avignon police headquarters. The two policemen in the car with us remained on the wharf to guard us, as promised.

We went straight to bed. I awoke about seven hours later, and Ghislaine served a wonderful meal Mathilde had prepared. I was halfway through when Janet walked in, yawning. Mathilde plied her with food, too, and soon both of us were feeling a lot better.

"I think we have to have a meeting with Jean-Loup," Janet suggested. "We need to hire him as a bodyguard. He's obviously ex-Special Forces, though there's no way he'll ever admit that to us."

"Do we tell him everything?" I asked.

"Everything. If he's to protect us, he needs to know all the facts, without any exceptions," Janet said.

"And I've no doubt that he's absolutely discreet and can be trusted not to blab."

"But will he leave the barge and work for us?"

"We'll have to see. If the barge owner has hired him just for this trip, then there'll be no problem. Obviously when the police release us, we're going to have to leave the barge and hide elsewhere. That means that his services will no longer be needed here. There's no point in the *Marie Curie* having a guide if the passengers have permanently left the barge.

"It'll be harder if he's on a long-term contract of some sort, or if he has to give a month's notice," Janet went on. "But it'll certainly help if you make him an offer he can't refuse."

***

We'd asked Jean-Loup to join us for dinner. As was our habit, we'd asked Mathilde to recommend an Avignon restaurant, and she'd suggested that we try the Brasserie Gachet, presumably named after the doctor who'd looked after Vincent van Gogh in Avignon. As with her previous recommendations, her suggestion proved extremely successful.

Over the meal, we told Jean-Loup everything that had happened with the di Campione gang, starting with the explosion in Goran's Bottle Shop. We'd almost finished telling him about the trade of prisoners at the abandoned airfield in rural New

South Wales, when Jean-Loup interrupted for the first time.

"Now don't you tell me that they pulled the good old bomb-in-the-airplane stunt?"

I was stunned. "You mean that's been done before?"

Jean-Loup smiled. "It's been standard operating procedure when dealing with kidnappers, terrorists, and hostage takers for at least fifty years. You'd think that the bad guys would've realized that, but not too many crooks are intelligent. Anyhow, I'm sorry I interrupted you. Please continue."

We told Jean-Loup that the two remaining di Campione brothers, the identical twins Arcangelo and Domenico, had sworn vengeance, no matter what the consequences for them might be.

"Do you have a photograph of the twins?" Jean-Loup asked.

"Unfortunately not. I meant to get one, and somehow it slipped my mind. Now I can't get one without giving away our location, which I'm loath to do."

"But the twins know exactly where we are," Janet said. "That's why they sent the 'policemen' to the barge."

"Yes, but we're going to leave here for an unknown destination just as soon as we get permission from the police," I argued. "How would we get the photographs once we've left Avignon?"

Jean-Loup recommended that we decide what to do about the photographs after we'd agreed where to go next. It seemed that he was willing and eager to accompany us as a bodyguard. I'd not mentioned money or terms of employment, but these somehow seemed to be of secondary importance as far as he was concerned. On the other hand, I felt that it was important that our relationship be on a proper business-like footing from the start: once a financial planner, always a financial planner. I offered a salary to Jean-Loup. He nodded his head and changed the subject at once.

We finished our dinner, and I suggested we return to the barge. For once, the idea of sitting in an Avignon café drinking coffee and cognac didn't appeal to me at all, perhaps as a consequence of what had happened the previous night. Instead, I paid the bill, and we walked slowly through the shadows of the lamp-lit streets of the old city of Avignon in the direction of the barge.

As we neared the vessel, I saw that two new policemen were on duty. I gave them a good look. Both had short hair and their uniforms were impeccable. Most reassuring. They saluted us as we passed them, and we nodded back. The three of us walked along the gangway and stepped onto the forward deck.

Then an unusual thing happened. A silver Renault Laguna drew up near the wharf and two Muslim women got out and walked towards the barge. I knew they were Muslims because they were wearing black burqas. That is, they were covered from head to toe with a loose covering; all that we could see as they approached us were their eyes. And the reason that this was unusual is that France has banned the wearing of the burqa in public.

The reaction of the police was equally unusual. They'd been stationed on the wharf to protect us from kidnappers; this was clearly their primary duty, in all probability their sole duty. But seeing the women in burqas for some reason enraged them. I'm not sure if it was a case of Islamophobia on the part of both policemen, or whether they were outraged on behalf of liberated French womanhood. Whatever the reason, they started charging towards the two women, shouting *"Interdit! Interdit!"* I later learned that *interdit* means "forbidden;" the policemen were telling the women that the law in France prohibits the wearing of a burqa in public.

As the policemen neared the women, bulges appeared under both burqas in front of the women's right hips. Then they fired the weapons they'd hidden under their burqas. We were standing on the forward deck right next to the glass doors to the salon. The silenced pistols made popping sounds, and both policemen fell to the ground, where they lay motionless. Jean-Loup yelled to Janet and me to get down. He drew a handgun from a holster hidden under the jacket that he always wore and fired at the burqa-clad women.

His first shot hit the woman on our right, who stopped firing and fell to the ground in a sitting position. Bright red blood poured from her chest through her black burqa. Then she fell onto her side. The woman on our left trained her gun on us. Jean-Loup was standing, fully exposed. He turned his gun on the woman still on her feet and fired off a few rounds, but apparently to no avail; I think that the second woman was standing too far away. Janet and I were lying on the ground, looking through the spaces between the handrail stanchions on the side of the deck. The burqa-clad woman ignored Jean-Loup and lowered her gun, aiming it directly at Janet and me. One bullet hit a handrail. A second bullet hit a stanchion.

There was no third bullet. Either she was out of ammunition or her gun had jammed. She sprinted to her car and jumped in. Her tires squealed and screeched as she drove away flat chat, as we say in Australia.

Jean-Loup rushed down the gangway towards the fallen woman, his gun at the ready. He shouted to Janet and me to get into the salon, and I quickly scuttled through the glass doors into the comparative safety of the barge's interior. Janet moved rapidly, too, but it was obvious that, unlike me, she was icy calm and fully in control of herself. Albert, the captain of the *Marie Curie,* ran forwards from the crew's quarters into the salon. Ignoring Janet and me, he rushed to the window, then took out his cell phone and dialed 17, the emergency number for the French police.

Within a surprisingly short time, several heavily armed policemen and two ambulances were on the scene. The police knew that, before they could do anything else, they had to disarm the woman lying on the ground so that the emergency medical technicians could tend to the recumbent policemen. Then they saw that the woman was motionless, clearly badly hurt in the chest. There was no possibility that she could pose any further danger to anyone.

The policemen nodded to the EMTs, who now rushed forwards to help the wounded police officers. From the salon I couldn't hear their words, but the faces of the EMTs said it all—both men were dead. Then they turned to the injured woman. They cut away her clothing to be able to apply pressure to her chest wound to staunch the bleeding. The burqa fell away and, to my complete surprise, the "Muslim woman" turned out to be a man who looked a lot like Gioachino, Claudio, and Ottorino di Campione.

CHAPTER TWENTY

The previous night had been a nightmare. But what had happened at Avignon police headquarters the night of the kidnapping was a mere picnic compared to what followed on the night of the shooting. Commissioner Delacroix was there, together with Dubois and Petit, and all three were hopping mad.

In order to be able to interrogate Jean-Loup, Janet, and me separately this time, they summoned two interpreters. I was escorted to an office where Dubois and Petit were seated behind a desk. They demanded to know why I hadn't told them the real reason we'd been kidnapped. They claimed that the two policemen would be alive if I'd told them the whole truth. I politely pointed out that the policemen were dead because they ran towards the burqa-clad women the way a bull runs towards the matador's red cape. Even if they'd known about the avenging twins, it wouldn't have made a difference of any kind.

Furthermore, I told them that we were trying to stay alive. The murder attempt on the Canadian train wouldn't have taken place if the room-service waiter at the airport hotel in Sydney hadn't worked out who we were from the police on guard outside our rooms. As far as I was concerned, the less we said about anything to anyone, the safer we were.

Then they wanted to know why I hadn't told them about our passports, Walter, Smith and Jones, and everything else. I replied that we'd left Australia because two groups of people were after us: Drugovi members and the di Campione twins. Clearly the di Campiones, who'd come after us themselves the following night, had orchestrated the previous night's kidnapping. If we'd discussed Bosnian Serb issues with Dubois and Petit, it would only have confused everything beyond all comprehension.

Eventually the two French intelligence officers calmed down, but they didn't apologize for their earlier attitude and the sometimes brutal remarks they made. They agreed that the Srebrenica massacre was a red herring, and they asked me to give a statement to Commissioner Delacroix that included every detail that related to the di Campione cocaine gang but excluded everything to do with Drugovi.

While I was giving my statement, Dubois and Petit interrogated Janet. When I finally finished, Commissioner Delacroix told me to go to an office to wait until he'd obtained a statement from Janet. In the meantime, Dubois and Petit were interviewing Jean-Loup. I never had the slightest doubt that our bodyguard would keep to himself all the information that Janet and I had shared with him over our recent dinner.

I sat in a small room under the incessant scrutiny of a young policeman who never took his eyes off me and hardly even blinked. I wondered if he thought his job was to prevent my committing suicide. He clearly didn't realize that, following the arrest of one of the di Campione twins and with the other on the run, presumably hotly pursued by the French police, suicide was the very last thing on my mind. On the contrary, I kept thinking of the old saying, "Today is the first day of the rest of my life." Janet and I would soon be able to go back to Sydney and investigate important crimes like stolen umbrellas and boy scouts who escort little old ladies across the street against their will. We'd live happily ever after, with a heavy emphasis on the word *live*.

I sat in that room with my minder for maybe an hour and a half. Then I was taken back to Dubois and Petit. Janet and Jean-Loup were already sitting in the office. Everyone looked tired. This was the second night in a row that the three of us had assisted the police in their inquiries, and Dubois and Petit looked no less exhausted than we did.

Petit did the talking, while the police interpreter provided a simultaneous translation into English of everything Petit said. "We've compared the statements that the three of you have given independently," Petit said. "There are only a few minor discrepancies, nothing of any significance.

"I have to tell you three things. First of all, Arcangelo di Campione is conscious after surgery, and the doctors say that, although he's in great pain, he's not as badly injured as we'd thought. The blood transfusion he's received has undoubtedly saved his life. We need to know how he and his brother found you. He'll give us that information. You should have no doubt about that.

"Then, there's a major national manhunt in progress to apprehend Domenico di Campione. There's no question that we'll catch him, and soon. And when we catch him, he'll talk, too.

"Third, the two kidnappers are currently being interrogated, one under arrest in the hospital, the other here in the cells. Again, we need to know how they found you. If they know, they will tell us. I assure you of that, also.

"I want all three of you to remain on the barge until we know exactly how the di Campiones located you. The barge will stay tied up at the wharf. The police guard will continue until we've taken Domenico into custody.

"I wish you a good night, or what's left of it."

And with that, Dubois and Petit left. We were taken to Commissioner Delacroix's office. He looked extremely sad; perhaps he was thinking of his two policemen who'd been murdered that night. He told us that a police car was waiting outside to take us back to the barge. Delacroix stood up, shook hands with each of us, and we left his office.

The young policeman who'd watched me like a hawk drove us back to the barge, where we found four policemen on guard. It was clear that the French authorities were taking no chances with Domenico still on the loose and having sworn to kill us no matter what the cost to him might be. With his twin brother badly hurt and under arrest, his criminal urge for vengeance had probably redoubled.

As we walked onto the barge, I saw Aurora's rosy fingers thrusting through the dark clouds hovering over the horizon. Reflected in the water of the Rhone, the dawn scene looked like a French Impressionist painting. Unfortunately, I was too tired to appreciate the glories of nature; I needed to crawl into my bed at once.

I woke after some eight hours of dreamless sleep. I showered and dressed. As I entered the dining room, Ghislaine greeted me and pulled out a chair. Instead of sitting, something made me look out the window onto the wharf. Now six policemen were there, all armed with Fass 90 assault rifles. Ghislaine pointed to the other window. Directly across from our barge, a police launch was stationary in the water. It was lying at anchor on the river, parallel to the *Marie Curie* and some thirty yards away from us. I could see several heavily armed police on board.

"What's going on, Ghislaine?" I asked.

"I don't know, *Monsieur* Damon," she said, "but while you were sleeping a senior police officer arrived and informed us that all six of us have to stay on the barge. In addition, none of us is allowed to go on deck under any circumstances whatsoever, especially you and *Madame* Janet. As he left the barge, more policemen arrived, and the launch took up its position next to us on the river."

Janet joined me while I was eating dessert. I told her what had happened. The two of us tried to work out why the barge was now exceedingly heavily protected. None of our suggestions made any sense. After all, if four policemen had been considered sufficient to protect us when we'd arrived on the barge at the break of day, why were there now six heavily armed police on the wharf and at least four more on the launch?

Then Jean-Loup joined us, yawning and still half asleep. We told him what had happened, and we asked him if he had any ideas. He just shook his head, excused himself, and went aft to the crew's quarters to get some food.

The rest of the day passed quietly. Janet and I sat in the salon, reading. Albert popped in, apparently to check that all was well. We smiled at him and he left the salon, only to return at hourly intervals. Ghislaine tried to ply us with food and drink, and Mathilde pulled out all the stops when cooking dinner for us.

But the mood on the barge was somber. All six of us were constantly aware that the previous night, on the wharf where our barge was moored, the di Campione twins had murdered two policemen who'd been charged with protecting us.

***

The next morning Ghislaine woke us. She told us that the police were waiting to take us to Commissioner Delacroix's office. Janet and I dressed hurriedly. I grabbed a croissant and Janet took a *pain au chocolat* from the pastry bowl in the kitchen. Jean-Loup was waiting for us in the salon. Together the three of us walked past the heavily armed policemen towards two police cars parked on the wharf. We all got into one of the vehicles. As we sped off, the other car, with four policemen aboard, closely followed us. The sirens blared as we raced to Avignon police headquarters.

We ate our breakfast on the way, trying hard not to drop puff pastry on the upholstery and floorboards, but with little success. When we walked into Commissioner Delacroix's office, we were in no way surprised to see Dubois and Petit there too, together with an interpreter whom we'd not seen before. We all sat down, and Janet and I accepted their offer of coffee.

Petit spoke. "Yesterday we asked you to provide a statement regarding the di Campione cocaine gang, but we explicitly stated that you were to exclude everything to do with Drugovi. Today we want a statement from each of you describing in the fullest detail all your interactions with the Bosnian Serbs. There's no need to mention anything about the di Campiones; you gave all that information yesterday."

I was stunned. "But I thought we'd all agreed that the entire Bosnian Serb issue is totally irrelevant. What's going on? And why are there so many policemen guarding the barge? And why are none of us allowed on deck? And there's a police launch anchored just off our barge. Why?"

It was as if I hadn't spoken. Petit merely reiterated, "We want a detailed statement from each of you regarding Drugovi. *Monsieur* Ogilvy, give your statement to the Commissioner. *Madame* Maitland, please come with me; I will show you where you will wait."

I was surprised to hear the Commissioner call her '*Madame* Maitland,' because I knew that he knew that Janet was unmarried. I later discovered that the social norm in France is to use *mademoiselle* for a young woman and *madame* for someone of Janet's age or older, irrespective of marital status.

Through the translator, I told the Commissioner the whole story, once again beginning with the explosion at Goran Pekić's bottle shop. I described the series of events in Sydney that culminated in the arrest of the participants in the Srebrenica genocide. Then I gave a detailed account of what had happened in Banff, starting with the Western Canada Sightseeing brochure on my bed and ending with the attempt on my life in the dining saloon on the train.

Commissioner Delacroix asked me how Drugovi had found the two of us. I explained that a room-service waiter, a member of Drugovi, had spotted us in Sydney. The Commissioner asked a few more questions, none of which seemed particularly relevant. Then it was Janet's turn, while I sat in the same office as before, but this time with a different policeman to watch over me. A much older man, seemingly close to retirement, he looked at me with sympathetic eyes, but he never took those eyes off me for an instant. Again, it was unclear to me why the policeman was observing me that closely.

Then the three of us were escorted to an office where Dubois, Petit, and Delacroix were waiting with the interpreter. This time Dubois did the talking.

"Yesterday morning Arcangelo di Campione refused to talk. We were most unhappy with that decision and informed him that we were withholding all painkilling drugs until he told us the full story. After two hours of agony he gave in. He informed us that your barge captain, Albert, has a son, Bertrand, who's a medical student in Padua because he was turned down for admission by the French medical schools where he'd applied. Father and son are extremely close and talk frequently by phone. Albert innocently told his son all about the two passengers who'd rented his barge for their exclusive use. Bertrand isn't a particularly good student, but he's a superb mimic and has major comedic talents. He put together an act for an 'open mike' night at a Paduan comedy club in which he depicted two rich tourists on a French river barge: an Englishwoman and an Australian man."

Dubois explained further. "Italy is riddled with small-time drug dealers, low-ranking members of the di Campione cocaine gang. One of them happened to be in the audience that night. Domenico and Arcangelo had gotten the word out to the whole organization that anyone who spotted either of you would be handsomely rewarded. In fact, the bounty is so large that the French and Italian drug distribution networks have declared a temporary truce. Their members at all levels are cooperating in every way they can to lay their hands on the money.

"Anyhow, the drug dealer put two and two together, and after the show, he visited Bertrand in the green room, where he praised Bertrand's performance to the hilt. He took Bertrand to a café and bought him drinks, ostensibly to thank him for his unforgettable performance. When the alcohol had suitably softened Bertrand up, the drug dealer asked him what had given him the idea for his superlative act. Suspecting nothing, Bertrand told him all about his father and the *Marie Curie*.

"This information quickly reached Domenico and Arcangelo. It was easy for them to find the location of your barge. They put on the burqas in order to lull the police guards into a sense of false security. Their idea was to get close to the guards and shoot them with their silenced pistols, then rush aboard and kill the two of you. Even if you'd heard the popping sounds of the guns as they fired at the policemen, the twins would've been close enough to the barge at that time to make countermeasures extremely hard.

"Their plan was foiled by the reaction of the policemen on seeing two 'Muslim women' in public covered from head to foot in burqas. They rushed towards the twins. As a result, the shooting started far enough from the barge for Jean-Loup to have time to draw his pistol and shoot Arcangelo. We still have no idea exactly why Domenico fled. As you suggested, perhaps he was out of ammunition, or perhaps his gun had jammed. His silencer may have had something to do with it. We don't know, but we'll certainly find out when we have him in custody.

"In any event, we have police all over France searching for Domenico. I've no doubt at all that we'll soon have him behind bars."

I responded, "And the sooner the better. I can't wait to return to Sydney."

There was a long silence. The three French law-enforcement officers looked at one another quizzically. It seemed that they couldn't decide who should respond to my remark. In the growing silence, Delacroix spoke up.

"There's been a major complication. We interrogated the two bogus policemen as soon as we could. First, we spoke to the one who drove the SUV, but he wouldn't talk. The injured man also refused to say anything, but then we told him what we'd told Domenico: no painkillers for his badly broken arm until we had a detailed statement from him. Unlike Domenico, it didn't take long for him to start singing like a canary.

"He told us that he and his partner were approached by a gangster known as Pepe the Bishop; I've no idea how he acquired his nickname. Pepe promised them a large sum of money, half of it up front, to grab both of you and bring you to his home, which isn't far from Avignon.

"In fact," he added, turning to me, "that T-junction where you started shouting about 'kidnappers' is only about a mile from Pepe's house. It's a good thing you caught on when you did. A minute or two later and it would've been too late.

"Pepe apparently didn't say why he wanted the two of you to be brought to him, and the two 'policemen' didn't ask. The man with the broken forearm then informed us that Pepe provided them with the police uniforms and the seven-seater SUV, and told them where to find the barge.

"Now we had enough information to detain Pepe. We searched his house and discovered that Pepe the Bishop is a Bosnian Serb. We asked him if he'd been at Srebrenica. He freely admitted to being a Bosnian Serb, but categorically denied that he'd been anywhere near Srebrenica at any time whatsoever. Nevertheless, we sent his picture to the International Criminal Tribunal for the Former Yugoslavia in The Hague, but we haven't heard anything back yet.

"Soon after we asked him about Srebrenica, Pepe the Bishop told us that he wanted to make a full confession. He stated that a strong-arm man named Borislav Daničić had contacted him. The Padua comedy club has two tickets at every performance set aside for the local newspaper, *Gazetta di Padova*, in the hope of getting a review and, therefore, free publicity. The theatre critic enjoys a good laugh and, if there are no plays for her to review, she goes to the comedy club. It turned out that Bertrand's act was so good that she wrote it up for her paper.

"Her review appeared in print two days later, and Borislav Daničić read it. He immediately realized that Bertrand might've been portraying the two of you. Unlike the clever drug dealer who bought drinks for Bertrand and then learned everything he wanted to know with no difficulty, Daničić used violence to get the information he wanted. He went straight to the comedy club with a fellow hoodlum. They cowed the club manager into providing them with Bertrand's address, found Bertrand at home in his student lodgings, and threatened him with physical harm unless he told them everything. Bertrand is small like his father, and although he's not highly intelligent, he knew precisely what would happen to him if he didn't answer all their questions in the fullest detail. Consequently, once again he revealed everything he knew. He answered all the questions they asked him, including where his father's barge could be found.

"Daničić then contacted Pepe and ordered him to kidnap you. Daničić instructed Pepe to contact him in Padua the moment you two were in Pepe's clutches. Pepe then confessed that he approached the two phony policemen, offering them lots of money, half of it up front, to kidnap the two of you. He also conceded that he gave them police uniforms and the SUV. However, they used their own guns.

"We strongly suspect that Pepe's 'full confession' is just an attempt to throw us off the scent of Srebrenica and Drugovi. Pepe admitted that he paid the bogus policemen while at the same time stating that he agreed to carry out Daničić's 'orders'—that was the exact word he used—without mentioning money. That leads us to believe that both Pepe the Bishop and Borislav Daničić are members of Drugovi. Furthermore, we think that the instruction that Daničić actually gave to Pepe was to kill you both the moment you were safely in his house, but we have no proof of that—yet.

"We then returned to the two phony policemen. We confronted the driver with the statements that his injured partner and Pepe made. Realizing that the game was up, he also gave us a statement. He's extremely self-serving, but the bottom line is that it's incontestable that the kidnapping attempt was initiated, orchestrated, and paid for by Daničić and Pepe. They are both Bosnian Serbs, who may or may not be members of Drugovi.

"And that was why we increased the guard on the wharf and brought in the police launch to protect you on the water side of your barge. At that time, we didn't know too much about Drugovi, but we didn't want to take the slightest chance. After all, two of our policemen are dead, and we certainly didn't want any more casualties of any kind.

"We then contacted the Italian police and told them what we knew. We gave them a copy of Pepe's statement, together with the statements from the two 'policemen.' Their confessions strongly corroborate most of what Pepe told us. Once Borislav Daničić is in Italian police custody, we'll meet with you again to decide on how to proceed.

"In the meantime, Daničić is free and Domenico di Campione is also still on the loose. Consequently, the police guard stays in place and you will all remain on the barge and will not venture onto the deck.

Please ask your chef to provide us with a list of supplies she needs, and we'll do our best to assist her."

CHAPTER TWENTY-ONE

The next morning, the police once again came to the barge to take us to the police station for further interviews. As before, Dubois, Petit, and an interpreter were with Commissioner Delacroix in his office. They all looked exceedingly grave, even the interpreter, an elderly woman with gray hair incongruously in pigtails. This wasn't a good sign.

It was clear that, before we arrived, Petit had been chosen as the spokesman.

"There were some developments yesterday," he began. "We've spoken to law-enforcement agencies in Australia, Bosnia and Herzegovina, and Canada. We've also been in touch with the International Criminal Tribunal for the Former Yugoslavia in The Hague. What we've learned is that Drugovi— 'comrades'—isn't just, as you were told, an organization consisting of the members of the Bosnian Serb Army who massacred the Bosniak prisoners. It's much larger than that. It also includes sympathizers.

"We've learned that Goran Pekić wasn't at Srebrenica, but he was definitely a member of Drugovi. Also, do you remember that we told you that Pepe the Bishop declared categorically in his statement that he'd never ever been anywhere near Srebrenica? Well, it appears that he was telling the truth about that. But he's undeniably a member of Drugovi, too, which is why he obeyed Borislav Daničić's orders. Incidentally, they've locked up Daničić in Padua. The Italian authorities will probably extradite him here to face kidnapping charges, together with Pepe and his two strong-arm men. Once Daničić has served his sentence in France, we'll deport him to Bosnia to face murder charges. Yes, Daničić was at Srebrenica."

"Are we going to spend the rest of our lives on the run from Drugovi?" I asked Petit.

"We really can't say. On the one hand, law enforcement officials all over the world are arresting more and more 'comrades,' including many who were at Srebrenica. Also, the hatred that spawned the genocide seems to be abating in the Balkans, because it appears that only a few of the sympathizers are younger men. In addition, the capture and trial of the Bosnian Serb General Ratko Mladić, after he hid from the consequences of his actions for nearly sixteen years, may eventually result in the dissolution of Drugovi. All that is excellent news. But on the other hand, it's always possible that a member of Drugovi will recognize you, and the consequences of that may well be fatal to you. Overall, in our considered opinion, it's unlikely, but not impossible, that you'll face any further danger from Drugovi."

After a pause, I asked them the obvious question. "What do you suggest we do in the short-term? We obviously can't spend the rest of our lives on the barge."

"No, you can't, for numerous reasons," Dubois said. "Here's how we see the situation: Domenico di Campione is on the run. In order for him to kill you, he has to find you while simultaneously eluding a nationwide dragnet. That means that you need to act in such a way that will make it hard for him to find you, while making it easy for us to find him should he come after you.

"If you were to go back to Australia, we don't think that you'd achieve either objective. He'll quickly find out where you live and where you work, which will probably prove fatal for both of you. Also, with all due respect to our esteemed colleagues in your country, the Australian police are unlikely to pursue Domenico as single-mindedly as a police force of which he's just murdered two members. Our advice to you is therefore to stay in France until we've captured Domenico. We feel that you'd be safer in small towns and villages, and that you should try to stay away from larger towns and certainly from cities. Of course, we expect you to let the local police know where you are in case we need to provide protection rapidly. I'll give each of you a card that you can show to the police that will make the process extremely quick and efficient."

We thought about his suggestions for a moment. Then I replied, "I believe that Jean-Loup is willing to act as our bodyguard. Is that correct, Jean-Loup?"

Our former guide nodded stiffly.

"In that case, *Monsieur* Dubois, speaking for myself, I'd certainly be prepared to follow your advice. Janet, what do you say?"

"I agree."

"Then that's settled."

Dubois then turned to me. "I believe that you said you have a cell phone that you use exclusively to communicate with Detective Chief Inspector Tregethick in Sydney?"

"Yes, but I don't use it for more than thirty seconds at a time."

"I understand," he said. "Would you please give us the number, in case we need to communicate with you in an emergency."

Both Dubois and Delacroix wrote down the number I gave them.

"Now, if one of you needs to get hold of me, use this." Dubois handed each of us a card. A telephone number was the only thing printed there. "The people who answer that phone know how to contact me twenty-four hours a day, seven days a week."

Next, I turned to the four Frenchmen. "Do any of you have a suggestion where in France we should go?"

"For practical reasons, I'd like to suggest that you stay here in the Vaucluse," Commissioner Delacroix said. "You're currently in the region of Provence-Alpes-Côte d'Azur or PACA, which consists of six *départements*. Please be kind enough to look at this map on the wall behind me. Here we are in Avignon, the *préfecture* of the Vaucluse *département*. There are no other large cities in the Vaucluse and therefore the police in our *département* report to us here in Avignon. We're better acquainted with all aspects of the case than any other agency in France. Dubois and Petit are currently based in Avignon, and I strongly suspect that they'll remain here until Domenico is taken. That means that, from the viewpoint of police procedure, it'll be to our advantage to have you stay here in the Vaucluse. If you wish to explore other parts of Provence, I can't stop you, but I'd strongly urge you to avoid large cities like Marseilles, Nice, Toulon, and particularly Aix-en-Provence."

Jean-Loup, who hadn't said anything for long while, suddenly spoke up. "I know it's a big city, but why 'particularly' Aix-en-Provence?"

Delacroix smiled. "Because Aix is known for its superlative pastries, especially pastries made with chocolate. If Domenico, who knows your interest in fine food, were to find out that you were in Provence, the place where he'd set an ambush for you would be Aix-en-Provence."

"Fine," I said, "we'll stay in the Vaucluse. After all, it's the only *département* named after a suburb of Sydney."

My attempt at Australian humor went down about as well as a clown at a funeral. Not even Janet could manage a grin.

***

Because Petit and Dubois wanted us to get out of Avignon undetected, the entire operation proved to be quite complex. At the outset, Delacroix phoned one of the policemen guarding the wharf to tell him to go on board the barge. He was to tell Ghislaine to pack our suitcases and to instruct Albert to sail the barge about five miles south to an otherwise deserted wharf. When the barge arrived there, the crew took our suitcases off and loaded them into the trunk of a dark blue unmarked police car.

Next, the police set aside a gray unmarked car for our use. Petit told us that the electronic equipment on the gray police car would make it easier for them to track us than if we drove an ordinary rental car; I assumed that there was some sort of transmitter hidden in the bodywork that could be activated remotely. Also, in case of emergency, Janet or Jean-Loup would be able to use the equipment in the car to contact the French authorities. The police drove the gray car to Château de Raymond, a wine farm about twelve miles north-east of Avignon, and parked it inside a large shed.

Then the dark blue car also proceeded to Château de Raymond, where it joined the gray car inside the shed. With both cars inside, they closed the shed doors. Meantime, Jean-Loup, Janet, and I traveled from Avignon police headquarters in the back of a black police van. More precisely, they drove the van into the courtyard of the police station and closed the heavy doors to the courtyard; it was now impossible to see into the courtyard from the street. Next, we emerged from the building and climbed into the closed back of the van. The police drove us in the van from Avignon directly into the shed at Château de Raymond. Only after they had once again shut the shed doors did we get out of the vehicle. A helpful policeman took our luggage from the trunk of the dark blue car and put it into the trunk of our gray car. We climbed into the gray car, they opened the shed doors one final time and off we drove. Unless someone had been watching the shed through binoculars, we'd managed to get out of Avignon undetected.

Janet drove us towards the village of Maîtreville. Jean-Loup was riding shotgun, and I was sitting in the back seat. After we'd driven for about an hour, Janet suggested that we stop for lunch. She hadn't said one single word since we left Avignon, and that probably meant there was something important that she wanted to discuss with us.

We went into a bistro in a small village just off the D900, the main road along which we'd been travelling. We sat down in a corner, away from other people. We ordered our lunch, and then I turned to Janet.

"Tell me, what's on your mind?" I asked.

"I have four questions," she replied. "Question One: Where does Drugovi get its funds? Question Two: How many gangsters do you know who read theatre reviews? Question Three: How did Drugovi and the Culbertson twins know we were in Banff? And Question Four: Why did the di Campiones and Drugovi try to kill us one day apart in Avignon, both times using disguises?"

"I've no idea what you're getting at," I replied. Jean-Loup seemed equally confused.

"Fine, let's start at the beginning. The ODESSA organization financed the escape of thousands of former SS-officers from Germany to South America by means of Nazi gold, as well as money and valuables they'd stolen from concentration camp victims. But where does Drugovi get its money? For example, Pepe the Bishop offered the two phony policemen a large sum of money, half of it up front, to kidnap us. Where did Pepe get that kind of money? Some of the 'comrades' are on the run and probably aren't earning any money at all. In fact, unless they receive regular funds from Drugovi, they'd probably starve. One or two of the 'sympathizers' may be multi-millionaires, but I doubt it. Again: where does Drugovi get its funds?"

"Where?" I replied.

Janet ignored me. "Now let's look at Question Two. In his confession, Pepe the Bishop said that Borislav Daničić read the review of Bertrand's comedy act in *Gazetta di Padova,* and that was how he traced us. Does that make any sense to you? Can you imagine a strong-arm man waking up in the morning, walking to his favorite café for breakfast, picking up a copy of the local newspaper that he finds lying on one of the tables, and opening it to the theatre page as he sips his first cup of espresso for the day? If he wanted to know which horses were running that afternoon at the local racetrack, of course I could believe that. If he turned to the obituary column to read about the guy whom he bumped off the previous day, I could probably accept that, too. But the theatre page? No way, no how."

"Just how did Daničić find out about us?"

Janet ignored me again.

"And third," she asked, "How did Drugovi and the Culbertson twins know that we were in Banff? Damon, you know how Drugovi found us there, but Jean-Loup may not know all the details. A room-service waiter at the Lord Berkeley Hotel in Sydney saw the police standing guard outside our room and put two and two together and informed his superiors in Drugovi. Then they used the Canadian National Airline passenger list to find our new names and track us to Vancouver. The wife of a Drugovi member found the reservation that Marcelle made for us, and they followed us to Tweedsmuir House in Banff and from there to the Western Canada Sightseeing train. The Drugovi assassin drove from Banff to Kamloops and joined the train there, disguised as a replacement attendant, and tried to kill Damon with the syringe.

"But how did the Culbertson twins track us to Banff? Yes, we know that the Culbertson twins were recruited by someone who called various theatrical agents in Vancouver. But how did that person find out about us so that he could recruit Jethro and Jett Culbertson and instruct Sam the 'movie director' to trick them into following us? And Damon, you found the Western Canada Sightseeing materials from Drugovi on your bed during the same week in Banff that the Culbertson twins followed us around Banff National Park and onto the Western Canada Sightseeing train at the behest of the di Campiones. Why?"

By now I knew that I wouldn't get an answer; this time I kept quiet.

"Now let's turn to the fourth question. Drugovi tried to kill us one night in Avignon using phony policemen, and the di Campiones tried to kill us the next night, masquerading as devout Muslim women. Is all this coincidence? Doesn't this bother you at all?"

"I agree that you have some good questions. But do you have any good answers?" I responded.

"Well, try this on for size," Janet shot back. "Suppose that the Drugovi comrades are secretly cooperating with the Italian cocaine gang. That would answer my first question: Where does Drugovi get its money? The answer is that they're involved in cocaine smuggling."

"Wait a minute," I interrupted. "Just suppose that you're correct. And just suppose further that there really is cooperation between the cocaine gang and Drugovi. Why does this cooperation have to be kept secret? Why can't Drugovi simply operate as a branch of the cocaine gang?"

"I knew you were going to ask that," Janet replied. "For last hour it's been bothering me, too, but now I have the answer. The members of Drugovi are ultra-nationalists. For some ultra-nationalists the end justifies the means, no matter what—think of the Nazis or the Stalinists. But the majority of the members of Drugovi would be horrified at the idea of dealing in cocaine, irrespective of how the organization used the resulting profits. Key leaders of Drugovi cooperate secretly with the cocaine gang, but the rank-and-file members either have never wondered where the funds are coming from or, if they ask, they're told that funding is a matter for the higher echelons. Does that make sense to you?"

I nodded.

"Now," Janet continued, "for my second question: Does Borislav Daničić read the theatre page in *Gazetta di Padova?* The answer is, of course not. The whole idea is quite preposterous. I'll tell you what really happened. Arcangelo di Campione confessed that a small-time drug dealer was present at the open mike performance at the comedy club in Padua and witnessed Bertrand's act. He plied Bertrand with alcohol and found out all about us. He then informed his bosses in the cocaine gang; the information eventually reached Domenico and Arcangelo.

"I believe that the Italian cocaine gang then tried to find a way to inform Drugovi where we were without revealing the secret connection between Drugovi and the cocaine gang. My guess is that someone in the gang phoned Borislav Daničić anonymously and told him that the local Paduan newspaper had printed a review of a comedy act, and that Borislav should get certain information from Bertrand. Borislav then passed on the information that he'd forced out of Bertrand to Pepe, a fellow member of Drugovi. At that time, he repeated verbatim to Pepe what his Drugovi informant had told him about a non-existent review in *Gazetta di Padova.*

"Next," Janet went on, "do you remember my third question: How did Drugovi and the Culbertsons know we were in Banff? The answer is along the same lines as the answer to the second question; the Culbertsons knew because someone in Drugovi told them. And I've just told you and Jean-Loup how Drugovi found us there.

"Lastly, I'll answer my fourth question, which is: Why did the di Campiones and Drugovi try to kill us one day apart in Avignon, both times using disguises? The answer is obvious. They operated at the same time in Avignon because both groups knew that we were there; they're actually the same group. And they used disguises because they realized that, after all that's happened, we're extremely suspicious at all times."

My mouth dropped open and I was speechless with admiration for a while. Then I congratulated Janet on her brilliant analysis. I added, "But we have to let Dubois and Petit know about this. How do we do that?"

Jean-Loup spoke up. "We have Dubois's card. If you'll give me your throw-away cell phone, I'll arrange to meet him and Petit back in the large shed at the château in an hour's time."

CHAPTER TWENTY-TWO

When we arrived back inside the shed at Château de Raymond, Petit and Dubois were waiting next to a big black Citroën. They looked worried. Jean-Loup had obviously told them how urgent our meeting was. However, I gathered that he hadn't told them that we had good news for them, information that would surely help them to break the case.

Dubois said that for security's sake we should sit and talk in their car with the shed doors shut. When all five of us were settled, Janet methodically explained her theory. Unlike the official interpreters, who were professional simultaneous translators, Jean-Loup had to translate sentence-by-sentence from English into French. I could see that this frustrated Janet, who would've preferred to talk without interruption, but then again there was no alternative.

On the other hand, the frequent breaks helped Janet to formulate her thoughts clearly. The result was that by the time she was finished both Petit and Dubois had accepted Janet's hypothesis. It explained all the unexplained facts and didn't contradict anything that we knew to be true. Best of all, it simplified the task of the French and Italian law-enforcement officers. Rather than having to trace all the members of two totally independent gangs, they could now concentrate their forces on the one combined gang.

By now it was late afternoon. We piled back into our car, they opened the doors of the shed, and off we drove. "Next stop Maîtreville," I said to Janet, who was driving.

"I've a better idea," Jean-Loup said. "I suggest we cancel our reservation in Maîtreville and stay in Colline de Sainte Agathe for the next week."

"Why?" I asked. "I thought you and the police chose Maîtreville because it's safe."

"Colline de Sainte Agathe is as safe as Maîtreville, but it offers an opportunity to bring this whole affair to closure. I'll explain over dinner."

"Janet, Jean-Loup saved our lives. I'm certainly willing to go along with his change of plans. How about you?"

"I'm happy," Janet replied.

Jean-Loup proceeded to make three phone calls. As far as I could determine, the first call was to reserve three rooms for us in Colline de Sainte Agathe, and the second was to cancel our accommodation in Maîtreville. The third was to inform the police that we'd be staying in Colline de Sainte Agathe.

We arrived at Colline de Sainte Agathe just over an hour after leaving the shed at the château. Following Jean-Loup's directions, Janet parked the car in front of an imposing two-story building bearing the sign *"Chambres d'Hôtes."* I'd seen the sign in quite a few places in France, but I still had no idea what it meant.

"Welcome to Maison de Sainte Agathe, the nicest bed and breakfast in Provence," Jean-Loup said.

I was utterly stunned as a mullet, as we say in Australia. On the one hand, you know my attitude to beds and breakfasts. Calling an establishment a *chambres d'hôtes* doesn't change anything; after all, if you put lipstick on a pig, it's still a pig. On the other hand, as Janet had only recently reminded me, Jean-Loup had saved our lives. As far as I was concerned, that meant that if he thought that we should spend a week in a *chambres d'hôtes* then we would do precisely that. Accordingly, I said nothing. In fact, I didn't even roll my eyes when Janet glanced in my direction, let alone utilize my highly developed and exceedingly sophisticated miming skills.

We entered Maison de Sainte Agathe, where the proprietor, Alphonse du Maurier, met us. He was a tall, thin Frenchman wearing a shapeless gray suit, a white shirt, and a bow tie. Regarding the panoply of colors and outrageous pattern of his bow tie, the less said about it the better—you can use your imagination. In fact, I still get nightmares just thinking about that bow tie. Nearly as bad, du Maurier saw the world through a gold pince-nez on the bridge of his nose.

Monsieur du Maurier made a lengthy and effusive speech. Unfortunately, it was in French and when it finally rolled to a halt, Jean-Loup reduced the whole megillah to one word, namely, "Welcome!"

This draconian pruning of his interminable discourse didn't faze *Monsieur* du Maurier one iota. On the contrary, he beamed at Janet and me, and then started another endless peroration. When the bell finally rang for the end of round two, du Maurier turned to Jean-Loup and bowed. Jean-Loup bowed back, and then turned to Janet and me, and said, "*Monsieur* du Maurier says that you're most welcome here."

In reply, we mumbled appropriately. Jean-Loup however, rose to the occasion. He'd reduced *Monsieur* du Maurier's interminable opening discourse to only one word and his subsequent address to a single sentence. Now he transformed our muttered English responses into rolling Gallic encomia. In fact, his translation into French of our brief responses was almost as long as *Monsieur* du Maurier's two dissertations put together.

When Jean-Loup finally ran out of steam, *Monsieur* du Maurier bowed to Janet. Janet bowed back. He bowed to me. I bowed back. Then Alphonse du Maurier said in flawless English with only the merest hint of a French accent, "My old friend Jean-Loup can certainly talk the hind leg off a donkey, can't he?"

Needless to say, after the tensions of the past weeks, this excursion into pure French farce caused us to dissolve into hysterical laughter. I was laughing so hard that I was unable to breathe, never mind speak. And the other three were equally helpless with unconstrained mirth. Eventually, after some minutes, relative peace reigned.

Alphonse showed us to our rooms. In its own way, much to my delight, Maison de Sainte Agathe was just as wonderful as Tweedsmuir House. In particular, when I tried out the bed in my room it proved to be exceedingly comfortable. Also, there were no notices whatsoever in our bedrooms. In fact, the only notice in the whole place was in the second kitchen, the one that Alphonse du Maurier was kind enough to make available for use by his guests. Best of all, there were no china figurines anywhere. This was enormously encouraging.

Alphonse suggested that we eat our dinner that night at the Restaurant du Mistral, virtually across the road from Maison de Sainte Agathe. He said that the chef specialized in authentic Provençal dishes. Following Alphonse's advice, we started with pistou soup; *pistou* is the Provençal word for "pesto," a paste of made from the local olive oil, garlic, and basil. Next, we ate Grand Aïoli, a dish of salt cod and vegetables served with a garlic mayonnaise. Our main course naturally had to be lamb. We asked for roast lamb with Provençal herbs and, yes, it was heavy on the garlic. For the cheese course, our waitress suggested two local cheeses, Picodon and Banon; both were delicious. And in case you were wondering, we washed all this down with a truly excellent Châteauneuf-du-Pape.

When it came to dessert, Janet specified "anything without garlic" and I concurred. The waitress nodded and disappeared. About fifteen minutes later she was back with a laden tray. It seems that she'd misunderstood Janet; she thought she'd said "everything without garlic." However, neither Janet nor I were upset, or even disconcerted. On the contrary, we each tasted just a little of the Calissons d'Aix, an almond-paste pastry; the pithivier, which turned out to be a puff pastry pie with a fruit and frangipane filling; a cake made with lots of Muscat de Beaumes de Venise; and a dessert made with three kinds of chocolate, plus chocolate mousse and fresh cream. Jean-Loup took one look at the panoply of high calorie, high cholesterol, high fat offerings and instantly decided to skip the dessert course entirely. Which was a great pity for him.

When the coffee and cognac arrived, Janet and I turned to Jean-Loup and said, "Okay, why did you bring us to Colline de Sainte Agathe rather than Maîtreville?"

"As we drove along the D900, did you notice that there are two kinds of villages?" Jean-Loup asked. "The modern villages are built on the side of the main road, but the older villages are constructed on the tops of high hills. There are two reasons for this. First, during the Dark Ages, when those villages were founded, they didn't want to build houses on arable land, which was limited and precious. But much more importantly, the villages that were started many hundreds of years ago were built on high ground and surrounded by thick walls for protection against attacks by marauding bands and invasions by local warlords. In a sense, each mediaeval village was a fortress built on top of a hill.

"There's more than one entrance to some of those villages," Jean-Loup continued. "Others, however, are like Maîtreville and Colline de Sainte Agathe in that they have exactly one road leading up from the plain, and the gateway where that road enters the village is the only opening in the village wall.

"You'll recall that your original belief, endorsed by the Canadian and French law-enforcement agencies, was that there's a minimal threat to the two of you from Drugovi. After all, they're rounding up more and more 'comrades' all over the world. On the other hand, we unanimously agreed that the real danger to you is the killer Domenico di Campione. There's a nationwide hunt for him. Everyone also agreed that it's highly unlikely that he could possibly know where we are now. That meant that if we were holed up in a village like Maîtreville with one road and one opening in the wall, we'd probably be safe from Domenico. We'd simply stay in Maîtreville until the French police can track him down and take him into custody, and you two could then return to Sydney.

"Today, however, Janet realized that Drugovi might not be a spent force after all. It seems that Drugovi is in an unholy alliance with the Italian cocaine gang led by the di Campione brothers or, more precisely, by Domenico di Campione, the only brother still alive and at liberty. Even though they've arrested a number of members of Drugovi lately, there may well be enough remaining 'comrades' and 'sympathizers' for the organization to remain a viable component of the cocaine gang, even though most members will be unaware of the secret partnership. In particular, if a former member of the Bosnian Serb Army who's now working as a waiter in a Provençal restaurant were to notice the two of you, then that information might well reach the ears of Domenico.

"What I'm trying to say is that, even though it *seems* unlikely that you'd be attacked by Drugovi hit men, the members of that organization have served and probably will continue to serve as additional eyes and ears of the cocaine gang. If a Drugovi comrade or sympathizer sees you, Domenico will surely learn of it.

"For law enforcement, the fact that Drugovi is a component of the cocaine gang is good news, because now they have only one gang to smash, not two. But for you and Janet, it's truly bad news because, with a network of Drugovi members spread around the world and almost certainly present here in France, the probability that Domenico will find you is now that much greater."

"That all makes good sense," Janet said, "but you still haven't explained why you wanted us to stay in Colline de Sainte Agathe rather than Maîtreville. You said that both Maîtreville and Colline de Sainte Agathe are essentially walled fortresses with just one entrance. But why are we here and not there?"

"All I'm going to say now is this: Were Domenico to find you, you'd better off here in Colline de Sainte Agathe rather than Maîtreville. If, as we assumed earlier, the probability of Domenico locating you is almost zero then it wouldn't matter where you were. But it now seems that Domenico may well hear about you via Drugovi. If that happens, you're better off here for reasons that I'd prefer not to share with you yet."

"Why not?" Janet asked.

"Because if you knew the details of the plan that I've drawn up to save your lives, it probably wouldn't work. My plan relies on your not knowing my plan."

And that was that. No matter how hard Janet and I tried, we simply couldn't convince Jean-Loup to say another word about the subject. Frustrated, I paid our dinner bill and we went across the road to bed at Maison de Sainte Agathe.

The next morning brought two surprises. One was somewhat expected; I'd had an excellent night's sleep on the truly comfortable bed I'd carefully inspected the previous day. But the other surprise was completely unexpected.

I went down to breakfast. Midway through the meal I realized that this was probably the best breakfast I'd ever eaten. In particular, the peach tart was the most sublime example of a fruit confection I'd ever experienced. When Alphonse du Maurier came into the dining room bearing more coffee, I went into raptures over the tart and asked him about it. Alphonse extremely reluctantly admitted that he'd baked it.

In the meantime, Jean-Loup had come downstairs and joined me. As always, he was far too wide-awake and cheerful to be a good breakfast companion. On this occasion, he sat down just as Alphonse spilled the beans regarding the identity of the peach tart baker. Jean-Loup turned to me and exclaimed, "Didn't you know that for twelve years Alphonse was the head chef at the Vanguard Palace in London?"

I was totally taken aback, and stammered a few words. Jean-Loup got up from the table, walked to the buffet, and came back with a big slice of the peach tart. He ate a large forkful, then turned to Alphonse and just smiled. And Jean-Loup's beatific smile conveyed far more about the glories of that peach tart than my effusive praise had done.

Janet joined us a few minutes later. Neither Jean-Loup nor I said a word to her about the peach tart. We waited until she'd taken a slice to eat with her second cup of pressed coffee. With the fork carefully held in her right hand, Janet slowly lifted a piece of tart into her mouth.

"Why are you two staring at me like that?" she demanded.

Then the peach pie interacted highly favorably with her taste buds and a look of pure bliss appeared. And Janet immediately appreciated why we'd been gawking at her with a look of expectation on our faces.

After breakfast we went for a walk through the village, which was founded in Roman times. Several of the buildings appeared to be many hundreds of years old. For example, the village church is Romanesque, not Gothic. Also, we saw a notice on the thick stone ramparts surrounding the village stating that they date from the thirteenth century.

Overall, the village was in a state of excellent repair. There's no question that the locals have a strong sense of pride in their beautiful village, and there was no sign of any essential maintenance work that had been postponed. Jean-Loup mentioned that the population of most of the hilltop villages of

Provence has been steadily decreasing since the end of the Second World War because many younger people are moving to the towns. As a consequence, the average age of the inhabitants is increasing because more and more Provençal villagers are now retirees. Older people in general have less money and less energy than younger people, but that was in no way reflected in the buildings of Colline de Sainte Agathe. In particular, the ramparts were in superlative shape. They looked as if they were strong enough to fend off a battalion of tanks, let alone an insane killer bent on revenging his brothers.

I noted with great satisfaction that there was indeed only one way into Colline de Sainte Agathe. The road started climbing the hill and then turned sharply to the right as it approached the single gap in the fortifications. But just before it entered the village, the road turned equally sharply to the left. As a result, if Domenico decided on a frontal attack, his car would be slowed by the two severe bends. Alternatively, Domenico could try to sneak up the hill on foot, but he'd have great difficulty climbing the thick, lofty stone walls in excellent condition that totally surround the village. Yes, he could try to throw a grapnel onto the top of the wall and then climb the rope to reach the fortifications. But that seemed somewhat unlikely. Just because Domenico was a psychopathic murderer didn't automatically mean that he embodied the skills of James Bond. All in all, our stroll through the village of Colline de Sainte Agathe turned out to be surprisingly reassuring from the viewpoint of our physical security.

After we'd traversed what seemed to be all the streets of Colline de Sainte Agathe, Jean-Loup led us to a café with an outdoor terrace that looked out over the vineyards and farmlands on the gently rolling plain below the village. Over coffee and cake, Jean-Loup laid out his suggested strategy.

"My suggestion to you both is that we lie low here in Colline de Sainte Agathe until the police find Domenico di Campione. That shouldn't prove to be any sort of hardship to you. You've comfortable accommodation in Maison de Sainte Agathe, the breakfasts are the best you'll ever enjoy in your whole life, there are great restaurants here—last night's meal was just a sample of the wonderful food in this village—and many of the cafés and restaurants have terraces like this one that overlook the glorious countryside.

"The one weakness in this strategy is that they don't staff the police station here in Colline de Sainte Agathe on a full-time basis. A police officer comes here twice a week for about three hours, and that's it. On the other hand, that's the state of affairs in all the other hilltop villages too. Quite frankly, there's usually no need for a permanent police presence in this part of Provence. However, the local government is aware that emergencies can and do arise. To able to respond quickly, there are mobile units all over the *préfecture* that can be summoned in case of a crisis.

"Our mutual friend, Commissioner Delacroix, has made very sure that all the law-enforcement officers in this area are fully aware of the situation. In addition, our other good friends, *Messieurs* Dubois and Petit, have taken precautions of their own. All this has been done as discreetly as possible with all information being imparted on a strictly need-to-know basis. Janet, I don't have to tell you that even the finest police forces in the world have a few rogue cops who sell information to the bad guys or trade information in exchange for drugs or sex. There's no doubt that everyone has taken the greatest care to ensure that you're protected should Domenico come here, while taking every precaution to prevent Domenico locating you in the first place."

As usual when it came to police matters, Janet replied before me. "Jean-Loup, I agree with almost all of what you said. The key point is that we need to stay safe while the French police find Domenico, and living here in Colline de Sainte Agathe is an excellent way to achieve that.

"However," she continued, "I do have a major concern. If the police find Domenico then our worries are over, and we can go back to Sydney. But what if Domenico is holed up as securely as we are? What if he's decided not to make his move until he learns where we are? In that case, we'll have to stay imprisoned here in Colline de Sainte Agathe for the rest of our lives. From what you just said about the village, I gather that Colline de Sainte Agathe is a luxurious prison in every possible way, but for us it's a prison nonetheless.

"Damon and I have been through this once before. We hid in Lyons for a month. We saw all the sights, we ate the most wonderful food, and we drank some truly glorious wines. But after a month we were bored to tears.

"What happened was that we were so well hidden in Lyons that there was no way that members of the Italian cocaine gang or Drugovi could possibly have spotted us. I strongly suspect that the same thing is going to happen here. We're going to stay here in paradise, waiting for the police to get their hands on Domenico. My intuition tells me that Domenico isn't going to come searching for us. Instead, he's going to stay in some extremely safe place until he receives reliable information as to precisely where we are, and *then* he'll come after us with a vengeance. But while we sit here lolling in the sun in extreme luxury, absolutely nothing is going to happen.

"Here's my suggestion. Let's decide on a time period, one full week, say. We'll give the French authorities seven days to locate and arrest Domenico. If they find him, wonderful! If not, we're going to have to emerge from our place of concealment to lure him out of hiding."

"Just a minute, Janet," I protested, "I've no intention whatsoever of setting myself up as bait for Domenico. And that's nonnegotiable."

"And what, pray, is the alternative?" Janet asked. "Again, if the police get him then we have no worries. But if a week goes by or a month or a year or whatever period you decide and Domenico hasn't yet been captured, are you prepared to go back to Sydney with Domenico still on the loose? Now that *would* be setting yourself up not just as bait, but as a target.

"What I'm suggesting," Janet added, "is that we decide how long to give the police to find him. And if after that time they still haven't apprehended him then we've no choice but to use ourselves as a lure to tempt Domenico out of hiding. Of course, we'd do it in such a way that police sharpshooters would surround us at all times. And Jean-Loup would be at your side, of course."

"I think there's one vitally important factor you've both overlooked," I replied. "Since leaving Sydney I've been attacked by a murderer dressed in a uniform extorted from a Western Canada Sightseeing train attendant, by two phony policemen, and by two bogus pious Muslim women. How are the police sharpshooters going to detect Domenico in time?

"Jean-Loup, you've saved my life twice and I'll never forget that. Never ever. But even you were initially fooled by the two 'women' in black burqas."

Jean-Loup nodded but he didn't say anything.

"And Janet," I continued, "I certainly take your point that unless the police find Domenico soon we'll have no alternative but to set ourselves up as targets. But with Domenico's propensity for disguises, my very real fear is that he'll be able to kill us both before Jean-Loup and the police realize that Domenico is within shooting range.

"To take an extreme example, suppose we were to go to Paris and sit at a front-row table at an open-air café on the Avenue des Champs-Élysées watching the passing throng stroll by. And suppose further that a nun wearing a traditional religious habit were to walk up to our table and ask us for alms for orphans in Central Africa. Would the police shoot her on sight for the simple reason that she might just happen to be Domenico in disguise? Obviously not. But what if 'she' just happened to be Domenico, once again in religious drag?"

Neither Janet nor Jean-Loup said anything.

"Domenico is smart enough to realize that armed guards are going to think twice and three times before they shoot anyone in ecclesiastical garb. I'm sure that's why he and his brother turned up in burqas. And that's why I gave the specific example of someone dressed in a nun's habit. It's one thing to talk about an abstract concept like freedom of religion; it's quite another to be concerned about people who appear to be devout proponents of a religious faith tradition but who are actually certifiably insane murderers in disguise."

Again there was silence. Both Janet and Jean-Loup knew that I was right. But none of us could come up with a reasonable solution to the very real predicament in which we found ourselves.

There was a long silence that lasted for at least five minutes, probably longer than that. Then Janet spoke up.

"For now, why don't we follow Jean-Loup's advice? That's to say, let's stay here under cover for a week. As Jean-Loup pointed out, we have every creature comfort imaginable. We're lucky enough to be in a truly beautiful part of the world. The sun is shining. Let's eat, drink and be merry."

I looked at Jean-Loup and he looked at me. From the expression on his face, it was obvious that we'd both recalled the same two biblical verses that we'd learned as children in Sunday School. The one, taken from the Book of Ecclesiastes, states that "a man hath no better thing under the sun, than to eat, and to drink, and to be merry." The other was a statement of the prophet Isaiah, "Let us eat and drink; for tomorrow we shall die." But some sardonic wit had conflated the two verses, yielding the dark and foreboding combination: "Let's eat, drink, and be merry, for tomorrow we die."

CHAPTER TWENTY-THREE

W hat should've been a relaxing week of fun for Janet, Jean-Loup, and me turned out to be tension-ridden from morning to night. All three of us were now completely convinced that Domenico wouldn't be found until Janet and I had emerged from hiding and a member of Domenico's gang or someone from Drugovi had observed us. We all knew that our continuous reveling in the luxuries of Colline de Sainte Agathe, eating and drinking to our hearts' content, was a complete waste of time. And we fully recognized that the only way the issue could ever be resolved would be if Janet and I set ourselves up as sacrificial lambs.

Nevertheless, all three of us pretended that everything was fine. We consumed Alphonse's unrivalled breakfasts with apparent gusto. We seemingly enjoyed the lengthy stroll around the entire village that we undertook every morning. Then came coffee and cake in one of the several cafés with terraces that overlook the fertile Provençal plain, brimming with orchards, vineyards, farmlands, and meadows, with hazy mountains as a distant backdrop. Lunch was taken at one of the many outstanding restaurants that were crammed into that hillside village. After our predictable postprandial promenade, we appeared to relish our afternoon coffee at another café. Towards evening we went to a bar for an apéritif. We almost always chose to drink Muscat de Beaumes de Venise. We never opted for champagne—our mood was far too gloomy for that. Then came dinner at another of the wonderful restaurants of Colline de Sainte Agathe, accompanied by wines of an equally high standard. And so to bed.

Each of us knew precisely what the other two were thinking every waking minute of the day. And yet, by some unspoken accord, we never mentioned the topic of Domenico di Campione for the entire week.

Now the time had come to face reality. A phone call to Commissioner Delacroix merely confirmed what the three of us had known from the start: despite a nationwide manhunt, the police hadn't found the slightest trace of the missing drug lord.

The inevitable time had come to bait the trap. The problem, of course, was that Janet and I were to be the lure.

There was no question that the initial step had to be a council of war with the French authorities, because they needed to guard us continuously. As good as he was, Jean-Loup couldn't be expected to be on duty twenty-four hours of every day. Jean-Loup phoned Commissioner Delacroix again to ask for a meeting that the three of us and various members of the French law-enforcement agencies would attend. Jean-Loup told us afterwards that he'd very briefly outlined the purpose of the meeting and had suggested the large shed at Château de Raymond as a possible location.

Two hours later Delacroix called back on my emergency cell phone. I handed it to Jean-Loup. There was a brief conversation and then Jean-Loup hung up the phone and returned it to me. He said, "We meet tomorrow morning at ten in the shed."

During the previous week I'd dozed fitfully, but I'd usually managed to get a couple of hours of reasonably deep sleep each night. But now I lay awake, tossing to and fro like a cork on the surface of Sydney Harbour buffeted by the Southerly Buster as it roars in from Antarctica. I must've dropped off towards dawn because I was asleep when Alphonse knocked on my door at half past seven.

I tried to wake up by having a colder shower than usual but with little real success. I shaved and dressed like an automaton. I'm sure that Alphonse provided us with a truly outstanding breakfast but I ate it the way a condemned man eats his final meal. By nine o'clock, we were on route D900, heading back to the Château de Raymond.

When we arrived at the large shed, we found that half of it had been fitted out as a meeting room; the other half was now a parking garage. An outsized table had been placed near the far wall of the building. About twenty men and women were in the shed, most of them in uniform, both police and military. We recognized Commissioner Delacroix and also Dubois and Petit, but we weren't introduced to any of the other participants.

We were all quickly ushered to the table. At each place there was a microphone and a set of headphones. A uniformed interpreter sat at a small desk behind us, providing a simultaneous translation of the proceedings into English for us when the French police, army, or national security personnel spoke, and into French whenever Janet or I spoke.

Commissioner Delacroix opened the meeting by repeating what Jean-Loup had told him on the phone. He then suggested that I address the meeting. I briefly explained that Janet and I felt that the only mechanism by which we could lure Domenico di Campione out of hiding would be if a confederate told him where we were. In other words, the sole way that could possibly lead to closure would be if we were to be the bait for a trap.

The meeting went on all morning. During the initial session, each participant made one of the same two points. The first school of thought was that it was out of the question for foreigners to offer themselves as murder victims. Apart from ethical issues, the ramifications of our deaths would be politically devastating. My impression was that, for those speakers, covering their behinds was much more important than arresting Domenico.

The other school of thought could best be described as a Gallic version of the Latin proverb *dulce et decorum est pro patria mori* (it is sweet and fitting to die for one's country). The main thrust of their remarks was that it's infinitely sweeter and incomparably more fitting to die for someone else's country, the French Republic in this instance. As speech after speech brimming with jingoistic fervor followed, I started to get the distinct impression that only by exerting extreme willpower were some of the participants able to refrain from ending their remarks with a heartfelt *Vive la France!* And I wouldn't have been the least bit surprised if everyone at the table had suddenly stood at attention and started singing *La Marseillaise* with patriotic passion.

What concerned me the most was that both camps were obsessed with our inevitable deaths. Not one speaker suggested that, although our willingness to sacrifice ourselves was indeed noble and altruistic, the police and army could at least make some attempt to protect us.

At eleven o'clock, they served coffee and pastries. When the meeting was called to order after the break, I pressed the button on my microphone and addressed the meeting.

"Every speaker seems convinced that Janet and I will be killed if we let Domenico di Campione find out where we are. But we can't go on this way. We cannot and we will not stay in hiding for the rest of our lives. The matter has to be resolved one way or the other. This is nonnegotiable.

"Then, not a single speaker has even mentioned the possibility that the police and military could protect us against Domenico. Also, no one has mentioned that certain precautions can be taken to avoid injury. For example, we could wear bulletproof vests.

"I'd like to suggest a specific plan of action, in two phases. In Phase One, Janet and I will ensure that Domenico finds out about us. In Phase Two, we'll trap him."

They looked at me as if I'd come from another planet. I went on, "In Phase One, we'd like a regular police patrol car with at least two heavily armed uniformed police officers to be stationed at all times inside Colline de Sainte Agathe, and another patrol car at the bottom of the road that goes down the hill, just before the intersection with the main road. At least two other members of the police force should guard the walls of the village night and day to make sure that Domenico doesn't try to climb in the back way. And if you could spare additional men and women, that would be even better.

"Janet, Jean-Loup, and I will frequently travel from Colline de Sainte Agathe to visit other villages in the area. We'll travel in a convoy of three cars, with our car in the middle, sandwiched between the two police cars. When we arrive at our destination, the police from both cars will escort us. Of course, we'll wear bulletproof vests under our shirts at all times.

"The result will be that everyone in the vicinity will know that Janet and I are staying in Colline de Sainte Agathe, heavily guarded by police. With all the drug dealers in France looking for us to get their hands on the huge reward that Domenico di Campione has offered, the news will inevitably reach his ears. He's desperate to kill us. Yes, he's a criminal psychopath, but I think that he's sane enough to realize that he'll be unable do anything during Phase One. If he tries to attack us inside Colline de Sainte Agathe, or on the road, or in another town or village, he knows that he'll definitely fail, even though he'll certainly be disguised, probably as an ecclesiastic of some sort. Instead, he'll wait until the police decrease their presence to a point when an attack becomes viable.

"At that point we'll have him. The trick of Phase Two will be to retain the same number of guards but to replace uniformed police by plainclothes police and patrol cars by unmarked cars. It's unlikely that an informer will realize that the strength of the guard will not have decreased. Once the news gets through to

Domenico that you've reduced or even lifted the protective cordon, he'll strike and try to kill us."

Having said my piece, I turned off my microphone and sat back in my chair. As I relaxed, it seemed that every person around that table wanted to reply. Delacroix had to bang on the table repeatedly for order. Finally, there was silence. Delacroix then went around the table in a clockwise direction, inviting each participant in turn to respond to my plan.

Much to my surprise almost everyone thought that the plan was workable. A number of objections were raised, but the law-enforcement participants answered all of them. In fact, neither Janet nor I had to respond. It was soon clear that the French authorities were going to implement our plan, albeit in a modified format. Most of the suggested improvements were relatively minor, but there was one major change that they made that I'll tell you about later.

After nearly an hour of discussion, some of it quite enthusiastic as more and more people saw the advantages of the plan I'd laid out, Commissioner Delacroix spoke again. He stated that what was needed now was detailed planning for Phase One. Once Phase One was underway, planning for Phase Two could begin. He asked Janet and me to return to Colline de Sainte Agathe and to stay inside the walls until he was ready to start Phase One. In the meantime, he'd make every effort to procure bulletproof vests for us right away. Also, the police would increase their presence inside Colline de Sainte Agathe as soon as possible.

Commissioner Delacroix declared the meeting adjourned. Janet and I took off our headphones, rose to our feet, stretched, and then we walked over to Commissioner Delacroix to thank him. The fact that we spoke to him in English wasn't a problem, because we were able to convey our sincere gratitude despite the language barrier. Next, we warmly thanked Dubois, but his colleague Petit had already left the shed while we were talking to Delacroix.

Jean-Loup joined us. We got into our car and headed back towards Colline de Sainte Agathe, stopping en route for lunch at a roadhouse. Our mood was one of elation, almost exultation; the depression of the last week had totally lifted. Bearing in mind that I'd just proposed exposing us to the murderous rage of Domenico di Campione, you might think that the three of us would've been quaking with fear, but that wasn't the case at all. I suspect that the reason for our high spirits was that we realized that the nightmare was coming to an end, one way or another. I knew that all three of us were unmarried and we had no children, which meant that our attitude was perhaps a little more foolhardy and rash than it should've been. On the other hand, Janet and I had been on the run for months, and we needed some sense of finality.

CHAPTER TWENTY-FOUR

That night we had a celebratory dinner at the Restaurant du Mistral, the place where we'd eaten on our first night in Colline de Sainte Agathe. We invited Alphonse du Maurier to join us as our guest. As on that initial meeting, he and Jean-Loup had us in stitches. Fortunately, Janet was capable of ensuring that our mirth didn't exceed the acceptable bounds of propriety; no Englishwoman worthy of the name would tolerate behavior in a restaurant that might in any way mar the pleasure of other diners.

The next morning, we resumed our sybaritic pursuits as we waited for Commissioner Delacroix to commence Phase One of my plan. As we strolled through the village, we were delighted to observe that some pieces of the stratagem were already in place. We saw a police car parked in the street in front of Maison de Sainte Agathe with two large uniformed policemen sitting in the front seat intensely scrutinizing the passers-by. As we strolled past the police station after lunch, we saw that the door to the main room was open even though it was Wednesday and ordinarily a police officer was there solely on Mondays and Thursdays and then only from nine o'clock until noon. Then we spotted two soldiers with automatic weapons walking along the top of the wide stone wall of the city, stopping regularly to peer down the hillside. On our way back after dinner, we noticed that the lights were still burning in the police station. And finally, when we arrived back at Maison de Sainte Agathe, a bulky package was waiting for each of us— our bulletproof vests had arrived.

The following morning all three of us wore our bulletproof vests under our shirts to breakfast. Alphonse raised one eyebrow when he saw us but he didn't say anything. I wondered just how much Jean-Loup had told him. When we first met him, Alphonse had referred to Jean-Loup as an "old friend." Alphonse certainly didn't have anything like the physique of a Special Forces soldier, and Janet and I therefore assumed that they'd met some other way, perhaps at school.

We spent the morning wandering around the village in high spirits. We ate lunch at a restaurant with a sunny outdoor terrace that overlooked the road that led up to Colline de Sainte Agathe. We'd hardly started our main courses when we saw a police patrol car park at the bottom of the hill about twenty meters before the intersection with the main road. It was gratifying for us to know that the police were methodically putting into place more and more components of Phase One of the plan.

In the middle of our coffee, Jean-Loup's phone rang. The conversation was lengthy and almost completely one-sided; our bodyguard hardly said a word. By the time Jean-Loup hung up the phone, his coffee must've been cold. He hurriedly drank down what was left in his cup and then turned to us.

"That was Delacroix. Phase One starts at midnight tonight."

I had to restrain myself from jumping to my feet and cheering. I could see that Janet was as delighted as I was.

Jean-Loup went on: "The authorities have made a clever addition to your plan. Do you remember the small market that they held last Friday here in Colline de Sainte Agathe? Actually, virtually every historic village and town in this region has its own weekly market. In fact, the day of the week on which each village holds its market hasn't changed for hundreds of years.

"The police think that, in order to increase the chance of your being observed, we should visit a different market each day, accompanied by uniformed police, of course. Tomorrow is Friday, which means that there's a market here and also in Payrouge. Obviously, there's no point in our going to the Colline de Sainte Agathe market. Instead, tomorrow morning at nine we'll drive from here to Payrouge. Our car will be sandwiched between the police car parked below and the police car parked up in the village. And the remaining police and the soldiers will remain on duty, just in case Domenico tries to sneak in here while we're gone.

"When we get there, wherever we walk we'll be escorted by the police officers who'll have accompanied us to Payrouge in their two cars. Delacroix considers it highly unlikely that Domenico will make any sort of attempt during Phase One, but neither he nor anyone else involved in this operation is prepared to take the slightest chance."

Day One of Phase One dawned darkly. Angry black clouds covered every square inch of the sky. During breakfast, all the electric lights burned in the dining room, but the room still seemed murky and gloomy. The dim light outside cast a pall on our mood, and there was no spring in our steps as we walked to our car. As we drove along, the sky cleared somewhat, and this caused our spirits to rise just a little. Janet remarked more than once about the influence of weather on mood.

Payrouge turned out to be a fair-sized town about ninety minutes away from Colline de Sainte Agathe. When our convoy arrived there, we encountered an issue that everyone had overlooked: there was no parking to be had. Eventually we split up, with one police car finding a parking space in a street not far from the market square, while Janet and the other police driver ended up on a rough field on the edge of town. I, for one, was concerned that the sharp stones over which we drove might cause a flat tire, but fortunately all went well.

With the cars finally parked, the three of us, accompanied by two visibly armed policemen, made our way towards the market square. Using their walkie-talkies, the two sets of police managed to find one another and thereby double the number of our guards to four.

On the way to the market, we discovered just how huge it was. The various stalls were arrayed not only on the square itself, but also in many of the surrounding streets. This had the unwanted side effect of reducing the small number of parking spaces in the town to almost none. There were even more stalls on some of the broad footpaths of streets that were lined with regular shops. The result was that Payrouge on Market Day was crowded with sellers and buyers. We were about to be exposed to a broad audience.

The market was partially organized. The town square was divided into a section for fruit and vegetable sellers, an area for butchers and one for fishmongers, and a sector for other food sellers. The other half of the square was reserved for clothing stalls. But there were locations, especially in the side streets, which contained what seemed to be a random collection of stalls.

As we approached the square, we noticed a farmer who was selling three kinds of cheeses that he made. We sampled all three, of course. One variety in particular was truly outstanding and its taste seemed very familiar. We asked the farmer about it, with Jean-Loup interpreting. The farmer explained that he wrapped the cheese in chestnut leaves when he matured it. We asked him the name of the cheese and he said, "Banon."

Janet remembered that that was one of the two cheeses we'd greatly enjoyed on our first night at the Restaurant du Mistral. However, this Banon was even better than the one in the restaurant, and we bought some for Alphonse.

Next to the cheese seller, a high-powered salesman stood in front of a stall laden with boxes of steak knives, which seemed to have incredibly sharp serrated blades. The knives were sold in sets of six, with handles made of stainless steel, bone, cattle horn, or wood. In fact, there were other choices for the handles as well. But regardless of the material with which the handle was made, every knife was decorated on the top with a metal bee, the symbol of Napoleon Bonaparte.

Janet and I were greatly impressed by the style of the sales pitch, even though it was delivered in rapid-fire French and we therefore didn't understand a word. Standing only a yard from us, the salesman overheard me making a remark to Janet about the bee on the knives. He instantly switched to fluent English with a foreign accent. He explained that soldiers from the town of Laguiole, where the knives are made, had exhibited such bravery during the Napoleonic wars that Napoleon gave them the right to use his symbol on their knives.

When the Payrouge incarnation of Ron Popeil finally stopped to take a breath, we asked him where he'd learned to speak such excellent English. He said he'd been a seaman for twelve years on British freighters. We were so taken by his spiel that we bought box containing half a dozen of his ultra-sharp steak knives to take back with us to Sydney.

The next stall sold pastries. Neither Janet nor I can ever resist pastries. We bought one each for ourselves and a selection for the policemen guarding us. As far as I could make out, French policemen are firmly forbidden to accept gifts of any kind whatsoever. They are also positively prohibited from eating on duty at any time at all. However, I soon learned that both these rules are, as Hamlet put it, "a custom more honour'd in the breach than the observance." Consequently, the police who accompanied and guarded us were gracious enough to accept the pastries that I offered them and to enjoy them along with us. While we were all eating, the dark gray nimbus clouds started to drift away and the sun came out.

Other sellers on that street sold wooden toys, children's clothes—mainly hand-knitted outerwear—and assorted hardware. We didn't stop at any more stalls until we reached the main square. It was now eleven o'clock, time for morning coffee. There were three cafés on the square with outside tables. We were careful to choose one that had two vacant tables together right on the edge of the square. We pushed the tables together, arranged seven seats around them, and made sure that Janet and I were seated facing the square. This was just one of the many opportunities we took to get noticed that morning in the hope that word would get out to Domenico that we were in Provence.

After our midmorning refreshments, we walked to a line of stalls on the wide footpath in front of a row of shops. Most of them sold prepared foods, like jams and preserves, pâtés, and the like. Best of all, the stallholders encouraged tasting of their wares.

I walked up to the pâté stall and helped myself to a small piece of pâté de foie gras on a toothpick. It was absolutely scrumptious. I was about to buy some for Alphonse when there was a sharp crack followed by a loud boom.

I naturally assumed that a bomb had gone off. I was about to throw myself on the ground when the heavens opened. Realizing that protection of a different kind was needed, my next reaction was to take cover under a nearby awning until the rain was over. Our security detail, however, had other ideas. They immediately realized that everyone would run to take shelter, and we'd all be packed like sardines under such cover as we could find. That would make it almost impossible for Jean-Loup and the police to protect us. As a result, they rushed us back to our car while the cloudburst continued unabated.

The downpour was of Biblical proportions. In fact, I firmly expected the farmers in the vicinity to be lining up their animals two by two. Our clothes were soaked when we finally arrived back at the car, and I quickly learned that bulletproof vests are not waterproof. During the hurried aqueous retreat from the market, Jean-Loup and the police had agreed that, on reaching our cars, we'd immediately drive back to Colline de Sainte Agathe, a wise decision in view of our sodden state. Much to my surprise, the drenching rain didn't let up for a single moment on the homeward drive.

We'd almost dried out by the time we reached Colline de Sainte Agathe. The one police car left us when it reached the bottom of the hill, and the other accompanied us to Maison de Sainte Agathe. We went inside; gave the Banon cheese to Alphonse, who thanked us profusely; and changed out of our damp clothes. Over lunch we tried to evaluate the success or otherwise of our excursion to Payrouge. It was obvious that many people had observed us. What was less clear was whether the appropriate people had made a careful note of the fact that we were in Provence.

That evening over dinner, I raised something that was bothering me. Apropos of nothing, I turned to Janet and asked, "When you were living in Manchester, where did you do your grocery shopping?"

Janet appeared to be a little taken aback by the question. "There was a large supermarket just around the corner from my flat," she replied, "and they usually had everything I needed."

"But I'm sure that your work as a Detective Superintendent took you all around Manchester and beyond. Did you ever shop at other supermarkets too?"

"Certainly. If I found myself outside a supermarket and I needed eggs or bread or whatever, I'd pop in and buy whatever I needed. I wasn't married to that one supermarket. I'd shop wherever it was most convenient at that time. Why?"

I ignored the question.

"But aren't there open-air markets in and around Manchester like the one we were at today at Payrouge?"

"Yes, there certainly are, although they are mostly much smaller in scale. Why are you asking?"

Once more, I sidestepped Janet's question.

"And did you shop at those markets?"

"Almost never."

"Why not?"

"Well, the supermarkets had everything I needed. Their prices were generally reasonable, and the quality of the meat and vegetables was excellent. And the fruit was really good too. Most supermarkets had convenient parking. As a result, it was almost always quicker and easier to pop into a supermarket. Oh, I forgot to mention, our supermarkets are open from really early in the morning until quite late at night, which meant that I could shop when I had the chance."

"Precisely. But why are we going to weekly open-air markets when most people never set foot in them? Surely we should be going to the supermarkets of Provence?"

Jean-Loup spoke up. "But Damon, this is France, not England. Over 50 percent of French people refuse point blank to buy meat, fish, eggs, vegetables, or fruit in a supermarket. For some reason, they're convinced that buying stuff that's been lying out in the sun in an open-air market is infinitely superior to what the supermarkets sell. And that view is particularly strongly held here in the small country towns of Provence.

"Also, the lofty racks of supermarket shelves that line each aisle make it difficult for people to see you, other than those shoppers who happen to be in the same aisle as you. And customers in supermarkets are generally intent on finding the next item on their shopping list. They rarely look at other shoppers.

"But most important, it would be really hard for me to protect you in a supermarket. If you're spotted by Domenico, all he has to do is hide around the corner of the aisle you're on, and when you get to the end of the aisle, that'll be it.

"Rather than venturing into a supermarket, I strongly urge you and Janet to stick to the traditional open-air markets of Provence."

CHAPTER TWENTY-FIVE

The neighboring hilltop village, Roquesan, held its market on a Saturday. It was only a fifteen-minute drive to a charming hamlet basking under the summer Provençal sun. The village market was small, filling perhaps half of the large parking lot next to a church. This time we had no trouble finding parking, because the market was badly attended.

Most of the stalls displayed local produce, but the row right next to the church contained an eclectic mix of vendors. When we reached the first stall we saw that it consisted of a disorganized pile of mixed hardware. The stallholder had lumped the various items higgledy-piggledy on the trestle table. It would be hard for someone looking for a specific component to locate it in the chaotic jumble.

At the second stall we greeted the farmer who'd made the Banon cheese that he'd sold to us the previous day. We realized that, in addition to the local vendors at each market, there were a number of individuals who made a living selling their goods at a different market each day of the week.

We moved on to the third stall, and there we were delighted to see our friend from the previous day, the steak-knife salesman. Janet, Jean-Loup, and I shook hands with him while the four new policemen just looked on. After his success the previous day, the salesman now tried to sell us a dozen knives with gold-plated handles, but we politely thanked him and moved on to the next stall, where African violets in pots were on display.

After we'd walked up and down all three rows of stalls I suggested that we return to Colline de Sainte Agathe. I felt that the whole trip had been a waste of everyone's time because of the small number of people present at the Roquesan market. Nevertheless, in the car going back to Colline de Sainte Agathe, Jean-Loup pointed out that the more people who saw us, the more likely it was that we'd be spotted by an informant.

"Even if only a hundred people saw us today in Roquesan, that makes one hundred more people than the thousand or two who saw us yesterday," he declared. "And it all adds up."

Janet and I weren't convinced. The whole object of the exercise was to be noticed by the "right" people or, more correctly, the "wrong" people, and to us it seemed unlikely that the bad guys would be at a tiny market like the one at Roquesan.

The next day was Sunday. The markets that were held on that day were in villages that were located far from Colline de Sainte Agathe. Accordingly, I suggested to the others that we drive to Gigondas, a village with great restaurants that's well known for the wonderful red wine made there. But Jean-Loup was quick to point out that four policemen sitting and drinking coffee in a café in Payrouge was one thing. But four policemen in uniform eating Sunday lunch in a gourmet restaurant in Gigondas and drinking the local red wine at about two hundred dollars a bottle was quite another. Consequently, we spent the day quietly in Colline de Sainte Agathe, noting the continual presence of police and soldiers.

Monday meant market day in Maupassant, another relatively large town in the region. As before, we left promptly at nine o'clock, and an hour later we found ourselves in a monumental traffic jam on the edge of Maupassant. There was no apparent reason for the major congestion, but that didn't prevent the drivers of large trucks from sounding their horns and gesticulating threateningly with their fists even though, under the circumstances, both activities were totally futile. After nearly an hour the traffic cleared, and we drove on.

The police had learned from our experience in Payrouge. This time they'd arranged for three parking spaces to be set aside for us. But they hadn't reckoned with the Maupassant market goers. Three elderly pickup trucks, their bodywork dented and rusting, occupied our reserved spaces; the orange plastic cones that the police had used to reserve our parking locations lay on their sides some distance away.

The drivers of our three cars started hunting around for parking. We were lucky to find a place quite close to the market but the two police cars had to hunt elsewhere for somewhere to leave their vehicles. I suggested to Janet and Jean-Loup that we remain inside our car until the police could join us, but Jean-Loup reminded us that during Phase One the police were accompanying us only for show. We therefore decided to walk slowly towards the market as we waited for our police escort to catch up with us.

We turned down a side street and found a line of stalls. We were clearly getting close to the market square, and we slowed down even more. Standing at the first stall was the cheese maker, whom we greeted like the old friend that he now was. Next to him lay the disorganized pile of hardware. And the high-pressure steak-knife salesman manned the third stall.

A crowd of at least twenty-five potential buyers surrounded him, listening spellbound to his rapid-fire patter. When he spied us, he waved an arm in greeting and then gesticulated to the crowd to make room for us to come to the front. Somewhat embarrassed, we made our way through the throng where we each shook hands with the steak-knife seller.

He resumed his pitch in French. He picked up a knife that was lying apart from the others and demonstrated the sharpness of its blade by carefully running the index finger of his left hand over the serrated blade. I saw that the cutting edge appeared to have been sharpened on a grindstone. The salesman, whose powers of observation were remarkable, noticed that I'd seen the extra-sharp blade. He said, in English, "It's sharp, isn't it!" and plunged the blade into my left side, the least protected area of the bulletproof vest he'd spied under my shirt. The steak knife was aimed directly towards my heart.

***

The aramid fibers in my bulletproof vest saved my life. I'd always thought that bulletproof vests protect the wearer from bullets but provide no defense against knives. However, when a vest contains aramid, a long-chain synthetic polyamide, it also protects against blades. It's even effective against the specially sharpened Laguiole steak knife with which the salesman had stabbed me.

I'm sure you're extremely worried about what happened to me, so let me quickly reassure you and tell you that only the tip of the blade pierced my skin. In more detail, as the knife salesman tried to push his knife through my bulletproof vest, Jean-Loup and Janet simultaneously tackled him. Janet grabbed the knife and Jean-Loup broke his arm; Jean-Loup seemed to be making a habit of breaking my assailants' arms.

As the two of them wrestled him to the ground, the four policemen came running up. They quickly had the situation under control. Once they had the steak-knife seller in handcuffs, one of the policemen radioed for an ambulance, which rushed me to Maupassant Hospital. When we arrived there, I was quickly taken to the Emergency Department, where my bulletproof vest was removed and a technologist X-rayed my chest. The emergency physician found a tiny puncture wound in my side; it was located about three inches below my armpit. There was one infinitesimally small drop of blood. The doctor disinfected the miniscule wound and put on a Band-Aid. Unfortunately, all the Band-Aids in the Emergency Department were decorated with characters from French comic books. The one she applied to my side had two characters on it; the doctor hesitantly put forward that they might possibly be Tintin and his dog Milou. She was considerably more knowledgeable regarding best-practice medical procedures, however, and informed me that I had to have an antitetanus toxoid injection, as a precaution. The site of the injection bled another Lilliputian drop of blood. Immediately the casualty nurse applied another Band-Aid, this time bearing a picture of *Capitaine* Archibald Haddock, a friend of Tintin's, according to the nurse, who appeared to be considerably better informed in that regard than the doctor. By this time, Jean-Loup and Janet had arrived at the Emergency Department. They took me back to Maison de Sainte Agathe accompanied by the two police cars, with both cars blaring their sirens. We therefore had no trouble with traffic jams getting out of Maupassant, and we raced back to Colline de Sainte Agathe in fine fettle.

I kept telling everyone that I was fine and I assured them that I wasn't in a state of shock. On the other hand, I certainly was in a state of intense curiosity. In fact, we all had questions: Who was the knife seller? Why had he stabbed me? Had he reported our presence to others? If that was the case, had anyone informed Domenico yet? And if the man who'd stabbed me had obeyed someone's orders and reported us, why had he taken action himself?

The three of us had discussed these questions all the way home. We got absolutely nowhere other than generating a whole heap of unlikely hypotheses. When we arrived back at Maison de Sainte Agathe, we mutually agreed that we'd refrain from discussing the stabbing until we had some firm data.

At about eight that night, Commissioner Delacroix phoned Jean-Loup to ask the three of us to meet him at nine the following morning at the Colline de Sainte Agathe police station. When we arrived there, we found Delacroix accompanied by two detectives from Avignon. All three of them were friendly enough, but they certainly didn't look happy.

Through Jean-Loup as translator, Commissioner Delacroix began by saying how sorry he was that I'd been stabbed. He was most solicitous. I was pleased that he didn't raise the issue of who, if anyone, was to blame for the fact that Janet, Jean-Loup, and I had become separated from our police escort.

Delacroix then informed us that he'd come to share with us such information as the police now had. Regrettably, they hadn't learned very much. Since his arrest, the steak-knife seller had refused to say a word.

Police investigators had gone through all his possessions with a fine-tooth comb. They'd found two interesting documents. The one was an expired passport in the name of a Bosnian Serb named Gojko Rovčani, who'd been killed in 1997 in a high-speed car crash on a country road between Banja Luka and Kneževo. However, the photograph in the passport was of someone who only vaguely resembled my assailant. The other was an Ordinary Seaman Certificate issued in 1998, also in the name of Gojko Rovčani. The steak-knife seller had told us that he'd worked for twelve years as a seaman on British ships, and an Ordinary Seaman Certificate is needed for that job. The photograph on the certificate definitely looked like the knife salesman. Unfortunately, the detectives hadn't yet found any papers that contained the real name of the man who'd tried to kill me.

The only other useful discovery was a prepaid cell phone that someone had recently used to make a several calls to a number beginning 387, the country code for Bosnia. The police had traced the number and found that it, too, belonged to a burner phone. However, their two calls to that phone number had gone unanswered. These were the only facts that the French police had established. Everything else was conjecture.

At this point Delacroix paused and conferred quietly with the two detectives he'd brought with him to Colline de Sainte Agathe. Then he turned to us.

"We're operating under a number of hypotheses. I'd like to discuss these hypotheses with you, and I would warmly welcome any input you can give us, both positive and negative.

"First, we firmly believe that your assailant was a Bosnian Serb. All the evidence points in that direction. I assume you agree?"

All three of us nodded.

"Second," Delacroix continued, "until we have evidence to the contrary, we're acting under the assumption that he was a member of Drugovi. We find it interesting that our calls to the 387 number weren't answered. A common practice among gangs is that they won't answer a phone unless they recognize the caller's number. For that reason, we called the 387 number using the assailant's own cell phone. The fact that our two calls from that cell phone were ignored leads us to believe that someone in Bosnia knew in advance that the steak-knife seller was going to make an attempt on your life. If he'd succeeded and had got away, he'd have sent some sort of message to Bosnia. Obviously that message wasn't sent, and as a result the telephonic communication channel between the assailant and Bosnia was immediately shut down. In fact, a gang member in that country has in all probability already destroyed the SIM card for the 387 number. Accordingly, our working hypothesis is that the steak-knife seller was indeed a member of Drugovi.

"Was he at Srebrenica? We don't know yet. We've sent two photographs of him to the International Criminal Tribunal for the Former Yugoslavia in The Hague. One is the photograph on his Ordinary Seaman Certificate. The other is the mug shot we took yesterday after arresting him. Up to now, we've heard nothing from The Hague. We expect to receive a reply later today. When it comes, I'll share it with you. Do you all agree that it's likely that the assailant is connected in some way to Drugovi?"

Again we all nodded.

"Third, we're acting under the assumption that Domenico now knows that you're somewhere in Provence. Our reasoning is that, if the Drugovi leaders know where you are, then they've surely shared that information with the Italian cocaine gang. Does this make sense to you?"

For the third time we all nodded. A shiver went down my spine.

"Given that we're assuming that Domenico is now aware of where you are, we would like to start Phase Two right away and slowly replace uniformed police and patrol cars by plainclothes officers and unmarked cars, as we all agreed."

Delacroix turned to me. "However," he continued, "yesterday an attempt was made on your life. Even though the perpetrator is in custody and we're all but certain that no similar attempt will be made until it seems that we've lifted the protective cordon, any watcher would get most suspicious if our reaction to the assassination attempt were a *decrease* in protection. On the contrary, we have to *increase* the uniformed presence for a while.

"Here's the plan. Tomorrow we want you to go to the market at Fleury-en-Provence. Three police cars and a total of seven officers will accompany you there. They'll be heavily and ostentatiously armed. Phase Two will start two days after that. At that time, we'll scale the protection back to two patrol cars and four police in uniform. The day after that, the patrol car parked near the intersection with the main road will be replaced by an unmarked car stationed outside a farmhouse at the foot of the hill. Two plainclothes officers will man the unmarked car. Two days after that, the patrol car parked outside this police station will be replaced by another unmarked car parked near the police station in the village square.

"By the time Phase Two is complete, I'm sure that you'll be thoroughly sick of markets. But walking through markets certainly seems to be a really good way of getting noticed, as we saw yesterday."

"*Monsieur* Delacroix," I asked, "wouldn't he expect us to keep a low profile now? Won't Domenico get suspicious if we continue to visit markets?"

"On the contrary," he replied, "he would regard it as strange if he heard that you and *Madame* Maitland stayed away; it's well known that the tourists who come to Provence flock to our markets. And there's no reason why you should avoid going out in public. After all, Domenico surely knows that we've arrested the knife seller and that we're providing you with police protection in the highly unlikely event that there are other assassins out there."

Turning to me again, Delacroix said, "*Monsieur* Ogilvy, let me say once again that we're all most upset that you were attacked yesterday, but at least you weren't badly hurt. A few more days and we should have our man securely in custody, and you and *Madame* Maitland will be safe."

And with that, the interview was over. We thanked Delacroix and went off for our morning coffee and a pastry.

CHAPTER TWENTY-SIX

The next three weeks were a haze of markets, markets, and more markets. I don't recall specifically where we went or what we saw. Instead, each day's market just blended into the next. We even drove for what seemed like hours to get to Sunday markets. Unfortunately, as I told you before, none were held within a reasonable distance of Colline de Sainte Agathe.

As ordered by Commissioner Delacroix, the police presence increased in response to the knife attack, then decreased back to its previous level. Then, slowly, uniformed police officers and patrol cars were replaced by plainclothes cops and unmarked cars. Eventually we reached a point when there were no police or army personnel to be seen, not even standing guard on the thick stone walls of Colline de Sainte Agathe. From then on, we drove to markets in a discreet parade of three cars, with at least five hundred yards between the unmarked car in front and our car, and between our car and the unmarked car behind. The fact that all three drivers were following the same route made it easy for them to follow one another, even when the car in front wasn't visible. When we reached the day's market we parked our three cars as best we could. Then the four plainclothes men and women ambled over to our car and the seven of us walked around the market in an informal group.

As far as we were concerned, it would've been hard for any but the most skilled observer to realize that we were now under plainclothes protection. Nevertheless, our never-ending visits to markets didn't bear any fruit. There was no sign whatsoever of Domenico. We even tried asking some of the stallholders who moved from market to market where they would be selling their goods the next day, and then we turned up there. But nothing worked.

As I said, three weeks went by. I was too bored to be frightened. Then I realized what must be happening; I'd been too clever by half. I'd assumed that, during Phase Two of my plan, any watchers would be fooled into thinking that police protection had been lifted. But what if I was wrong? What if even the least competent of watchers had noticed that four armed plainclothes officers accompanied us, if not surrounded us, at all times? What if the unmarked cars had fooled nobody?

After returning from what seemed like the thousandth market, I called Janet and Jean-Loup into the living room of Maison de Sainte Agathe, where I shared with them what I've just told you regarding the failure of Phase Two.

"So where do we go to from here?" Janet asked.

The answer was obvious: "Aix-en-Provence," I replied.

I explained my reasoning. "Do you remember what Commissioner Delacroix said about Aix? It was something along the following lines: 'If Domenico knew you were in Provence, he'd set an ambush for you in Aix-en-Provence.' What we have to do now is meet with Delacroix and tell him that his protectors have evidently been spotted."

Jean-Loup arranged a meeting for the following morning at the Colline Sainte Agathe police station. This time Dubois and Petit accompanied Delacroix, and the commissioner had brought his own interpreter along, a stocky middle-aged woman named Alexandrine. Clearly, he and his team considered that this would be an important meeting. I strongly suspected that, behind the scenes, higher-ups in the French security forces were involved, and perhaps even the Foreign Ministry as well.

The office at the back of the Colline de Sainte Agathe police station was crowded. It was a warm and sticky day, and the ventilation in that small room was definitely suboptimal. However, none of the seven people crammed into the office noticed the heat or the humidity, because we were all obsessed with the task of smoking out Domenico di Campione.

Petit opened the proceedings. He summarized the activities of the past few frustrating weeks in one sentence: "Despite our best efforts, Domenico is still at large."

I spoke next. I pointed out that I wasn't prepared to spend the rest of my life playing cat and mouse with Domenico. Rather, the matter had to be resolved one way or the other. "I propose that Janet, Jean-Loup, and I travel to Aix-en-Provence. We'll walk the streets in such a way that it'll be unambiguously clear to any watcher who sees us that we're under no police protection of any kind whatsoever. Hopefully the news will get to Domenico. He'll emerge from hiding, and he'll try and kill me. And, equally hopefully, Jean-Loup will be able to stop him."

An intense three-way conversation between Delacroix, Dubois, and Jean-Loup now ensued. Alexandrine, skilled as she was at simultaneous translation, was unable to keep up with the discussion because Dubois and Jean-Loup spoke alternately while Delacroix kept talking continuously in parallel with their dialogue. As far as I could make out, Dubois was rehashing the first of the two arguments that various speakers had made at the beginning of the large meeting in the shed at Château de Raymond; he kept saying that it was politically most unwise for two foreigners to offer themselves as lambs to the slaughter. Jean-Loup repeatedly countered that Janet and I had no choice, and that we could not and would not continue our current way of life. I never did find out what Delacroix was saying. However, the fact that he was unable to switch out of continuous talking mode into listening mode showed the extreme strain under which he was laboring.

Realizing that we were getting nowhere, Jean-Loup stood up. "This has gone on long enough," he declared. "You've absolutely no authority whatsoever over Janet and Damon. Yes, you certainly have the power to deport them, but if you do that I will go to the newspapers. This isn't a matter of national security, it's merely drug dealing, and the papers will definitely publish the story."

There was a stunned silence that seemed to last forever, but probably went on for only about ten or fifteen seconds. Then Dubois spoke. "Will you please excuse the three of us?" he asked exceedingly politely through Alexandrine, the interpreter. Dubois, Petit, and Delacroix then left the meeting, leaving Janet, Jean-Loup, Alexandrine, and me behind in the office. For the first time I noticed the hot, stuffy air. I could hardly breathe.

"I'm going outside," I said. "Please call me back inside when they return." And I walked through the main room of the police station onto the village square. I saw the three officials standing under a shady oak tree near the police station arguing vehemently. Wanting to keep right out of their way, I strolled to the far side of the square. I sat on one of the three benches located under another oak. I don't believe that they noticed me, because they were far too deeply engrossed in their intense discussion. After a minute or two, Janet, Jean-Loup, and the interpreter joined me.

The overall situation might have looked amusing to a bystander. On one side of the picturesque village square, two men and two women were sitting on two benches under a large tree, silently enjoying the heat but not the humidity. On the other side, three senior French officials in suits and ties were in a heated dispute under another tree. Dubois, Petit, and Delacroix eventually stopped arguing. One of them looked around and saw us, I think it was Petit, and he nudged the other two. All three of them walked over to us.

"We've come to a decision. Shall we go inside?" Dubois asked. His politeness was even more pronounced than before.

"Can't we talk out here?" I asked. "It's really much more pleasant than in that stuffy office, and it's clear that there's no one else around."

I could see that all three of them were extremely uncomfortable with that suggestion, but none of them wanted to say anything untoward. After looking questioningly at one another, the three men sat down on the third bench. Petit looked around carefully to be quite sure that we were still alone, and cleared his throat.

"We feel that the French police and security forces have let you down. We haven't yet been able to come up with a plan of our own to trap Domenico di Campione; the plan we've been following is the one that you suggested at our joint meeting in the large shed at Château de Raymond. I realize that this may sound somewhat melodramatic to you, but from our side the honor of France is at stake.

"As Jean-Loup pointed out," Petit continued, "we cannot stop you from going to Aix-en-Provence in order to lure Domenico out into the open. We have the greatest respect for Jean-Loup and his proven ability to protect you. Nevertheless if Domenico somehow manages to disable Jean-Loup then the two of you will be sitting ducks."

"That is correct," I replied, somewhat stiffly. "But we feel that we have to take that risk to resolve the issue."

"We understand that and we respect your viewpoint," Petit continued, after carefully checking yet again that there were still no eavesdroppers in the immediate vicinity. "However, we would like you to give us one more chance, but with the odds tilted considerably more towards you."

This time I did not bother to respond. On the one hand, this was the first time that the French authorities had put forward any sort of proposal of their own. However, their motivation was the honor of France rather than a decisive statement of intent to bring the whole affair to a successful conclusion. It smacked of desperation. Nevertheless, out of politeness, the least we could do was to hear them out.

Petit continued. "Our idea is to increase the odds in your favor by substituting a specialist police officer for *Madame* Maitland here."

This suggestion came like a proverbial bombshell. I glanced at Janet. She appeared to be as stunned as I felt. Jean-Loup looked interested.

"Please continue," I said.

"Dubois and I know of a woman with dual French and British nationality. Her father, a Parisian by birth, was transferred to the London office of a large French insurance company—he was about twenty-five years old at the time. While he was there, he met an Englishwoman and married her. Their daughter, let's call her Véronique, was educated in England and France. She speaks both languages like a native. When she finished school, she went into the same sort of line of work as Jean-Loup here.

"If you and *Madame* Maitland would give your consent, we'll escort *Madame* Maitland to Paris to meet with Véronique. We think that after a few days in one another's company Véronique will be able to imitate Janet sufficiently to fool the drug gang. If *Madame* Maitland agrees, she'll show Véronique her clothes, and we'll arrange to acquire similar—if not identical—clothing for Véronique. We have access to excellent make-up artists and wig makers, and Dubois and I feel confident that Véronique will be able to masquerade most successfully as *Madame* Maitland.

"Once both *Madame* Maitland and Véronique are satisfied with Véronique's portrayal, Véronique will join you and Jean-Loup. Of course, if you agree to this plan, both of you will have to be extremely careful to refer to Véronique as Janet at all times."

The plan sounded perfectly feasible to me, but Janet had other ideas.

"*Monsieur* Petit," Janet said, in her dangerously calm voice that invariably means trouble, "once Véronique has been installed in my place, what happens then?"

"Well, with two trained bodyguards, *Monsieur* Ogilvy will be able to be seen at events that would be too dangerous with just Jean-Loup to protect him."

"Such as?"

"Well, for example, if the three of you were to go to a football game, Jean-Loup would probably be able to protect you only on one side. But if *Monsieur* Ogilvy were to sit with Jean-Loup on one side and Véronique on his other side, he would be protected on both sides."

"And if, at an exciting point in the game, Domenico were to sneak up behind him, what then?" Janet asked.

Neither Petit nor Dubois could think of an answer to that one. Commissioner Delacroix didn't seem able to help out, either. Petit changed the subject as quickly as he could manage.

"Another example then. Currently it would be dangerous for you and *Monsieur* Ogilvy to go dancing because, even if Jean-Loup were seated on the very edge of the dance floor, the two of you would be dangerously exposed on all sides. But Véronique could go dancing with *Monsieur* Ogilvy, because she would be armed."

I could see that Janet was perilously close to exploding, but I decided that, with my extreme lack of tact, it would definitely be much safer to let her handle the whole situation.

"*Monsieur* Petit," Janet said, slowly and quietly, "where does a woman keep a gun while she dances?"

The silence this time lasted much longer. Neither Dubois nor Petit was able to come up with a reply of any kind. And again, Commissioner Delacroix didn't seem to have an answer either. Alexandrine just smirked. Jean-Loup had a look on his face that said, *I'm keeping right out of this one.*

By this time even Petit and Dubois had realized that they'd entered a minefield without a map, and they therefore looked most relieved when Janet spoke up once more.

"*Monsieur* Petit, it seems to me that the purpose of your plan is to increase the number of weapons protecting us. One way to do that would be for you to get three police specialists: one pretending to be me, one pretending to be Damon, and one pretending to be Jean-Loup."

"Surely Jean-Loup could protect himself?" Dubois replied, rather unwisely venturing even deeper into the minefield.

"And then who's going to protect the real me and the real Damon while your policemen are pretending to be us?"

Again silence. The look on Petit's face made it clear that he wished that he and his colleague had never raised the subject of Véronique. Dubois seemed to be praying that the village square at Colline de Sainte Agathe would split open to enable him to plummet to the center of the earth. And Delacroix's face said, "I told you guys that this was a really, really stupid idea."

At this point in the proceedings, Janet's British upbringing took control. Keeping her voice and demeanor as charming as she possibly could, she spoke again.

"*Monsieur* Petit, we all appreciate that you put forward your suggestion of having Véronique masquerade as me with the best of intentions. You and *Monsieur* Dubois are incontestably concerned about our safety, as is Commissioner Delacroix, and having a female version of Jean-Loup to protect Damon was an admirable idea. But there's a much simpler way of raising the level of security.

"As you know, I was a police officer for twenty years. I passed all the marksmanship tests. Rather than having Véronique impersonate me, why not issue me with a weapon?"

The silence this time was palpable. Petit looked at Dubois. Dubois looked at Petit. Neither said a word to each other. Neither face moved a micron, not even their eyes. Yet it was clear to all of us that the two Frenchmen were communicating with one another. Delacroix just sat there impassively.

Eventually Petit and Dubois came to a decision. "Will you please be kind enough to excuse us for just a brief moment?" Dubois asked.

We nodded and smiled, and the three officials got up from their bench and walked slowly back to their corner of the square.

At this point, Jean-Loup finally entered the conversation.

"Do you know how to shoot?" he asked me.

"I grew up on a sheep farm in New South Wales. At that time, the dingo had the legal status of a pest, and that meant that farmers were told to eradicate any wild dog they encountered. And I shot my first rabbit when I was seven."

"With a rifle, I assume?"

"Yes."

"Any handgun expertise?"

"Unfortunately not."

Jean-Loup shrugged. Only a Frenchman can express such depth of feeling by raising his shoulders and eyebrows while turning his palms upwards and his ends of his mouth downwards. I think they learn this gesture in the cradle and practice it at least three times every day, if not more often.

He turned to Janet. "As far as Dubois and Petit are concerned," he said, "the honor of France is at stake. When they come back, I'm certain that they will authorize you to carry a gun. At that point, it would be most productive, I think, to suggest that you meet with Véronique to acquire body-guarding tips from her. I've worked with police officers trained in your country, and I know for a fact there's very little that you could pick up from Véronique. But from a viewpoint of diplomacy, I think you might consider suggesting that you 'learn' from her."

Janet nodded enthusiastically, and was about to thank Jean-Loup for his excellent suggestion when the three Frenchmen returned. This time Dubois was the spokesman.

"*Madame* Maitland," he said courteously, "you have made an excellent suggestion. We would be delighted to authorize you to carry a weapon of your choice. What handgun would you like?"

"*Monsieur* Dubois," Janet replied with warmth in her voice, "it has been a number of years since I fired a gun. Would it be possible for me to meet with Véronique at a shooting range, and for her to suggest what sort of handgun I should use? At the same time, I am sure that there are a tremendous number of important skills that I could learn from her."

Both Dubois and Petit smiled warmly. Their body language revealed gratitude and relief.

Dubois replied, "What an excellent suggestion, *madame!* The police have a first-class shooting range in Avignon. I'd be delighted to escort you to Avignon, and you could spend as much time as you need with Véronique, I'm sure that she's only too willing to share her experiences with you."

Now it was my turn to speak.

"*Messieurs*," I said, "there is no question now that Domenico knows where we are. Do you therefore think that it would do any harm if Jean-Loup and I were to accompany Janet to Avignon? Janet would be able to get admirable advice from Jean-Loup as well as from Véronique. And I'm sure that I'd learn from them both what not to do when Domenico comes for us."

Janet had totally charmed Dubois and Petit with her suggestion. My request was also warmly received. By clearly deferring to Véronique and Jean-Loup, the French experts, Janet and I had established a strong rapport with the representatives of the French authorities.

The next day the three of us drove to Avignon police headquarters. Véronique had taken a high-speed train to Avignon from Paris the previous evening and was waiting for us when we arrived at headquarters. She cordially welcomed us back to the city. Dubois and Petit had thoroughly briefed her and she seemed to have a keen grasp of all the critical issues. Best of all, she made it clear from the start that her primary goal was to ensure that we stayed alive and unharmed when Domenico came after us.

Véronique turned out to be delightful, friendly, cooperative, and eager to help us in any way she could. The only unfortunate moment occurred when we were joined by Petit and Dubois and they saw Véronique standing next to Janet. As we say in Australia, Blind Freddie could have seen that there was no way that Véronique could possibly have impersonated Janet. Janet was six inches taller than Véronique. Janet has an oval face; Véronique's face was distinctly round. Janet is thin; Véronique was obviously carrying excess weight, especially around her hips. Differences in hair color and styling could easily have been fixed, and Véronique could have used contact lenses to change the color of her eyes. But the primary determinants, height and build, were so mismatched that any attempt at passing Véronique off as Janet would instantly have been detected.

Of course, no one even hinted that the original proposal was preposterous. We all just continued to converse amiably until the two men politely excused themselves and left the four of us. None of us said a word. Even I realized that there was no need to comment in any way.

After the initial meeting, Véronique suggested that we all go to the police shooting range. Janet turned out to be an excellent shot, and she was delighted in every way with the pistol that Véronique strongly suggested that she use.

After ninety minutes at the range, we returned to police headquarters. Commissioner Delacroix had set aside a room for the four of us. A sandwich lunch was laid out, and we got right down to business. Again, I don't want to irritate you with unnecessary details. Instead, I'll just say that I spent a day and half in that room learning everything I could from Véronique and Jean-Loup about staying alive. They quickly agreed that it would not be a good idea for me to carry a weapon, because in the heat of the moment I'd probably do more harm than good. Rather, I learned how to assist my two bodyguards, Janet and Jean-Loup, to defend me against Domenico. They drilled me repeatedly as to what to do, and perhaps more importantly, what not to do.

Véronique gave Janet detailed instructions in body-guarding techniques. At no time did Janet indicate that she was familiar with what was being said, even though afterwards she told me that she'd had practical experience of almost all of the techniques and tricks of the trade that Véronique shared with her, aided at times by Jean-Loup. As far as Janet was concerned, we needed to have Petit and Dubois on our side, and she was willing to do whatever it took to ensure this.

After lunch on the second day, it soon became clear that both Jean-Loup and Véronique had run out of things to teach us. It was time to go. We thanked them both profusely, especially Véronique, and the three of us returned to Colline de Sainte Agathe for one final night. There was no need to mention that the next day our destination would be Aix-en-Provence.

CHAPTER TWENTY-SEVEN

We packed our suitcases, I settled our remaining bill with Alphonse du Maurier, and Janet drove us from Colline de Sainte Agathe to Aix-en-Provence. We checked into the Hotel Splendide, which indubitably lives up to its name.

The hotel is situated on Cours Mirabeau, one of the most beautiful streets I've ever seen. It's wide. The broad footpaths are planted with plane trees. It has beautiful fountains. At the western end of the street is a major traffic circle graced by a large fountain, La Rotonde, with three huge statues on the top. Halfway along Cours Mirabeau is an old moss-covered fountain that emits natural hot water from underground. The locals claim that it dates back to Roman times. And at the eastern end is a fountain depicting René of Anjou, known locally as Good King René because he brought Muscat grapes to Aix about six hundred years ago.

On the first day, we strolled from our hotel to La Rotonde. We sauntered around the traffic circle, and then ambled up the left side of Cours Mirabeau, stopping at a pavement café to sip a cup of coffee. We continued our excursion all the way to the statue of Good King René where we crossed the street and strolled back slowly on the other side. On the way, I noticed a bakery, Boulangerie Saint-Étienne, which had the most scrumptious looking pastries and cakes displayed in its shop windows. We bought one each and tried them on the walk back to the hotel. We decided that a return trip the next day was absolutely obligatory.

Accordingly, around half past ten the next morning, we crossed Cours Mirabeau and made a beeline for Boulangerie Saint-Étienne. As we walked towards the shop, I noticed a Franciscan nun coming towards us. My initial impression was that she was a typical member of her order. She was wearing the traditional religious habit: a white coif and wimple covering much of her head and neck, a black veil over her head, and a full-length black tunic. Over her tunic she wore the requisite black scapular, a full-length garment the width of her shoulders that covered her front and back but was open at the sides. Her gaze was lowered; her eyes seemed to be fixed on a point on the footpath about two yards in front of her. She appeared to be somewhere between thirty and forty years of age, but it was hard to tell because her coif, wimple, and veil masked much of her face.

However, there were a number of aspects of the approaching nun that worried me intensely. She was striding towards us, which meant that her gait was unquestionably not that of a contemplative nun. Next, what I could see of her facial features seemed oddly masculine. Also, the overall shape of her body, swathed though it was in her tunic and scapular, appeared to be masculine too. And finally, I couldn't see her hands, which were under her scapular; she could well have been harboring a gun.

I nudged Jean-Loup, who seemed to have shared my misgivings. He'd already partially drawn his pistol out of its underarm holster; I could see the bottom of the handgrip emerging from under the navy-blue blazer he habitually wore. Janet had reached into her bag and started to pull out her handgun, as well.

The three of us stopped and eyed the nun, who kept advancing directly towards us. It almost seemed as if she was marching in double time, so fast did she stride. As she neared us, I could clearly see that she wasn't wearing a pectoral cross on her chest. Now I was starting to panic.

But the figure in black never took her eyes off the footpath. As she passed us and continued determinedly towards the La Rotonde fountain, her head never moved; her gaze was inexorably fixated on an imaginary moving point on the footpath that marched in step with her, some two yards in front.

When the nun was at least a hundred yards beyond where were standing, Jean-Loup slid his pistol back into its holster, Janet let her gun fall back into her bag, and I started to breathe again. By common unspoken consent we bypassed Boulangerie Saint-Étienne and walked straight to Café Boniface on the next corner, where we indulged in spirituous liquor. More precisely, I had a double single malt Scotch whisky—yes, you know exactly what I mean—and Janet and Jean-Loup each had a glass of sparkling mineral water because armed bodyguards don't drink alcohol.

When we'd all had an initial swallow, I turned to Janet and Jean-Loup. "Who was that man?" I demanded.

"What man do you mean?" Janet asked.

"The one dressed as a Franciscan nun. Who did you think I meant?" I retorted angrily. "Was that Domenico di Campione?"

"That *was* a Franciscan nun," Jean-Loup said very calmly.

"But she didn't have a pectoral cross; I could see that very clearly," I protested.

"Only a Franciscan abbot or abbess wears a pectoral cross," Jean-Loup replied. "I would've been extremely suspicious if she'd been wearing one, because she certainly seemed too young to be an abbess."

"And why was she walking so fast?" I retorted, still rather too argumentatively.

"I've no idea," Jean-Loup responded, still extremely calmly, "but perhaps it was because she was in a hurry to get somewhere. That would tie in with the single-minded look on her face, too, and the way she kept staring at the pavement that way."

"But she looked like a man," I protested.

"Many women have a masculine facial appearance," Janet replied. "They can compensate for it by sporting an extremely feminine hair style. When a nun wears a traditional religious habit, however, her hair is covered by her coif. As a result, it's not unusual for a nun to appear to be somewhat mannish."

"But her body was also masculine," I insisted.

"She was wearing a billowy tunic and a loose scapular, which meant that there was no way that you could've deduced too much about the shape of her body," Janet said. "I think that your imagination perhaps roamed a little too freely—fully understandable under the circumstances, of course.

"And there was something else," Janet added. "I've been trained to spot if someone is carrying a concealed handgun. One of the signs is that the suspect may adopt a rather awkward posture, focused on the weapon rather than their center of gravity. So, unless the nun was holding a gun in the middle of her torso, her hands hidden under her scapular, it was unlikely—but not impossible—that she was armed."

And there the conversation came to an end. The fact that Jean-Loup and Janet had both undeniably drawn their pistols certainly reassured me. Clearly, I wasn't the only one who'd suspected that something decidedly untoward was afoot when we noticed the nun striding directly towards us. But it now seemed that the whole incident had been a false alarm.

We finished our drinks, but none of us felt us like returning to Boulangerie Saint-Étienne. In fact, in the light of what had just happened in front of the bakery, it was unlikely that any of us would ever want to go back there. This meant we needed to find a new but equally outstanding source of pastries in Aix.

That afternoon we decided to try the some of the side streets that radiate from Cours Mirabeau. After wandering somewhat aimlessly, we found Maison Fondant. The French word *maison* means "house" and *fondant* means "melting," and Maison Fondant specializes in melt-in-the-mouth chocolate pastries. The chef, Lucien-Pierre Charbonneau, combines dark and milk chocolate with chocolate mousse and chocolate cream and chocolate fondant and chocolate ganache and chocolate liqueur. He also uses other ingredients, of course, but his primary aim is to create chocolate confections of a standard unrivalled elsewhere in the world. His skills in tempering, molding, and sculpting chocolate are unmatched, to such an extent that Charbonneau deserves the Grand Cross of the Legion of Honor, The Supreme Order of the Chrysanthemum, the Nobel Peace Prize, the Bharat Ratna, the Congressional Medal of Honor, and the Victoria Cross, as well as the Collar of the Bolivian Order of the Condor of the Andes.

A really attractive feature of Maison Fondant is that, unlike Boulangerie Saint-Étienne, it incorporates a café where clients can sample Charbonneau's confections. The specialty of the house is Charbonneau's drinking chocolate. I still dream of that drinking chocolate almost every night.

After trying a variety of Charbonneau's products and then expanding the sampling space to include more of his masterpieces, I decided that I'd spend the rest of my life in Aix-en-Provence. Or bring Lucien-Pierre Charbonneau back to Sydney with me. Either way, I'd die happy. The problem, of course, was that through the actions of Domenico di Campione, I might achieve this outcome considerably sooner rather than later.

For the next few mornings, we walked up Cours Mirabeau, down Cours Mirabeau and then, having made every effort to be seen, we headed for Maison Fondant. The word *headed* doesn't adequately convey the sense of devotion that accompanied my daily pilgrimage to that chocolate Mecca. Maison Fondant became the center of my existence, its confections my very reason for living.

We were privileged to meet the master chocolatier himself, Lucien-Pierre Charbonneau, as well as many of my fellow chocoholics. What surprised me was that the Aixois who were as addicted to chocolate in all its glorious forms as I am were almost universally as thin as rakes. It just didn't make sense. We all came to worship at the shrine of chocolate every morning. We all drank the same drinking chocolate and we all ate the same pastries and cakes, and yet some of them looked almost anorexic. No one could possibly describe Janet or me as overweight. After all, we carefully watch our caloric intake and we exercise regularly. But compared to our fellow devotees, we looked like round chocolate truffles, whereas they looked like skinny chocolate-coated pretzels. When I pointed this out to Janet, she simply dismissed my observation as yet another of life's little mysteries.

The excellence of Charbonneau's chocolate partly made up for the total lack of constructive outcome of my new plan. Our purpose in coming to Aix-en-Provence was to flush Domenico out of hiding. But a week after the false alarm with the Franciscan nun, still nothing had happened. Undoubtedly a new strategy was needed. I told Janet and Jean-Loup that we'd hold a council of war in Maison Fondant the following morning.

We arrived there and we each ordered a favorite pastry together with Charbonneau's unmatched drinking chocolate. While we were waiting for our food, more of the regulars arrived, and we greeted one another like the old friends that we'd become. Then the door of Maison Fondant opened and a man in his thirties struggled to walk in aided by a crutch that he gripped in his right hand. He'd clearly been in a serious accident of some kind. His left foot and ankle were heavily bandaged, and his left arm was in a triangular sling. The top half of his head was also bandaged, and there was a large flesh-colored Band-Aid on his right cheek. You could feel the waves of sympathy from the customers seated at the tables and those waiting to be served at the counter.

The badly injured man worked his way with great difficulty towards an empty table next to ours. His crutch reminded me of something, but initially I just couldn't work out what it was. Then I remembered. After the nun had passed us on Cours Mirabeau, Janet remarked that one sign that someone is carrying a concealed handgun is if their posture appears to be centered on their weapon. It's natural for a person using a crutch to lean on the device and use it to support as much of their bodyweight as possible. But the injured man's posture seemed to be centered on his sling.

I shouted to Jean-Loup and Janet, "Watch out! Sling!"

But Janet was a step ahead of me. She'd already opened her handbag and was drawing her pistol at the same time as the "injured" man flung away his crutch and immediately grabbed the revolver that he'd hidden inside his sling. The two fired at the same time. I heard one loud bang and an echo. And Janet and Domenico di Campione both slumped to the floor.

CHAPTER TWENTY-EIGHT

Domenico had been clever. He'd hidden his weapon in his triangular cotton sling, and he fired through the fabric without drawing his revolver. But we'd been clever, too. Janet was wearing a bulletproof vest, but Domenico wasn't. Janet was badly bruised by the impact of the bullet, which knocked her to the floor. Domenico was stone dead.

For the next three days we submitted to endless interrogations conducted by the French police and security services. Each of us was grilled individually. For some reason, a wide variety of different officials from diverse agencies all felt that it was essential to hear our story first-hand and in detail, starting each time with the explosive destruction of Goran's Bottle Shop and ending with the Wild West-style shoot-out in Maison Fondant.

No one would explain to us why this never-ending series of interrogations was necessary. After all, Delacroix, Petit, and Dubois already knew every detail of what had happened to us. They'd spoken to Walter in Sydney, as well as to Smith and Jones in Vancouver. That meant that they'd been fully briefed on everything that happened to Janet and me from the time that Mrs. Martha Wigram had walked into our office. Notwithstanding this, even Delacroix, Petit, and Dubois insisted hearing our story once again from the very beginning, as did all the other police and security personnel.

Furthermore, it was absolutely crystal clear to every official that none of us had committed any wrongdoing whatsoever. Nevertheless, other than not being locked up, as had happened to us in Connickville police station, Janet and I were treated almost as if we were criminals. When we finally arrived back in Sydney, we asked Walter why the French police had behaved this way towards us, but neither Walter nor the more senior colleagues that he consulted were able to explain it. Or, if they knew why, they weren't prepared to share that information with us.

While guarding us night and day, Jean-Loup had saved our lives twice. He'd freed us from the kidnappers before Pepe the Bishop or Borislav Daničić could kill us, and he'd fought off burqa-clad Arcangelo and Domenico di Campione before they could shoot us. It's hard enough to express your gratitude to someone who's saved your life once. When it happens twice, it's all but impossible. As a token of our indelible indebtedness to him, I decided to offer Jean-Loup a job working with Janet and me in Sydney. His response left me speechless.

"Thank you very much, I certainly do appreciate your kind offer," he said, "but I live with my wife and six children in Carcassonne in south-west France, and I really must be getting home to see them."

We'd lived with Jean-Loup for weeks and weeks, but at no time did he mention that he had a wife, let alone six children. The behavior of the French police was puzzling, but Jean-Loup is a total enigma to me.

Janet and I flew back to Sydney within a few hours of the French officials permitting us to leave. We've been back here for a month now, and I'm delighted to be able to tell you that both the Italian cocaine gang and Drugovi have left us alone—for now.

AFTERWORD

This story is a salute to the superlative Rocky Mountaineer train, which we have fictionalized into the "Western Canada Sightseeing" train.

All the characters in *A Case of Wine* without exception, and in particular the hosts at the beds and breakfasts, are imaginary and bear no relation to any actual person, living or dead. With the exception of Harry's Café de Wheels, we made up the names of all the restaurants mentioned in this book. All other commercial establishments, including hotels, beds and breakfasts, businesses, shops, and shoppes, are equally fictitious, as are the airlines, train companies, and newspapers. Furthermore, every crime-related issue, without exception, is completely fabricated.

We stress that all the actions we have ascribed to Australian, Canadian, French, and Italian law-enforcement agencies are totally fictional and are in no way intended to reflect actual actions of those law-enforcement agencies or those of any other law-enforcement agency.

Mullajumba, Prodica, Connickville, Maîtreville, Colline de Sainte Agathe, Payrouge, Roquesan, Maupassant, Fleury-en-Provence, and the Sydney suburb of Willowbrook are all figments of our imagination, as is Zongiri Council.

Because of its pyrophoric properties, and especially because it burns at an extremely high temperature, triethylborane is used before lift-off to ignite rocket engines, including the F-1 engine on the Saturn V Rocket and the SpaceX Falcon 9 heavy-lift rocket. It is also used in industrial processes as an initiator in radical reactions. It is effective even at low temperatures.

For information regarding Australian financial planners garnering 10 percent commissions, visit `en.wikipedia.org/wiki/Great_Southern_Gr oup`.

More details on RG142, the eight-day way to become an Australian financial planner, can be found at: `www.smh.com.au/business/banking-and-finance/cheating-rife-in-financial-planning-20140815-104gkn.html`

The title of this book refers to both the cardboard box containing a dozen wine bottles, as well as the ensuing police investigation. In addition, the title is a tribute to one of our favorite authors, Herman Charles Bosman, and especially his short-story collection entitled *A Cask of Jerepigo* (a case of wine), published in 1964 by Human & Rousseau, Cape Town.

Lastly, ODESSA (*Organization der ehemaligen SS-Angehörigen,* or "Organization of Former SS Members") is a real organization. Drugovi, however, is a figment of our imagination—as far as we know.

ACKNOWLEDGMENTS

We gratefully acknowledge the many constructive suggestions we received from Howard Aksen, John Gallo, Joe Kensell, the late Johan Koeslag, Jill Selikowitz, and Jane Wolfers, our early readers.

Fine art photographer Raphael Shevelev created the double portrait that appears on page 392. After seeing the work, photographic historian Dr. Anne Hammond wrote, "This is extraordinary. I don't know of any other photographer who has been able to merge two portraits into a double portrait . . . I think of the composite photograph . . . as combining and averaging the unique markers of personality, whereas you have preserved them and lovingly linked them . . ." We thank Raphael for once again allowing us to reproduce his masterpiece in one of our books.

As always, it has been a real pleasure to work with our publisher, Jennifer Chesak, of Wandering in the Words Press. Our developmental editor, Michael Mann, subjected the manuscript to his invariable meticulous scrutiny, and we thank him for his helpful comments, criticisms, and suggestions. And for the ninth time, we thank Jennifer for designing a remarkable cover.

SHARON STEIN

Sharon Stein is a pediatric radiologist. Born in Cape Town, South Africa, Sharon was a professor of radiology at Vanderbilt Children's Hospital in Nashville, Tennessee and an examiner for the American Board of Radiology. She is a former president of the Southern Pediatric Radiology Society. In 2009, Sharon moved to Sydney, Australia with her husband, Steve Schach, to be with their grandchildren. She is an accomplished cook and baker who loves to share her recipes and techniques. This is her sixth thriller co-written with Steve Schach; Wandering in the Words Press published the first, *Coopers Island*, in October 2013.

STEVE SCHACH

Steve Schach, a native of Cape Town, South Africa, moved to Sydney, Australia, in 2009, after twenty-six years as a professor at Vanderbilt University in Nashville, Tennessee. Before he began writing thrillers, Steve wrote thirteen best-selling software engineering textbooks, which are used in universities all over the world. Down Under, Steve intended to become a full-time grandfather, and limit his intellectual activities to solving cryptic crossword puzzles and avidly watching Sesame Street with his grandchildren. However, the urge to write proved to be far too strong to overcome. Wandering in the Words Press has previously published eight of his thrillers, most recently *Crossword Traitor* in April 2018, co-authored by Sharon Stein.

Sharon Stein & Steve Schach

www.ingramcontent.com/pod-product-compliance
Lightning Source LLC
Chambersburg PA
CBHW021428240626
47153CB00001B/74